Kitchen Sink Gothic

Selected by
David A. Riley
and
Linden Riley

Parallel Universe Publications

First Published in the UK in 2015
Copyright © 2015

Derek Edge and the Sun-Spots © Andrew Darlington 2011. An edited version was originally published in *Tears in the Fence #53*
Daddy Giggles © Stephen Bacon 2012. Originally published in *Peel Back the Sky*
Nine Tenths © Jay Eales 2012. Originally published in *Terror Scribes*, Dog Horn Publishing.
Cover artwork © Joe Young 2015

ISBN: 978-0-9932888-3-8
Parallel Universe Publications, 130 Union Road,
Oswaldtwistle, Lancashire, BB5 3DR, UK

CONTENTS

INTRODUCTION

M. John Harrison used the term kitchen sink gothic in association with Robert Aickman. After quoting John Coulthart's description of Aickman as having the "quotidian Britishness of Alan Bennett darkening into the inexplicable nightmares of David Lynch", he added: "I often return to BBC4's *The Golden Age of Canals*, which features Aickman as a broody, nerdy TE Lawrence of the waterways, for its footage of decaying tunnel entrances, drained locks & Kitchen Sink Gothic clutter embedded in wet mud."

Coined in the 1950s, Kitchen Sink described British films, plays and novels frequently set in the North of England, which showed working class life in a gritty, no-nonsense, "warts and all" style, sometimes referred to as social realism.

It became popular after the playwright John Osborne wrote *Look Back In Anger*, simultaneously helping to create the Angry Young Men movement. Films included *Saturday Night and Sunday Morning, The Entertainer, A Taste of Honey, The L-Shaped Room* and *The Loneliness of the Long Distance Runner*. TV dramas included *Coronation Street* and *East Enders*. In recent years TV dramas that could rightly be described as kitchen sink *gothic* include *Being Human*, with its cast of working class vampires, werewolves and ghosts, and the zombie drama *In the Flesh*, with its northern working class, down to earth setting.

It's an area of writing that fascinates me, especially coming from a working class background and having been brought up in a terraced street in a solidly Lancastrian mill town which any viewer of *Coronation Street* would recognise as typical of its type. My formative reading in weird fiction, though, came from middle-class Americans (Robert Bloch, Ray Bradbury and H. P. Lovecraft) or from upper middle-class British writers like M. R. James, Algernon Blackwood, the Bensons. etc. I always felt there was a place for working class horror fiction whose characters were more than merely just comic constructs.

For me, within the horror genre, kitchen sink gothic is the antithesis of Jamesian or Lovecraftian horror. There are no distinguished scholars. The settings are unglamorous, perhaps

5

unatmospheric *in the accepted sense of the word in supernatural literature*. And gritty.

I was reminded of my own occasional leanings in that direction after someone reviewed one of my stories (*Dark Visions 1*, Grey Matter Press, 2013): "*Scrap* by David A. Riley *could easily have been a kitchen sink drama*, depicting the lives of two brothers growing up in a poverty-stricken council estate in England."

Shortly afterwards I came across John Braine's novel *The Vodi*, listed by M. John Harrision as amongst his top ten novels: "Constructed round the fantasies of a recovering tuberculosis patient, *this novel was the defining moment of an as-yet-unreported genre, kitchen sink gothic*. One of my favourite books of all time, it doesn't seem to be in print with the rest of Braine's backlist." Fortunately, Valancourt Books rectified this situation, republishing it in paperback in 2013.

In the anthology you are now holding you will find stories that cover a wide range of Kitchen Sink Gothic, from the darkly humorous to the weirdly strange and occasionally horrific. I hope you find the genre as fascinating as I do.

David A. Riley, 27th July 2015

DADDY GIGGLES
Stephen Bacon

Someone has scratched the words *HOTLINE TO HEVEN* into the metal plate above the payphone in the hospital's reception. Despite the depressing nature of the sentiment – or maybe because of it – someone else has scrawled the message *Phone for BJ* next to a 6 digit number. Duffy wonders whether the initials represent an actual person or if it's shorthand for something else.

His boss delivers the conversation with implied iciness; *of course they'd cope without him for the following week - it was his mother, wasn't it?* The fact that Duffy hasn't bothered to visit her for the past fifteen years is left unsaid.

The café is on the top floor of the hospital, almost as an apology. Duffy pays for a plate of lukewarm chips and a stale breadcake, and takes a seat near the window. Views across gravel-topped roofs, adorned with a row of bulky air-conditioning units, does little to raise his mood. At one point three nurses enter with their lunches, chatting together with far too much humour than seems appropriate. Duffy rubs his eyes and watches the heavy clouds outside drift into solid formations. The plastic bag between his feet leans firmly against the skin of his legs.

It seems busier when he returns to the ward. The hospital is a real eye-opener. Life in London for the past fifteen years has left him cynical and embittered, yet a kernel of nostalgia has remained; yearnings for the simpler life that he believes still exists in his home town. But he is surprised by the level of neglect and squalor that has infested Renfield since he'd left for the bright lights; he'd noticed the boarded-up houses, the figures sheltering in dark doorways, the scantily-clad waifs loitering on corners. The streets that once radiated with promise now brimmed with filth and sickness. Even inside the hospital, sallow drug-addled wastrels gaze listlessly from their beds; blue fluorescent bulbs installed in the toilets to prevent junkies from locating their veins. He is reminded of that song from his childhood - *Life in a northern town.*

The doctor ushers him inside his bland office and explains the serious extent of his mother's health. Duffy accepts the information with resigned inevitability. The doctor seems annoyed by his indifference. Duffy nods and stands, offers thanks, and quietly leaves the office.

A powerful blend of polish and antiseptic tries unsuccessfully to mask the underlying stench of death and despair that poisons the ward. Duffy looks for his mother's name on the whiteboard that adorns the wall of the nurses' bay, and heads along the corridor. Eventually he reaches a door at the end with the name *Duffy* written on the plate. He listens for a moment, hearing only silence, then knocks quietly and enters.

She is beneath the covers, eyes closed, pipes trailing from her body to the machines loitering next to the bed, low beeps injecting the silence with intermittent noise. Duffy is shocked by how frail she looks. Blue veins stand out in her paper-thin eyelids, fluttering lightly in time with the hiss of the oxygen canula that flows from her nose. He approaches the bed and sits on a chair that is positioned against the wall.

Her lips look thin and blue and fragile. Her chest is rising and falling in a shallow quiver. Duffy's eyes trace the mottled angle of her face. The intervening years have taken their toll on her – that, and the ravages of disease. Duffy had prepared himself for the impact of seeing her in this state, but the sight is shocking nevertheless. His detachment almost falters.

Then she opens her eyes.

For a few seconds she just stares at him. Then she closes her eyes. "You've come."

"Mum." He waits until she opens her eyes and looks at him. Then he says, "You're dying. I didn't want to miss it."

She closes her eyes. The room is heavy with shuddered exhalations.

He takes something from the plastic bag and tosses it onto the bed. It is a tattered toy, a threadbare relic of his childhood. Grey stuffing bulges through rips in the stitching. The face of the creature is grotesque; uneven button eyes, lolling crimson tongue, lopsided chin, a tarnished brass bell clinging to the remaining cotton attached to its hat. Duffy wrinkles his nose at the dust that has been released into the air.

A vague light erupts in his mother's eyes. "Daddy Giggles."

She gurgles something that might be a chuckle. "Where'd you find it?"

"I've been to the house." He tries to keep his voice under control, tries to suppress the emotion. "I needed to see to the post. Cancel the milk. That sort of thing. Why'd you kept him?"

She seems to be thinking for a moment. Duffy realises she's trying to muster enough strength to shrug, but she finally gives up. "He's always lived in your room."

"It hasn't been *my* room for twenty years. Just another shrine to my wrecked life."

She licks her lips. "When was the last time I saw you? You didn't come to your dad's funeral."

"No." He purses his lips. "I had my own celebration in London. It was one of the best days ever."

Rain jewels the window like frozen tears. Duffy listens to the wind outside. "As soon as your funeral's over I'm going to burn that thing."

She glances again at the toy. "Why do you hate him so much?"

"You fucking know why."

She sighs. "I always hoped that you'd come back to see me."

"I haven't *come back to see you*." He swallows. "You realise you'll be in Hell soon, don't you?"

Her face turns ever so slightly towards the window. The light makes it look like her eyes are wet. "I love you. I've always loved you."

"Why did you let him do those things then?"

She manages to laugh feebly. "Dean, it's just a stuffed toy. How could it do *anything*?"

"It's evil."

The door suddenly opens and a nurse enters the room. She smiles at Duffy with a degree of humility and goes around the bed to press some buttons on the old woman's drip.

"How are you, Mrs Duffy? Feeling okay?" The nurse reads some charts that are stowed beneath the bed. "Has your son come to see you?"

The nod is barely visible but it's enough to appease the nurse. "Everything looks okay for now. I'll check on you later."

She leaves a fog of silence in her wake, although the machines do their best to break the discomfort.

"How could it be *evil*?" His mother jerks her leg beneath the covers. "It's just a toy - a stupid glove-puppet."

"We've been through this." Duffy avoids eye contact with Daddy Giggles. "That thing *ruined* my life. You let it."

The old woman frowns vaguely. Duffy continues. "I told you – it always came to me when you were on night-shift. It never happened when you were there, but I told you about it. I kept on telling you. Why didn't you stop it? You turned a blind eye to what it did."

"Dean, it couldn't possibly have done anything. I know you were unhappy at that time; perhaps it was –" She suddenly falls silent, and grimaces as a stab of pain wracks her body.

Duffy waits, his muscles taut with expectation, but the spasms diminish until she returns to normality.

When she speaks again, her voice sounds distant. "Dean…you were an imaginative child. I never knew what was real and what wasn't."

"Like you said."

"So perhaps you imagined the whole thing…"

"Mother, I had nightmares for years. I lost weight. I couldn't bear to be touched." He stands, the chair legs scrape harshly. "I was expelled from school. You remember the trouble I had. And you did fuck all."

"Dean, it's a kid's toy. Think about what you're saying."

They both glance at the lolling plaything. The wonky buttons give it an unconcerned expression, almost bored. Light reflects off its plastic hands, made smooth through time.

"When you're gone, that thing's going the same way – to the fire." Duffy glances at his watch. "Anyway, I'm going to get something to eat. I'll be back in the morning."

His mother takes a shuddering breath. "There's some bread in the freezer."

"I'll get my own bread, thank you." He turns and exits the room.

The nurse from earlier greets him and he explains he's heading home. She smiles sympathetically and pats his arm in a concerned manner. "Try to get some rest. We've got your mobile number – we'll call if we need you."

He takes the lift downstairs. Visitors prowl the corridors with thinly-contained emotion. Pyjama-clad patients huddle outside

10

the front door frantically sucking on cigarettes. The sodium lights give the car-park a surreal clarity that makes Duffy feel exposed rather than safe.

He drives back to his mother's house, hesitating after he has killed the ignition. The earlier visit was uncomfortable. He watches the darkness of the building for a few minutes, noticing the stickers in the corner of his old bedroom window. Somehow this makes him feel guilty. He slams the car door and enters the house. The familiar smell greets him, stirring memories from his childhood. He stands at the foot of the stairs and stares up into the darkness. When nothing appears, he walks through to the kitchen. The house is cold and depressing.

He opens a can of soup and warms it up in the microwave. Sitting on the sofa with the dish cradled on his knee feels like an act of rebellion; he remembers how his mother always insisted they ate at the table. At one point a drip falls from his spoon and splashes on the upholstery. He smiles to himself and leaves it to dry.

Afterwards he leaves the dish in the sink and watches some television. It feels weird to see reality programmes and 24 hour news in the house – when he was here last it was all New Romanticised pop stars and primitive computer graphics, *Jim'll Fix It* and *Roobard and Custard*. After several hours of staring at the screen he feels his eyelids beginning to droop. The prospect of going upstairs to bed feels abhorrent however, so he rests his head on the sofa arm and allows himself to drift.

The phone wakes him with a start. He snatches up the receiver and answers, listening to a nurse with a gentle voice advising him that he might want to return to the hospital. His mother's condition is deteriorating; she might not make it through the night. The nurse ends the call with reassurances that he shouldn't hurry, urging to take his time and remain safe.

By the time he is back in the car his heart is hammering. Damp hands grip the wheel. It is almost 3.30 am and the roads are silent, yet menacing. The few remaining vehicles in the car park give an impression of neglect. He hurries up to his mother's ward.

The duty-nurse greets him with muted dignity. She ushers him into a pastel coloured visitors' room and explains the situation; their expectations for the short time remaining, reassurances that his mother is comfortable. He nods and allows himself to be led to her room.

It looks identical to how it did earlier. She is sleeping. Her face has taken on a red pallor, almost reptilian. He takes a seat and watches while the nurse fusses around with the drip and writes things on the medical note. Then she leaves them alone.

Duffy waits until his mother dies. He sees her breathing becoming shallower. He notices the numbers rising on the attached equipment. The colour of the data turns red and the machine eventually beeps and activates an alarm. He resists the pressure to touch her hand, even when the nurses come in to take care of the situation. It is clear that she has breathed her last. One of the nurses rubs his back, a small gesture of humanity which seems inappropriate somehow. He fights to recoil from her touch.

Eventually they tell him he must leave while they attend to her. It sounds strange to refer to his mother as *'her'* now all that remains is a corpse, but he avoids commenting. He is led back to the visitors' room and the nurse scurries away to fetch him a cup of tea. Someone has placed a box of tissues on the coffee-table in front of him. Instead, he picks up a glossy magazine and begins flicking through it.

Presently the nurse returns with the tea. He takes a sip politely. It is far too sweet and milky. The nurse advises she'll be back shortly with some paperwork. She pats his hand, and leaves.

The scattered pile of magazines occupy him for a while, their content sufficiently trivial to hold his interest. He is just contemplating getting his Ipod out when the nurse returns.

She indicates where he is required to sign and he complies, eager to escape. She tells him he can return on Tuesday to register the death.

He nods simply. "Thanks for all you've done." He turns to go but the nurse's voice arrests him at the door.

"Oh – don't forget the bag." She hands him the carrier bag stuffed with his mother's effects. Numbly, he accepts it and wanders out.

The first signs of daylight are beginning to creep into the sky. Gathering movement in the streets unnerve him. Sounds are increasing all around. His car is waiting at the traffic-lights when he first hears the jingling.

Glancing down, he notices the carrier bag in the foot-well of the passenger seat. The juddering engine has shaken the monstrosity loose so that its button eyes scrutinise Duffy. He tries to swipe it away but the traffic lights thwart his plan. Impatient revs from the dustbin lorry behind force him to move. Daddy Giggles rocks slightly with the motion. As he drives, Duffy tries not be distracted by the intensity of its stare.

The house feels muted. Maybe it's because he realises his mother will never be returning. There's a languid atmosphere in the rooms, almost an exhalation of relief. He locks the door and collapses onto the sofa. The curtains are still drawn, the darkness conducive to sleep.

Duffy awakes much later. Pins and needles sparkle in the numb skin of his left arm. He rolls onto the floor and grimaces at the clock. Lunchtime.

His mouth is dry and sour, his tongue feels like a bloated slug. He makes a sandwich out of ham and cheese. He eats it at the kitchen table, staring through the window. The back garden is surprisingly mature, almost unrecognisable from the version in his memories. The shed in front of the hedge is faded, bleached by the weather and the ravages of time. He decides he will be frightened no more.

Without thinking, he pulls some bin-bags out from beneath the sink and hurries upstairs. His parents' room has been redecorated since he left, though he recognises his mother's old-fashioned taste in the new wallpaper. His father's possessions are long-gone. He gathers together his mother's belongings and stuffs them into the bag, trying to erase all trace of her; the paperback Mills and Boons, her glasses, a pair of threadbare slippers from the foot of the bed, even a dirty glass from the bedside cabinet. He hesitates before opening the chest of drawers that once belonged to his father, fearful of what he'll find, but they contain nothing more sinister than his mother's underwear. There are no signs that his father ever existed. At least, no physical signs; maybe the neighbours still gossip in hushed whispers.

Soon he has purged the room of all the things that he's afraid of. Numerous trips up and down the stairs leave him breathless yet exhilarated. He piles all the unwanted items in the centre of the back lawn. Then he takes a deep breath and plucks up the courage to visit his old bedroom.

The smell is unmistakeable. Familiar scents of Airfix paint and old comics greet him as he enters the room. It is identical to how he left it – even the 1980s posters, now faded, still cover the walls. His black and white portable television continues to gather dust in the corner. The original mattress sags on one side still, evidence of the countless nights he lay awake, listening for the sounds of approach up the stairs. How many times had he cried himself to sleep, how many hours had he spent shivering with disgust in the damp bed afterwards?

Rage injects his limbs with tremor. He surveys the location where his entire life began to unravel, and he feels nothing but remorse and a desperate need to obliterate the memories.

Trips up and down the stairs again. Dumping the past. Eventually he decides the pile in the garden is big enough so he stuffs crumpled balls of newspaper into the gaps at the bottom and then lights them, enjoying the sight of the orange flames that begin to spread through the pile. Soon the bonfire is raging, smoke rising into the afternoon sky like a monstrous grey serpent. The air is alive with pops and crackles.

It is a good feeling to be ridding himself of such nightmares.

There is a rack of bunched keys hanging on the kitchen wall. He grabs handfuls of them and tries them individually into the padlock on the shed door until one offers a slight give. The barrel is so rusted that he has to prise it open with a screwdriver. The latch springs back and the door opens with a creak of complaint.

Cobwebs have rendered the window opaque. Insect corpses litter the workbench and the lids of the jam-jars lining the shelves. Duffy tries the light and is surprised when the bulb flares into life.

He has to root around for a few minutes in the tangle of assorted timber beneath the bench, peering through the frames of cast-off DIY remnants and saved drainpipe sections before he finally finds what he's looking for. Unconcerned about the mess, he drags the dusty toolbox out into the centre of the shed, rattling the padlock. More locks. He laughs hollowly. It could almost be a metaphor for his father's life.

Rather than search for the key, Duffy lifts the sledge-hammer down from its rack and lets it drop onto the flimsy lock. The

14

sound is like a cymbal crashing. He bends and feels the rusted steel of the toolbox, pausing for a second as he thinks about the last time he looked in here, all those years ago.

That was the catalyst. That was the point when the horrors in here leapt out and exploded into Duffy's life, like when Pandora opened her box.

He draws a deep breath and opens the lid.

Dust and cobwebs. A dead woodlice. Nothing more. No photographs, no letters from those like-minded, no brown envelopes containing images beyond the realm of Duffy's childhood comprehension.

He feels cheated almost. He wonders who removed the evidence. *It's immaterial anyway*, he thinks. *That happened in another life.*

Outside on the lawn, the fire is declining. Heat clings to his skin like neglected ash. He walks back into the kitchen and returns with the carrier bag from the hospital. Tips them onto the fire. Several packets of tablets, a puzzle-book, a home-knitted cardigan, a pair of cheap reading-glasses. He glances round, puzzled. Then he looks back into the bag.

Daddy Giggles is caught on the plastic of the handle. He detaches it and drops the carrier bag, holding the toy up to examine it one final time.

The face is just as horrible as it's been in his dreams, made sinister by its child-like innocence. The tarnished brass bell catches the glow of the fire. Its jingle sounds subdued in Duffy's grip. The brittle plastic hands now appear benevolent – almost curled in the act of prayer. Duffy remembers the pain they once administered. He turns it upside down and examines the hole where one's hand was meant to slip, giving life to the puppet. The material is shiny through usage. He sniffs the cloth for one last invocation of darkness but there is just the scent of dust and stale sweat, nothing to conjure ghosts.

He tosses it onto the fire and watches the flames catch a hold of the cloth. It burns with an intensity that seems unreal. Eventually it is nothing more than a blackened ember scattered among the other discarded remnants of his childhood.

Duffy turns and goes back into his house. Overhead, an aeroplane breathes a languid drone as it crosses the sky.

1964
Franklin Marsh

"They'll be waiting for us."

Derek drained his Scotch, and put the glass back on the bar. He looked relaxed, confident and ready. His purple leather coat looked immaculate, as did the silver tonik suit, button down shirt, thin purple leather tie and Italian winklepickers. Matt finished his light ale. He was a slightly less expensive and assured version of Derek.

Lurch drained his pint, spilling some over his Fred Perry, staining it. He was a mess but six foot six, tough and frightened of nothing and no one.

Gerry slurped his own light ale but his throat tightened and he couldn't finish it. He was a slight, nervous individual, hoping his companions' hardness and confidence would rub off on him. It wasn't at present.

The quartet left the pub and headed up the sloping, cobbled road to the railway station. It was late, dark and turning cold. You wouldn't believe it was August.

Gerry inverted the bottle in his hand, spilling the beer down the road, willing his friends not to notice. The streets were deserted. Not even any nosey coppers.

As they neared the station, Lurch guffawed as he saw the motorcycles parked outside.

"Let's smash 'em!"

"Leave it," warned Derek quietly.

"Come on, Del. We…"

"Concentrate on the matter in hand," said Matt, easily.

Gerry couldn't help but admire them. The taste of sour beer was in his mouth. He felt sick, tired, sweaty. He was afraid to speak in case his voice broke, and the hand holding the bottle behind his back was trembling.

They entered the station. Some of the lights seemed to be out, pools of dark shadow concealing God knows what. The boys spotted a railway guard in a ticket booth beside the platforms. He saw them coming and closed the door quickly.

16

Gerry was about to smile when a roar of raised voices enhanced his fear. He was briefly aware of blurred figures leaping out of the blackness, tell-tale black leather jackets and slicked back hair registering as The Enemy.

A bicycle chain from nowhere struck him across his cheek and nose, stunning and stinging him. He fell back into his own personal darkness, wetness upon his face, still clutching that precious bottle.

He heard a gruff "Leave the kid," and tears stung his eyes, as rage enveloped his soul. He struggled to his feet, listening to the shouts, curses, screams and scuffling sounds. He climbed up onto a bench and tried to focus on the brawl, figures flitting from light to dark. Matt had seized the bike chain and successfully wrapped it around the assailant's neck. He heaved and the greaser choked and spluttered on his knees.

Lurch, the least sartorial, clever, pleasant member of the gang had come into his own. He had two of the Rockers by their jacket collars and was banging their ducks-arsed heads together.

Derek and the presumed leader of the rival gang faced one another on the platform. A toot from the dark made Gerry aware of an approaching train. Light glinted. Six inches of steel emerged from the Rocker's hand. Gerry's heart was in his mouth.

Derek calmly reached into that magnificent coat, his hand re-appearing filled with dark metal. Gerry's study of war films afforded him the knowledge that Derek was pointing a Walther P.38 at his adversary, a favoured weapon of German officers.

The greasy-haired blade-weilder's expression changed from victory to defeat. His mouth opened to scream as Derek pulled the trigger. A hollow click, and the Rocker's face resumed its former victorious set. He thrust forward with his steel, and Derek folded forward.

Gerry threw the bottle without thinking.

It hit the knifeman on the forehead, shattering as it did so. Pieces of glass fell away from the face, accompanied by a rain of blood. One stubborn piece remained embedded under the quiff, transforming the biker into a unicorn. He stepped back. Missed the platform edge. And fell beneath the approaching train.

"Run!"

It didn't matter who shouted. They ran. Through the darkened sea-side streets. Until they saw bright light from a café shining upon a herd of scooters. Blessed relief! And a lift home from the Chiswick Mods.

*

Stan the Man dropped Gerry off in Battersea. He'd cleaned up his wound but didn't feel he dare show his facial alteration at home just yet. Lurch and Matt had held court in the café, telling tales of daring, courage and violence. Gerry had watched Derek becoming paler and paler. White shirt now red, suit ruined worse than even Lurch could accomplish. A couple of Modettes offered to run him to the hospital. The crowd then agreed to disperse quickly, before Old Bill came sniffing around. Gerry had received a few shoulder slaps and compliments for his action, but he didn't enjoy it. He just felt numb, the Unicorn Rockers fall playing over and over in his head. The older boy's eyes staring directly at him from under the Brylcreem as he disappeared, the squeal of train brakes worse than fingernails on a blackboard.

Gerry climbed over the leaning fence, clambered onto the coalshed, and tossed gravel at the window. She opened it.

"Gez?"

"Mona."

"You been to Brighton?" Excitement in her voice. She moved back to let him scramble inside. She touched his cheek, and looked at his face.

"You've been hurt!"

"It's nothing."

He lay on the bed as she bathed his face with tissues and the contents of the water jug beside her bed. He'd felt exhausted on the journey back, but was now seized with an unexpected vigour.

They climbed into bed, and he took her with a savagery that surprised himself. She ended up in tears, from the scratches, bites, lack of affection and non-withdrawal.

He felt dazed. He loved her and had never acted like that before. She told him to get out, but he had nowhere to go.

*

A belting from his dad. Mona ignoring him. No sign of Matt or

18

Lurch (which was not necessarily a bad thing). Derek hadn't been seen.

Returning from work a month later, to be hauled inside the house, frogmarched to the living room, where Mona and her parents were sitting, sipping tea from his mum's best china.

Pregnant. Wedding. Wife and baby to live with your folks until things get sorted. Honeymoon in Minehead.

After the shock things improved slightly. His mum and dad cheered up, planning the reception. Long lost relatives agreeing to turn up. Old Smudge at the garage giving him a tanner a week raise "now you're to be a family man." Mona blooming. A great do. Getting pissed but not too pissed. Mona's lot stand-offish at first but gradually breaking down as the evening wore on. Matt and Lurch (who even looked almost smart in church) turning up. Matt told him Derek had survived but had "gone funny in the head". He was now a beatnik living in some Notting Hill garret.

"You wouldn't believe the state of him, Gez. Hair down 'ere, beard down 'ere. He's a right state."

Gerry was glad to hear that their former leader was at least alive, but for the first time in ages he thought of the Unicorn Rocker's face staring at him as he fell.

He performed on the wedding night, and next morning they were on the train to Minehead. It was really the last good week he had. They had a chalet to themselves. It was heaven.

The night before they returned, as Mona undressed he saw that she had started to show. He couldn't get it up that night. He felt sick and alone. And scared. They returned in a sombre mood. And he slipped into the normal routine.

Get up. Wash. Dress. Go to work. Lunch. Work. Come home. Dinner. Telly. Bed.

It was the last one that was the problem. As Mona got bigger, his fear increased. He told himself, it was stupid. But he was becoming convinced that whatever was growing inside her had it in for him. He kept seeing the Rocker fall under the train. It was a recurrent nightmare. He was hardly sleeping. He had other nightmares. He was waiting in the hospital, chain-smoking. Three men shared the room with him. They looked like Elvis Presley, Jerry Lee Lewis and Little Richard. They told him that the baby was theirs.

Gerry screamed at them to mind their own business (but he

couldn't deny their claim). He looked at them. A black man. A pervert who married a thirteen year old relation. And a greasy-haired hillbilly who slurred. He woke up sweating.

The one night he did fall asleep, Mona shook him awake. She took his hand and placed it upon her swollen belly. He felt the kick and screeched, falling out of bed. He saw Mona crying, and noticed the gibbering wreck in the mirror. But he'd seen it. He'd seen inside her. The slicked back hair. The black leather jacket. Tiny little Engineer boots, kicking at him. Trying to get out and get him. And a horn in the middle of its forehead. Made of glass.

He slept downstairs. They all got on at him. He became a zombie.

As the day approached, he became calmer. Everyone sighed. At last he was beginning to be a man.

Things couldn't have gone better for him if he'd tried. Mum and Dad got called away. Mum's mum was failing fast. He and Mona were alone. She was breathing faster. Her waters broke. He left her on the bed and went down to his dad's garden shed.

Hefting the axe, he returned to the house and climbed the stairs.

"It's starting, Gez!" Mona wailed.

I'll finish it, he thought.

DEREK EDGE AND THE SUNSPOTS
Andrew Darlington

Spots.

Sun-Spots.

Derek turns the glossy page. Then turns it back. There's something that draws his attention. A solar attraction. A stellar gravitation. The photo takes up the full page of the *National Geographic*. A feature documenting the latest astronomical data from Mount Palomar observatory. The beautiful clarity of the sun, the freckling of sunspots erupting down its right side, a contagion across the bottom curve, a few climbing its left side.

The waiting room is death-still. Afternoon light filters through the nets. A small enclosed garden beyond. There are dental wall-charts explaining cavities and the causes of tooth-decay. Cartoon toothbrushes with stern expressions. The disturbing whirr of the drill occasionally audible through the wall. The faint ghost of Mansion polish. When he'd first arrived and been shown in here by the receptionist there'd been an elderly lady in a headscarf who smiled a small quick smile up at him, a little nervously. She'd been called into the surgery soon after. And Derek was alone. With the pile of magazines. The *National Geographic*. The sunspots.

He looks up from the page. Everything is morgue-still. Nothing stirs. Faint sounds. Faint light. Nothing else. He pulls at the edge of the page, gradually applying a little more pressure. The sound as it tears free, fraying from top to bottom, seems unnaturally loud. Once detached he folds it, folds it again and shoves it deep into his jacket pocket. Places the magazine – yellow-cover up, back on the pile. Sits for a moment feeling queasy with apprehension. Then takes the *National Geographic* and conceals it under the other magazines, precisely midway down, between an *Illustrated London News* and a *Woman's Own*. And sits back again on the edge of the chair, waiting.

When the nurse appears to call him through, he stands up, certain she must hear the crinkle-sound of the stolen page as it settles in his pocket. Isn't there a curious expression on her face? He moves past her. The dentist is waiting…

On his way home he crosses the railway bridge. Looking down over the parapet at the silver parallels stretching away into sunhaze, glimmering away into the distances of other towns, and he notices the flood. A right-upper side tooth winces a little. Poked and prodded. At first the flood seems little more than an insubstantial shimmer of water, some way away. As he concentrates he can see how it extends in from the steep embankment where walls of smoky weed climb, in across the near-side sleepers, to surround a wide expanse of the tracks themselves, leaving them barely projecting like metallic scrawls across its still surface. The setting sun has turned the water bronze, so that it has no depth, although it must be deep enough to wade through until it spills over the rim of your shoes. Odd, there hasn't been rain. Well, not to speak of. As he watches more intently he can see the shapes of several tall birds poking and picking at the water, stalking through its glistening sheen with elongated legs. Stabbing with long beaks. Herons? Are there herons here? He'd never seen any before.

In his bedroom he fishes the page from his pocket and carefully smoothes it flat across his pillow. The yellow-hot disc of the sun glowing up at him, almost casting shadows. The blazing coronal loops stabbing into a black margin of space. And the pattern of sunspots. Like floating continents in the photosphere, each one the size of multiple Earths. Molten storm-fronts millions of miles across, intense with magnetic activity. Incandescent, 4000-4500 degrees Kelvin, set in a star a million degrees. The equivalent of a billion hydrogen bombs going off every second. Yet they form a neat constellation of spidery blemishes across the searing solar face. He looked at it for a long while. Couldn't quite work out why he'd brought it. What had made him tear the page out of the magazine and smuggle it home? Hell, if he'd asked they'd probably have given it to him anyway. He was kid. He was interested. That was good. That was to be encouraged.

*

Each morning, an hour and a half before school, Derek Edge would be reluctantly prompted awake by an alarm clock set on a bare wooden chair by his bed.

This morning, at first, his eyes don't focus. But he knows he's not alone. Something else is here with him, in the bed, sharing the pillow. He tried to ignore it, but it was too close. Something twitching with chitinous scales and flexing mandibles. A thingy, a fiendish thingy. Ticking, more geiger-counter than metronome. It was inescapable. A dry insectoid mustiness of dead earth and decay, rotting food and dark dampness. It must be inside the pillow, the feather pillow. There was something there. Something alive. He startles back warily. Perspectives adjust as he moves his head away. It's in the folds of his pillow. Smaller than it first appeared. Only a wood-louse. Skittering along the outer rim of a patch of moistness. Sipping his drool. Saliva that had leaked from the edge of his mouth as he slept, and it's feeding on it.

He watches. What if he hadn't woken when he did? Would it have crawled into his ear, laid its million eggs there, mutated or pupated or just munched some wax, chewed some eardrum? Or would it follow the drool-trail, tracking it to its source? Scuttling and skittering across the pillow-to-flesh divide, up the acne-cratered curve of his chin, towards the slightly parted lips, and the seeping strands of sleeping dribble? Up, over the lower lip, in under the upper lip, squirming through, drawn on each inhalation of snore-breath, to where the stream of spit pools? He might never have known. In fact, it might already have happened during previous nights. How many bugs had he swallowed over the months, over the years…?

Body-moisture cools along his spine, and on the sheet beneath. He reaches out, just a finger, and pokes at the louse. Then punches down into the pillow, creating a deep pit. It scrabbles and twitches. Then loses its hold and spins down into the pit he has created for it. Ha-ha. Gotcha. Spit-stealing bug. His two eyes look at the clock, willing it be wrong. But two ears detect the regular soft stir of its graduated motion. He reaches out to push in the stop. And waits as long as he dares. Savouring the warm comfort, putting off the moment. You can't shift into full consciousness in too precise a move. More a pleasurably slow blur. But not so long that sleep tempts and reclaims you back to stay. After a while he looks up at the luminous face. 06:30. He slopes up. Looks back at the bug. It's still there. "Chespius. I'll call you Chespius. After the ruler of the Dark Planet." He drops his legs over the edge of the bed. His feet touch the crumpled handkerchief lying there. He dresses in the half-light of his bedroom, carefully folding striped pyjamas over the chair-back. Sometimes he might tweak a look through the curtain-corner out into the stillness of morning. Beyond the steamed-up window set into its crumbling putty, beyond the yard and the wall, to see whether the rain is drumming steadily on the rooftops. But not this morning.

From the bedroom he crosses the landing, illuminated by a frosted glass window that casts long-legged shadows across the badly-painted walls. Past his mother's bedroom door. To the bathroom, an icy cave of pipes, tanks, and white-emulsioned walls. Water chuckles in the pipes. Linoleum smells of wax, with a reflecting gloss that looks other-planetary. Soap veined with the traces of other, earlier soaps, squeezed together to form a kind of endless composite soap. A bath overhung with strangely threatening drapes of white female underwear. Ridged hanging things that resemble windbreaks rented from Blackpool beach vendors, with dangling straps and catches, areas of brown-to-orange wrinkle-edged stains hinting at dubious womanly secretions and suspicious leakages, voluminous domes, padded and under-wired, edged with lacy softenings that are not entirely convincing, and seamed stockings, deflated things like shed snake-skins, dark bands at their usually unseen upper reaches, slips and the wide off-white expanse of underskirts that seem to billow like the mainsails of lost galleons. All this, with the suffocating taint of wash-day detergents, together exerting a repellent gravitation of mysterious unease. Guilty-scared of looking. But drawn.

The tooth on his upper-right side winces a little. He pokes at it. Then catches his reflection in the mirror. His face stares back at him critically. A gawky man/youth, his body – his thick chest, running to corpulence. Even with gut held in. Not exactly fat. Not exactly plump. But running to corpulence. His face a pasty shade of pale. A pale and indistinct comic-melancholy face. Pale like something sunless found under a stone. Indistinct, weak, vague, blurred at the edges, as though maintaining only the slightest connection to reality. As though the reflected image is fading too fast to be fixed. A second-hand echo, distant and remote. A shadow of some firmer – more decisive self. Protruding lower lip too. Plate-lipped. Duck-billed. Spoon-bill... "I'm not comfortable in this body. And this shit is for the rest of my life..." He comes up close to the mirror. Checks out his complexion critically. His round face. His acne. He can hear his mother's voice, the Old Lady commenting on his stutter, his acne. "Is acne ruining your life?" A pale speccy spotty-clock as cratered as the lunar surface. When the first astronauts orbit the dark side of the moon they'll find it tortured into the exact replica of... this image he can see in the mirror... Perhaps a smudge of "Medac" here? No, no help at all. Look at that spot, that one there, it's the size and proportions of an extra nose. How can you disguise that? No chance in hell. It's still a face that resembles a combustible planet. Each morning he's scared to look into the mirror for fear of seeing what new volcanic pustules have erupted overnight to further disfigure the lunar-cratered face-scape.

Fat. Grease. Dripping. Lard. It's all those fry-ups. All that chip-fat. Fried bread. It's all inside you, congealing there. Clogging up your internal organs with glutinous sludge. Gloopy putrid tides of it damming up your veins. Waxy layers silting up your arteries. Until there's nowhere else for it to go and so it's forcing its way outwards, towards the surface. Oozing through the pores in insistent yellow eruptions of pus. But how to stop it going in? She fries it up. You shovel it down. That's the way it works. Tell Mam...? You can rehearse the reaction. She'd be offended. "Oh, what I do's not good enough for you, is it? What's wrong with it all of a sudden?" Worse, she'd mock, make stupid embarrassing jokes about it. "Too much fat? Causing spots? Oh, Derek's becoming so particular about his appearance. Must be a girl involved. Who is this girl you fancy, Derek? Is that what it's all about?" And Auntie Jean, chipping in, "He's getting sensitive, as sure as eggs is eggs. That's hormones he's going through, not your cooking. You mark my words."

He looks again, scrutinises the pattern of erupting spots down the left side of his face, the couple on his chin, the few on his right side cheek. At first it doesn't connect. Something vital. Something significant. Then it does. Yes, the conclusion was inescapable. He paces back across the landing to his bedroom to retrieve the page. No mistake. The flecks of sunspots exactly chart the formations of acne on his face. Each and every one matches. He stands there with his mouth hung open. "Catching flies?" his mother said. What does it mean? It means nothing. How could it? Derek slopes shiftily to the dark descending stair-well, down through the eerily quiet house to the kitchen, and the smell of the previous evening's frying. The kitchen is painted dark green. With the pots sided, the big table is covered by a dark green crushed velour tablecloth. There are usually dishes in the sink festering as dawn-light plays over them, a chip-pan eternally full of congealing fat on the stove. An ancient wind-down wooden clothes-rack hanging by its system of pulleys from the ceiling, draped with discoloured underclothes, the mangle stowed in the corner, and a half-empty bottle of milk on the side-board, its silver-paper cap depressed out of shape, then replaced.

He stands still. Momentarily distracted. He reaches out to snick the radio on. The sound is blurred. Unfocussed. He spins the tuning. Stations flick by. The glimpse of a tune. A foreign voice. Then a calm news announcer riding the static-storm, "a freak outbreak of sunspot activity is thought to be responsible for the widespread interference affecting wireless and television reception. Experts today gave assurances that this, as well as the unseasonably warm weather will not persist..." before he, too, is submerged in distortion. Derek stares at the radio, willing the voice to re-emerge. It doesn't.

At length, his attention crawls along the work surface to the right of the wireless. There. That's what he needs. There are collectible cards in the tea packets, plastic submarines powered by baking-powder in the cornflakes, a white tornado in the scullery and... yes, matches. He slides the box open. Tips the few matches out into the trash. Half-a-dozen of them are dead. Why does she do that? Why does she stick the dead matches back into the box so you think there are more in there than there are? From the kitchen, gripping the box tight, he hares back up the stairs to his room. He's still there. Chespius. Trapped in circles and mounds of pillow. He uses the page from *National Geographic* to shepherd the louse into the matchbox. Snap it shut. He holds it up. Listens. He can hear the scrabbling. He peeps in. It's there. Snaps it shut again. As an additional precaution he folds the stolen magazine-page carefully around the box, into a kind of parcel, tight enough to provide camouflage, loose enough to allow Chespius to breath. Around the sides of the parcel the blazing coronal loops bend in around the creased planes of space. With the pattern of sunspots going from two to multiple dimensions. Altering the fabric of space-time. Finally, he hides the box in the bottom draw of his sideboard.

Each morning, Derek moves into the hallway, to where his bicycle relaxes against the grey wall, reflected by the large mirror in front of which – sometimes, he poses or pulls faces. A racing job with three-speed gears and turned-down handle-bars turned upwards in a gesture of defiant oddness. Although second-hand, it was still in good nick. He'd retrieve his newspaper sack from its place of concealment in the drawer beneath the mirror. It smells of newsprint, twine, and several other indecipherables. Depending on the time of year, as he emerges, pushing the bike, it would be dark, perhaps sultry with fallen rain, or grey with drizzle, or with sunrise just emerging, casting tall true shadows across the road from the park, stirring a thunderhead of clouds up into a vulgar morass of anaemic ochre. This morning is strange. So strange he pauses for a moment to watch it. A morning sky on fire from one side to the other. A huge flattened oval sun igniting cloud-stratum into rich layers of luminous gold. A warm humid sky... He might be a French Resistance Fighter, carrying messages of Allied liberation through sleeping Paris on the look-out for Nazi soldiers. Or the lone survivor of a nuclear holocaust setting out on an odyssey of exploration. Other times he's too tired to bother with fantasy, and merely moves out past the overgrown garden, lifting the sneck and out through the weary broken-hinged gate, peddling easily across the pavement, to bump down the kerb.

The Newsagent is about a quarter-of-a-mile away, across the park everyone calls the "rec". There's a path through the centre of the Park, a gradual rise made up of loose gravel the colour of nicotine sieved through dirty moonlight. It hisses beneath the tyre-spin. Sometimes, after night-rain, the pebbles glisten like fine gems, but when disturbed by the bicycle-tyre, you see their undersides are still dry. During autumn the morning path is covered by a slick layer of leaves that smell of slimy green wetnesses, and Derek dismounts to carefully remove snails from the path to rescue them from crushing feet. But other mornings he stands on them himself, feeling his weight on them, tensing the slight resistance, then the cracking open and small eruptions of green bubbling intestines. Or he might find himself riding over an abandoned condom, telling intimate tales of the previous evening. Now, he's almost midway across the rec when there's a sound, and movement in the trees. He looks up. At first the sky is too bright. even this early, to see. A dark intertwine of gaudy foliage etched deepest-green, yet glistening like a myriad prisms, near-black against it. But there are birds chattering and bickering at each other. A whirl of hummingbirds flickering across the gaps. Play-fighting in bursts of colour and long drapes of tail-feathers. He pauses the bike, leans up with one foot on the ground, and squints to see. Sitting alone straddled on the bike, he can see himself mirrored in the sky above, as though it's reflecting him, echoing back to him. And between him on the ground, and his reflection in the sky, there are shimmers of green birds with brilliant cockades. Curved beaks. Vivid blue birds with golden crests. Parrots? Parakeets? Surely not. Something deliciously and delicately gaudy escaped from the tropical gardens?

Something is not right. Back the way he'd come, at the ornate black-painted wrought-iron entrance gate there's a visitor's map of the rec. The coloured areas of the map faded into pale ghosts designating play-areas, pathways and lake. The glass mildewed and the wood-frame holding it in place moistly rotting. But he holds that map in the front of his mind. Laying it over the oddness he can see around him. This shingle path should continue in a slow upward curve between narrow sickly flowerbeds, through this elevated neck where this grove of trees marks out a kind of passageway between low walls intended to resemble the ornamental ruins of a castle, and then down a gradual dip to skirt – on one side, the artificial lake bordered by shrubs and rockery, and on the other by tennis courts encircled by high mesh fences, and further, to the far outer park gates. Adjacent to the gates there's a mysterious brick building on one side that no-one ever seems to use, and a brick-built turret on the other, a "folly". A lay-out so familiar it scarcely needs to register. Yet today, it was not as it should be. Today, it has an unfamiliar strangeness about it that he can't define. His right-upper side teeth wince a warning.

He freewheels through the narrow bottleneck between low walls mock-crenellated into ornamental castle ruins. The stonework is scuffed and tufted with dandelions, stones missing where kids have scrabbled intent on burrowing tunnel-ways through the dry scrubby bushes. Out the other side of the vermilion tunnel, looking down from the slight elevation, the grass – surely it still is grass? – has become green glass spurs in a ceaseless play of light. The huge flattened oval sun suffocating the sky igniting it all with a luminous quality. In its glow of pulsing light he can see Jurassic ferns and snarling vegetation. As though the colour-contrast on the TV has been turned up too high. He can see the tennis courts over to the left, but his attention is dragged sideways to the lake. There are dark shapes rippling through its usually sluggish water, and the surface glows as if hit by a vivid sunrise, or else reflecting some raging fire. Yet there's no raging fire, only the vivid morning sky ablaze from one side to the other. As he watches, something that might be a bird flits low across the sky-stained water, its jewelled wings almost brushing the still surface. And something beneath the surface quivers and moves in response to its darting shadow. The water smashes open and great snapping jaws rear up, spraying green slime and splinters of flashing light. The bird-thing dances aside with contemptuous grace, zips away, climbing clear, and circles back upwards towards the trees.

There's a comic-strip he'd once read, in which aliens from a super-hot world use a giant projector on an asteroid base to disrupt and intensify solar activity, raising the global temperature, adjusting Earth to super-hot conditions more to their liking, enabling them to take over. It's something like that. But it's also like, yes, that's it, it's like JG Ballard's *The Crystal World* where the trees begin to petrify into glittering jewels, yet simultaneously they're also awaking into new mineralised life-forms. In much the same way the "rec" has transmogrified into a garden of infinitely-coloured delight. A place where sprays of grass and spectral foliage in whorls and spirals of stone move like water over sand, stirred by the breeze. Where alligators with eyes of blind opals slip-slither beneath the glittering skin of dark water where more usually boys launch sailboats and girls feed bread to the ducks. Where a shrill chorus from jewelled birds

29

posed like heraldic designs chime in spasms of lyrical wonder. It's dazzling, entrancing, and he's both dazzled and entranced.

The world is changing. Stuff is happening. Strange stuff. Weird stuff with knobs on. It had begun when he stole those pages from *National Geographic* magazine in the Dentist's Waiting Room. Complicated by the appearance of Chespius. "Handramit!", a cuss-word he'd picked up from the CS Lewis book *Out Of Silent Planet*. Descending the slope he veers reassuringly close to the high mesh tennis court fences to where the path passes between the mysterious square building and the brick-built mock-turret, through the ornate black-painted wrought-iron gate. With an overwhelming sense of relief he skirts the gates to pedal into the main road. Warily, he glances left and right. Everything normal. A milk-float scurries, and the shops are still black-windowed in sleep. Five minutes down the road there's a light in the shop on the corner. In the window there are colour weekly magazines, comics, love-stories in pictures, and a brief selection of garish paperbacks.

Three bikes already there. Derek props his against the plate-glass, although he's been told repeatedly not to. As he does so, he can see his ghost-reflection in the shop-front. Only half-real. "Like I'm fading. Like I'm not quite here at all. Like I'm leaking away into some lost phantom-zone, becoming detached from the world." Into a doorway adjacent to the shop, he passes through a dark passage to where a fire-escape descends from the rented rooms above, and where occasionally flooding pipes empty water into mysterious grates. In the yard behind the shop is a lean-to piled high with boxes, stencilled with product-names and stuffed with bits of string, paper-clips, swept-up dust from the shop, and remaindered copies of last week's magazines. There's also a chipped and worn counter moved out from the shop during renovation, now used by Mr Clifford to arrange newspapers into separate piles for separate paper-rounds. As the kids wait, every now and then he pauses to slick vagrant strands of greased and slicked-back hair from his face, into place.

Derek waits his turn, sitting on the pile of boxes, reading a thumbed *Tit-Bits*. He speaks little, regarding the paper-girl with a kind of scared awe. She swears so expertly, and there are countless stories of furtive explorations. And two boys, both older – and bigger – than he is. He's vaguely intimidated by it all. "That's Derek, bet he's so scared he even looks under the bed before he gets in." "Naw. He always sleeps on the floor. Can't stand heights." At last he retreats back down the passage to his bike, bulging paper-bag across his shoulder, to mount, and wobble away at an angle to balance the unevenly-distributed load, or leaning it on the cross-bar sagging. Derek works a round of about two-hundred houses, in strict sequence. Down Regency Street, across Victoria Terrace, Victoria Avenue and Victoria Road, down Argyle Street and Hampden Villas into Park Square where he completes the round, and is within easy distance from home. A wide arc taking him around the outer perimeter of the rec. His eyes stray nervously to the house roof-tops, expecting at any moment to see eruptions of tropical birds rising from the transfiguring landscape that must, even now, be continuing, becoming more extreme. How can the Park-keepers deal with such changes? How will the world adapt? At intervals he pauses, rests his bicycle against a wall to glance through a paper before sliding it into a letter-box. Speed-reading lurid political scandal and diplomatic confrontations, reports of unseasonably warm weather causing heatstroke, and a girl in a swimsuit saying "Phew", industrial unrest, space-shots, adverts, juvenile delinquency, and cartoons strips of varying degrees of interest.

As he heads home, in an orbit around the rec, he has to cross the railway bridge. Steeling himself to gawp over the parapet at the metallic scrawls stretching away beneath a morning sky that's on fire from one side to the other. His right-upper side tooth winces a warning. He prods at it in nervous preoccupation. The huge flattened fried-egg sun is igniting a quivering haze over an expanding flood that had begun as little more than an insubstantial shimmer of water. It's now a lagoon. A tropical lagoon. As he watches more intently he can see the shapes of the tall birds stalking through its glistening inflamed sheen with elongated legs, they are not herons, but flamingos. Pink clouds of them. Rippling and rising into the air, circling, and alighting again to stab with long beaks.

Something must be done. The world is changing, overheating, a configuration of ingredients triggered when he stole that solar page from *National Geographic*. Then the discovery that the sun-spot formation matches his acne-pattern. Then the appearance of Chespius. But how to correct the situation? How

31

to make it come right? It was his actions responsible for setting these events in motion. He was guilty. He had to pay the price. There's only one way. A ritual incineration, a sacrificial offering. The package must be burned. The stolen solar photos now folded in around the matchbox, with Chespius within. All must burn. The pages charred into a swarm of fireflies. The ashes of the sun drifting like strange black snow. There's no other way.

The house is stirring. The fug of cigarette smoke already coiling. He pauses to get a glass of water from the kitchen, in case the funeral pyre gets out of control, then sidles up the stairs avoiding Mother and Aunt. This mission is too urgent for distraction. Into his room. The bottom drawer of his sideboard. The matchbox. "Chespius." Has he managed to escape? If so, how could he have managed to do it? Sometimes creatures have supernatural powers. How else...? What if the box is empty...? He folds the incriminating paper back, slides it open, and peeps in. No, Chespius is there. But rolled into a tight hard ball. Derek pokes it. No response. No movement. No uncoil of legs and hair-fine mandibles. Nothing. He rolls the ball around the inside of the box. Dead. Probably the immense wrap-around solar heat has sucked all the oxygen from the confined space, and he's suffocated. He'd not thought of that. He should have anticipated it.

What now? His tooth stabs unhelpfully. He sits for a long moment. Large plate-lipped mouth hung open. Staring into space. Catching flies. Him. The matchbox containing the wood-louse corpse. The folded solar page. The glass of water. The global crisis engulfing the planet. He looks from the matchbox, to the water, to the page. From the dead bug, to the page, to the water, to the matchbox. The solution is obvious. It's here. Staring him in the face. This is what he must do. There's no other way. A digestive penance. He picks up the page. Looks at the beautiful clarity of the sun, the freckling of sunspots erupting down its right side, a contagion across the bottom curve, a few climbing its left side. A choreography of acne. A mystic pattern with a terrible significance. He holds the page in both hands. Then begins tearing it into thin strips. Carefully rolls each strip into a ball. He rolls Chespius into an identically-sized worldlet of paper. Encloses them all in the matchbox, and shuffles it up and down, then left to right, hearing the soft spheres moving inside like colliding planets. Shuffling them. Then he retrieves them from the matchbox, and swallows them, gagging and retching, one by one, washed down with gulps of luke-warm water. The third one crunches unpleasantly with a faint taint of dry foulness. He feels sick. An urge to vomit it all back. At last he drains the glass. His stomach protests.

He sits still for as long as he dares. Doubling up in sudden stabs of pain as tides of digestive juice deluges leaping coronal solar flares in the depths of his gut. Feverish sweat breaks out across his forehead as the spasms intensify and contract. Digesting the sun. Digesting Chespius. But the next thing he does will be even harder. The next thing he does will determine if his scheme has worked. If his digestive tract has saved the world. Or if everything he knows and holds familiar will gradually warm up, through tropical, becoming unbearably hot as the sun-spot infestation destabilises the sun into nova. As his face erupts in reflecting patterns of spots, both answering and charting the outbreak. Until it all ignites and incandesces into blazing supernova ripping the solar system apart.

He steels himself to look out of the window. Terrified of what he might see…

BLACK SHEEP
Gary Fry

"I'm just a bit... nervous, that's all," said Billy, and his girlfriend pulled one of her faces.

He knew Trudy could be moody at times, and during the six weeks they'd been going out together, he'd learnt how to keep her on the right side of petulant. But this latest request – a meal with her parents at their house the following evening – had taken him by surprise, and he'd struggled to avoid upsetting her.

"But I come round here all the time," she said, waving an arm vaguely around his bedroom. Her saw her breasts jiggle beneath her tight top – at just seventeen, she was noticeably endowed – and this helped overcome his reservations. After all, he didn't want to risk losing Trudy to any other lad at sixth form college, did he?

"Okay, okay, I'll come," he said, shuffling a little closer on his bed and putting one arm around her shoulders. "But you have to give me another snog first."

"You're such a bad un, Billy," she replied, but was smiling in a way that suggested she hadn't meant it.

The bedsprings made loud noises as they groped and fondled. Billy squirmed and hoped his parents watching telly downstairs couldn't hear. He was used to being treated with disdain, while his younger sister Martine – out working and bringing money into the house – could do no wrong. "The bad un," he'd often been called, or sometimes the "black sheep of the family." But he didn't care about that. As soon as he'd got his A-levels and then a job, he was out of here, seeking new horizons. *Hasta la vista*, Mum, Dad and baby sis', cos you ain't gonna see me for dust.

He hoped Trudy would become part of those plans, and this was why he must get over his reticence about visiting her house tomorrow night. Before absconding with their daughter, he'd have to put in a good performance with her parents, showing he wasn't as dubious as he was often made to feel by his own.

He didn't know much about his girlfriend's home life, and

when, later that evening, he walked her back to the end of her street, it felt inappropriate to ask about it. He'd find out more the following day. He arranged to meet Trudy after college, kissed her on the lips (this was as far as they'd gone, but Billy was definitely working on that), and then watched her slender backside wiggle away through her clean neighbourhood, whose houses were all neat, attractive semis.

By contrast, his own street was flanked by grubby terraces and always littered. He sometimes found it hard to believe that Trudy found him desirable enough to date, but he supposed he was big, and he'd been told by other girls that he was "cute." Not that any member of his family agreed. As soon as he walked back inside that evening, they were on to him.

His dad, out of work, produced a wedge of cash Billy's sister had contributed from her wage this week. "At least one of you isn't a drain on the household," he said, his tone undeniably scornful.

"Oh, leave him alone, Keith," Mum added, her voice weary from a latest shift cleaning a local pub and all the cigarettes she smoked. The air in the lounge was thick with nicotine; Billy used his arms to cut a route to the foot of the staircase.

"That's right, you lazy runt," Dad called after him, searching for the TV remote-control unit on a couch smothered in scrunched up beer cans and a tabloid newspaper. "You go and take it easy. I mean, all that groping takes it out on a man."

"I'm going to do my homework," Billy replied, but knew as soon as he'd spoken that this was unlikely to impress his uneducated parents.

"We didn't need no education to get on in life," Mum said, and if there was any trace of maternal affection in her tone, it was quickly superseded by occupational bitterness. Then she added to her husband, "I suppose he thinks he's better than us now."

"I don't doubt that for a second, love." Dad had now located the remote-control unit and used it to turn over the set to catch the beginning of a Reality TV show. "Still, why the 'ell should we expect owt else?"

His heart aching, Billy left them and went upstairs.

Martine was there, hogging the bathroom as usual.

"Hurry up, Mart', I need a piss," Billy called through the closed door, having tried the handle and finding it locked.

"Sod off, Billy," his sister's voice came from inside, no less dismissive than their parents' had been. "I've been working. I'm filthy. I need a bath. And... I'm having one."

"But... but..."

"Why don't you go round your posh bird's house and use her bog? I bet she has two – one downstairs and one upstairs."

"I've been invited there tomorrow, as it happens," Billy replied, but kept his voice low as he paced back into his bedroom and quietly closed the door.

He stepped across to the mirror hanging in one corner and examined himself from head to toe, marvelling at how large he'd grown lately, developing a chiselled jawbone and dark, wavy hair. He was good looking, as many girls seemed to confirm. Maybe this would be his way out of such a squalid life. Perhaps he and Trudy could move away together, go to university or maybe another town and get jobs, start a new life, all unhindered by familial strains...

But he was making an assumption about Trudy's parents and any siblings she might have. She might even enjoy a happy home life, even though in Billy's admittedly brief experience, a happy family was like oral sex: everyone knew it existed but few got to participate in it.

He caught himself smiling in the mirror. It was good to keep a sense of humour about how he was treated by the three people who ought to love him most. But... something else was involved here, something he didn't quite understand. Then his smile faltered in the glass. Confused by what he only intuited, he stepped away and removed his textbooks to do more work for his A-levels. Maybe if he studied hard enough, acquiring knowledge in the process, he'd be able to figure out problems like this.

He tried doing so until he got tired. Later, after using the bathroom, he was typically ignored by all his family going to bed. But for the first time ever, something troubled him here, and when he checked his appearance in his mirror a final time, he saw little sign of the smile he'd always worn.

*

The following day, Billy attended college classes in English Literature and Psychology. In the first lecture, he and fellow pupils (including Trudy) discussed *To Kill a Mockingbird*. But despite a fondness for reading fiction (another reason his family disliked him), Billy was more interested in his other class.

This week the lecturer discussed in-group and out-group psychology, how people resorted to a mental process called "projection" to feel morally superior to others. This issue resonated with Billy, who'd been working lately on an essay with the same theme. He'd drawn on a lot of anecdotal evidence, but his tutor had said it ought to be supported by published literature. This had frustrated Billy – after all, what could be truer than real life? – but he'd acquiesced. He was determined to do all he could to get the highest grades possible.

At the end of the day, he'd become so absorbed in his thoughts that he'd almost forgotten where he had to go next. But Trudy, approaching him in the library, reminded him about that.

"You ready?" she asked, hugging him from behind.

He turned in his chair and must have conceded a reluctant glance, because then she grew petulant.

"You don't *have* to come," she added, giving him no chance to prepare a better response, let alone utter one. Then she gazed across the library, at another boy studying at a desk. The boy looked up and smiled… but then glanced away when he saw Billy also staring, with anger now on his face.

Billy turned to Trudy, threw his textbooks into his bag, and said, "Sure, let's go."

He'd just pictured his home and how unwelcome he was always made to feel there. Surely going to Trudy's place could be no worse than that, even if her parents turned out to be – as he half-feared – judgemental ogres. His girlfriend was all smiles and sparkling eyes as they left the building and strolled towards a bus stop. Once the bus arrived, they travelled through busy streets, drizzly and dark in the encroaching autumn. Billy hardly spoke, just kept reassuring hold of one of Trudy's hands, as if her presence lent him support for what would follow.

They alighted at the end of her street, five minutes' walk from his own. Now the thought of heading back there – to his private bedroom, if nowhere else – was even more tempting, but when Trudy threatened a sulk again, Billy accompanied her towards her house, in full view of anyone who cared to glance out through the front window.

But nobody appeared, allowing him and Trudy to advance up a wide driveway bearing a large saloon that ticked and cooled in the crisp evening. Trudy's dad must have just got back from work, Billy decided, sensing his heart rate ascend to unprecedented speed. Then they were at the front door, his girlfriend was opening it, and he was shepherded inside. After passing along a finely decorated hallway, they entered an equally stylish lounge, where a man and a woman were seated in leather chairs, each rather pert in posture, as if they'd been awaiting his arrival with the same kind of apprehension he now suffered.

"Mum, Dad, I'd like you to meet…" Trudy began, gripping his hand with obvious possessiveness, "… I'd like you to meet Billy."

"Hello there," said the man, a slightly balding, stocky guy in his late-thirties; he was dressed in the kind of suit Billy always imagined were worn by officious people: accountants, bankers or surveyors. He rose from his chair with mechanical promptness, occupying the pause left by his daughter's introduction with measured efficiency. Then he held out one hand for a shake, and Billy had little option but to take it, pump the arm inside the pinstriped jacket, and at last burble a reply.

"Nice to meet you, sir. And thanks for inviting me for tea… ah, I mean, dinner."

He'd made a bit of a mess of that, but this didn't trouble the grinning man. "Think nothing of it, young man. Besides, it isn't me you should thank. Allow me to introduce my better half. She's doing the cooking this evening. Me, I just toil at my desk believing that food on the table and clean laundry occurs by magic."

Billy reckoned his own dad also believed in such domestic conjurers… But then his attention was diverted to the short, attractive woman who'd just risen from the chair opposite her husband's. It was hard to believe the two of them had produced anybody as voluptuous as Trudy, but short of requesting a DNA test, Billy would have to accept it. A mental image of the act of coitus – the man still dressed in his responsible suit while his wife carried out housework – almost made him snigger as he shook the woman's hand. But he controlled himself enough to say, "Hi."

"Very nice to meet you," said Trudy's mum, and now that all the formalities were dealt with, Billy began to relax.

The woman – Polly, she was called – had soon retreated to the kitchen, and her husband – Alan – was fetching Billy a coke. Billy paced the lounge, relaxing more with every moment he survived in this strangers' home. Trudy had nipped upstairs, presumably to visit the toilet, and now, in the Sherlockian manner he'd acquired from books, Billy had chance to observe a few things about the family.

A few personal photographs were on display: his girlfriend at various stages of her upbringing, with pigtails and freckles, in leotard and leggings, on roller-blades and a bicycle. There were also several pictures of Polly and Alan, including one from their wedding where both appeared rather more satisfied than ecstatic (but at least – unlike in similar shots of his own parents' nuptials – they were clearly sober). No siblings were on display, and so Trudy must be, as Billy had suspected, an only child.

Alan reappeared, carrying a glassful of liquid that gurgled like an external representation of Billy's empty stomach. Having avoided food most of the day through anxiety, he now had a keen appetite. But that was when he was distracted by a number of amateurish paintings hanging on each wall. They weren't very good, and Billy was wondering whether they'd been executed by a family member Polly and Alan had refused to offend when Alan read his mind.

"I see you're admiring the artwork," he said, handing over the drink and then standing beside him to gaze at several poor framed efforts. One was a landscape, maybe the Yorkshire Dales, but its perspective was skewed and sheep in the fields looked like displaced clouds.

"They're... interesting," Billy replied, and that was all he felt up to. Tact had never been his forte.

But then Alan shared his secret. "I've never had a lesson in my life. It just comes naturally."

So he was the artist. It was good that Billy had reserved his judgement. He sipped from his drink, using the glass to mask unease on his face, but that was when Trudy reappeared and then Polly's voice summoned them elsewhere. "It's ready!"

Billy's girlfriend led him to the kitchen, the self-proclaimed master of oils and watercolours creeping along in tow. At the heart of this new room was a dining table, each place set with plates, cutlery, glasses and napkins. The napkins were white, like fleshless bone.

Billy was encouraged to sit with his back to the entrance, and the family gathered around him. A bowl of salad lay at the heart of the table, boasting tongs for tossing and oil for taste. Billy hoped something more substantial would be on offer and wasn't disappointed when Polly dropped the oven door to produce a tray of items she promptly brought across. These were kebabs on skewers… *Kebabs on skewers*, Billy thought with great hunger. *Result!*

After a little small-talk as everyone tucked in, Billy made some complimentary noises about the hospitality. He was feeling confident and wondered why he'd been worried about coming here. Trudy's parents seemed friendly and well-balanced, especially compared to his own unhinged folks.

"This is lovely, Polly," he said, after chewing another piece of meat from its hot skewer. "I hope you don't mind me asking, but is the meat cooked in a particular way?"

Perhaps he really meant to ask whether it been prepared in something other than a microwave or a frying pan. That was how all the food at his house was cooked, after all. But he remained silent as Polly, perhaps a little self-consciously, started to speak.

"It's been roasted in its own juices, Billy. The peppers give it zest." She hesitated, glanced at her husband, and then added, "But I don't mind telling you what the real secret is."

"Oh, come on, Mum," Trudy said, but her voice was amused. "A secret's no longer a secret if it's revealed, is it?"

"Don't be a prude, Trude," said Alan, and although Billy had expected him to be playful, it was disconcerting to realise that the man had sounded serious, as if rebuking the girl for some misdemeanour.

Billy returned his attention to Polly who, clearly perturbed by her husband's response, added more. "The secret is that the meat isn't mutton. In fact, it's…" She paused again, presumably for dramatic purposes, but then finished, "… it's goat."

Billy suspected that Polly had just prevented an escalating disagreement between Trudy and her dad, a habitual act of peacekeeping. The room grew silent… but then, maybe from a

40

room upstairs, a muffled sound of whimpering could be heard.

Was a pet in the building, possibly locked in a bedroom? But this thought did little to untangle the confusion mounting in Billy's mind.

"Goat?" he asked, an image of his family and the way he'd always been treated entering his mind. But he'd always been considered the black *sheep* of the family, hadn't he? Maybe he was getting confused by so many references to animals. Polly had mentioned mutton earlier, and although the meat most likely to come from a sheep was lamb, but she hadn't said that. Billy's scotched expectations might have resulted in these jumbled thoughts. Perhaps his textbooks could help him make sense of this, but not right now. He had to negotiate the curiously darkening episode.

"Yes, goat," Alan replied, and after gazing severely at his wife and daughter, he took another bite of this charred animal. Then, after swallowing and switching his attention to Billy, he added in a voice whose flinty tone was palpable, "Anyway, young man, you never told me when I asked. What did you think of my paintings in the lounge?"

At that moment, Billy dropped a piece of meat from his skewer. It fell into the white napkin he'd draped across his lap before starting to eat. The diversion gave him chance to think, and he took a while to retrieve the errant food on his lap. But after returning it to his plate, Alan's sustained stare forced him to respond to his question.

"Well..." Billy began, but his unease was clearly detected by Polly, who perhaps realised what a terrible artist her husband was. She smiled behind a glass of fruit juice as Billy mumbled, "... like I said, they're very... very..."

But before he could finish, Alan wrestled control of the discussion. "I've been painting for over *twenty* years, ever since my wife first got *pregnant*," he explained, and the emphasis he'd added to two key words made Billy realise that Alan had also noticed Polly's suppressed mirth.

Then Trudy intervened. "Do we have to discuss this?" When nobody replied, she turned to her mum. "Oh, *him* again. Always *him*."

She sounded as unhappy as her dad had grown, and at first Billy assumed she was sparing their guest from witnessing such family tension. But then he seized upon a troubling observation. Alan had claimed to have been painting for over twenty years, ever since Polly had first got pregnant. But whatever link there was between these facts – perhaps becoming a father had limited the time he'd had to practice his craft – it was secondary to another concern: Trudy was only seventeen years old. And so why had Alan said *twenty*?

Maybe the man had just chosen a random figure, a way of overdramatizing his point. He certainly had some issue with his wife. Billy saw how Alan looked at her, as if resenting her for ruining something he might otherwise have found fulfilling. But if that involved their only child – Trudy – why didn't he express similar resentment towards the girl?

It was too puzzling and unsettling to figure out, and Billy was relieved when Alan, after finishing the third of his kebabs, lifted his napkin, tossed it on the table, and then said stiffly, "Please excuse me." Moments later, he got up and backed away from the table, his arms snapping around his back. In his peripheral vision, Billy saw only a blur as the man swept out of the kitchen, into the hallway, and started thumping up the staircase.

Could Alan be envious of the attention Billy had given Polly's cooking after he'd ignored his artwork? Billy considered such a reaction childish, but nonetheless entertained it as a likely explanation for all he'd witnessed. But if that was true, what did Polly's pregnancy have to do with it? And why had Billy's girlfriend also grown churlish?

Just then, Billy heard another noise from elsewhere in the property. He'd thought the sound he'd detected earlier belonged to an animal, and this one left him in no doubt that it was something alive. He turned away, his unfinished kebabs shifting on his plate as he accidentally nudged the table. Then he listened more carefully to what sounded like a muffled expression of pain…

Trudy caught his gaze and then, smiling archly, said to both him and her mother, "Please excuse me, too."

Billy's girlfriend climbed from her chair, lifting her napkin without setting it on the table. Then, carrying it with her towards the hallway steps, she ascended with the same rigid determination her dad had demonstrated minutes ago.

Now Billy was alone with Polly, who had her eyes downturned. She'd plucked a toothpick from a receptacle beside the salad bowl and was rolling it between one finger and thumb. She looked as if she wanted the evening to end, her lips curled with what looked like frustration.

Once Billy had watched her for several seconds, perhaps prompting an explanation, she said, "They've never come to terms with it, either of them." Her voice was low and bitter, her eyes still tilted away from him. "Alan is resentful because he never had chance to fulfil what he considers his potential. And as for Trudy, well, she tries hard at school, but… but she was never as good as…"

Before she could finish, more footsteps pounded the stairs behind Billy. Then he turned again to detect who now approached in this domestic asylum. From his eye corners, he noticed a vague image in the hall, but that was when he noticed something alarming elsewhere. Although each diner had been served three kebabs earlier, Alan's plate now bore only *two* skewers.

That was when the man returned and sat down in his seat. His face looked less burdened than it had before his departure several minutes ago. Nevertheless, with inexplicable fright, Billy observed that he hadn't returned the errant skewer.

Billy snatched his gaze away, hearing more sounds from behind him. Moments later, he saw Trudy calmly retake her seat, also conceding less unease than she had earlier. It was as if whatever she and her dad had done upstairs had rendered them as affable as they'd been after Billy's arrival. Then Billy noticed that Trudy had failed to bring back her napkin.

What was likely to happen next? Was Billy expected to say something now? He was the veteran of many similar, if admittedly less surreal, encounters at his own home and had certainly developed a thick enough skin to deal with them. Then he drew breath and said, "I really enjoyed that meal. Thank you very much."

"Glad to oblige, son," Alan replied, his voice cheerful, as if his palpable resentment earlier had been the behaviour of another man.

"Mum is a domestic goddess," Trudy added, and then turned to Polly, perhaps hoping her reluctance to defend the woman earlier against her dad's envy could be repaired with this comment.

But Billy thought too much damage had been done. Indeed, seconds later, Polly stood from the table and, still holding that toothpick between finger and thumb, glanced at Billy. "You're a fine young man," she said, and then burst into tears as she left the room and stumped upstairs, from where Billy heard – he was certain now – *human* sounds of suffering.

"Let's return to the lounge and have some fun," said Alan, as if his wife hadn't just left the room in a flood of tears.

"Yes, *let's*," Trudy replied, and before Billy could agree or disagree – in truth, he wanted to leave and figure out what the hell was going on – he was shepherded back through to the living room as father and daughter conspired to draw him into their giddiness.

After a few minutes' merriment followed by curt enquiries into Billy's ambitions and scholastic potential, Polly reappeared. She'd cleaned herself up, almost certainly in the first floor bathroom. Her face was delicately powdered, her eyes dry, and she was grinning broadly. Then she slotted her comments into the unfolding conversation, as if she, her husband and daughter were a perfect family at play.

It didn't immediately occur to Billy to wonder what had happened to the toothpick Polly had been holding earlier and had taken upstairs… But after a tricky discussion about his own family, the issue was thrust into Billy's mind when he realised that he needed to use the toilet.

When Billy asked where the bathroom was, Alan said in a firm voice, "At the top of the steps, first *right*."

"Yes, right and *not* left," added Trudy, her tone as edgy as the cry of a new-born child.

And then, as if the comment underlined these weird instructions Polly finished, "We're in the process of… *revisions* up there."

But the word she'd used emphatically only made Billy feel even more apprehensive about going upstairs. If Polly had simply meant they were in the process of renovating a spare room and was self-conscious about how it looked, why hadn't she used the word "decorating"?

As Billy left the room – mindful of three pairs of eyes

44

watching – his thoughts returned to his concern during the meal. Why had Alan said twenty years when the seventeen since his daughter's birth was more accurate? The lack of mementoes in the lounge suggested that Trudy was an only child, and so might Polly have once suffered a miscarriage? Was this the thing her husband had never "come to terms with"? But that didn't make sense, because Polly had told Billy that her daughter had also yet to get used to this mysterious event. And what about the talk concerning Alan not fulfilling his potential and Trudy trying hard at school without being as good as –

After reaching the landing, Billy heard the same sound he'd detected downstairs... only louder now.

And it was coming from his *left*.

He glanced that way and saw only a shut door along the hallway, as quiet as a coffin's lid. From behind it, however, there came a soft moaning sound. Billy crept closer, cocking his ear that way. The noise was unsettling because it hinted at either something – a dog, perhaps – or someone being in pain. He briefly entertained the possibility of a person hidden deliberately out of view... but then realised he was being ridiculous. Then he retreated, turned right this time, and entered the bathroom.

After urinating, he examined himself in the mirror hanging on the wall. He recalled observing his expression last night, in the privacy of his bedroom, in what now felt like a comparatively uncomplicated house. His family was unkind and projected their failings onto him, but he could at least *understand* them. But in *this* family, he had to make a mental leap to assimilate its bizarre *mores*... Stepping away from the mirror, he realised that the smile he'd worn the previous evening had finally been erased. He was getting older now, and learning new things about life. The truth hit him the way the notion of death had when he'd been a little younger.

And then, after exiting the bathroom, he heard that moaning sound again, coming from behind the door at the end of the hall passage.

A quick look inside the room wouldn't hurt anyone, would it? Billy was interested in psychology, and thought he might pursue a career in a related profession. Satisfying his curiosity by establishing what made this family tick would be good for his studies, as well as his current anxiousness.

He paced forwards, reaching out for the door's handle.

Goat, he reflected, the thought prompting further recollections about the meal he'd suffered earlier and its weird rancour.

Then he turned the handle and pushed open the door.

Inside it was pitch-dark. The curtains at the rear were tugged laxly together, allowing a little moonlight to animate the figure in the room as much as the landing lamp behind Billy. At first he saw only a number of discarded photographs scattered across the threadbare carpet – each displayed a boy growing up to eventually become a bright-eyed young man – and a series of school certificates, all celebrating impressive academic achievements. Then, as Billy took one pace aside, the glow from the hallway illuminated more of the figure, bringing it into sharp focus.

It was a young man, and he was naked. He'd been tied by wire to a metal framework that held him rigidly upright. When he spotted Billy, his sluggish eyelids flickered, the pupils seeming to dilate. Billy tried to keep looking at the young man's face, but this proved impossible. He was soon forced to glance down and observe what damage his captors had inflicted on him.

There were wounds all over his pale flesh. Perhaps he'd been ensnared up here for years. Bruises and half-healed cuts covered every inch of his body. The kebab skewer that had gone missing from the kitchen when Alan had rushed upstairs was buried in the young man's upper left thigh. Blood wept in a ragged line to the knee, even though most had been soaked up by a napkin that somebody else – Trudy, of course: the victim's younger sister, just as this young man was his attacker's son – had wrapped around the wound.

Maybe the girl had at first wanted to keep her brother quiet by shoving the napkin into his mouth. But then, perceiving the man's unease, she might have had second thoughts. Even so, the victim didn't look as if he minded the pain involved in absorbing his family's projected dismay. When Billy glanced again at his face, he noticed something he hadn't spotted after first seeing him.

A toothpick was pinning together his lips, its points thrust through both wedges of flesh. His mum's domestic skills had certainly been put to good use here. But that similarly didn't appear to trouble this secret family member; he seemed content to do them all a good service.

Indeed, despite the silencing piece of wood, Billy recognised the broad smile on the victim's lips. After all, he'd recently worn an identical one, until he'd realised what damage families could do to a child.

JAMAL COMES HOME
Benedict J. Jones

Carole sat at the table with a glass of vodka and coke close at hand looking as washed out as the underwear hung over the kitchen radiator. The washing up was done but remained on the draining board. Carole looked at it and didn't care. She would put it away later. Where was he? Would he be home tonight?

"Carole?"

She turned, the voice pulling her from her thoughts, and looked at her friend Joan who had placed a hand over hers. Carole had known Joan for most of her life ever since they met at St Joseph's primary school in Dockhead.

"Sorry, Joanie. I was miles away."

Joan's mouth became a thin line and she nodded her head in sympathy.

"Your boy again?"

Carole nodded and she felt the tears well up once more. Sniffing them back she took a deep bite from her drink and then added more vodka. After pushing her stringy bleached blonde hair from her eyes she gestured with her glass to a framed montage of photographs on the kitchen wall showing a mixed race boy and girl in various stages of maturity from nappies to pouting teenage years.

"He's been gone three weeks now. Never been gone this long. Day or two maybe. But he always comes home when he's hungry or needs a bath."

Joan nodded, not mentioning that Jamal, Carole's son, also came back when he needed something to sell for his next pipe.

"They always do, don't they? Look at my boys. Kurt with the little ones and Terry seeing that girl he works with. They turn out alright in the end, Caz. It's just taking Jamal a bit to find out what he wants to do."

Joan made herself another drink.

"Least your lads never got on that stuff like Jamal."

"My two ain't no saints. They gave me their share of grief. Thank god they seem to have grown out of that now."

They sat in silence for a moment and stared at the walls.

"Want one?" asked Joan, offering her menthols across the table.

Carole nodded and then took the spark that Joan offered.

"Where do you think he is?"

There was nothing Carole could say. She shrugged in response and felt the tears come again – this time they could not be sniffed back. Joan's arms went around her and she held her friend close, shushing her as the sobs came loud and rhythmically.

"He'll be back, Caz. He always comes back."

Later, with fresh drinks, they sat; Carole with an eye on the frosted glass window in the front door while Joan played bingo on her 'phone.

"He was never any trouble when he was little."

Joan nodded

"I remember."

"Little sweet heart, no trouble, and then..."

"You seen what's on over at The Lord Nelson Friday night?"

"No, what is it?"

"That psychic, the one Rita told us about, Mrs Shandy."

"Oh, her. Yeah, I remember Rita saying."

"You fancy it then?"

"I couldn't, not with Jamal still out there."

Joan squeezed Carole's shoulder.

"He'll be back whenever he's done what he has to do."

She gave Carole a smile and Carole responded with a nod. Joan tossed back the last of her drink and collected up her 'phone and cigarettes.

"I best be off. I'll see you Friday."

"I'll get you a cab."

"Don't be silly, Caz. It's only across the estate."

"Still you know what it can get like."

"I'll be fine."

When Joan left Carole poured herself another drink and stared at the montage of her children for a long time before going to bed. She left the chain and bolts off the door so that Jamal could come in when he got home.

*

49

It's dark. Feel cold. The hunger's on me, gums itching and it burns behind my eyes. Try to see but there's only black. Want to go home, want to see the light and feel the sun on my face. Score some good shit and let myself feel everything. Don't want to be here.

*

Before the light of dawn coloured the sky over south London Carole was up. She walked around the flat. It didn't take long; her bedroom, bathroom, front room, kitchen and Jamal's room. She stepped inside. Squares in the dust on his side unit showed the ghosts on the television set and stereo he had taken away and sold. Looking inside his wardrobe she found a few cheap well-worn hoodies and jeans he'd bought from the market. It made her think of the days before the pipe when he took such care in how he looked. There were pictures, at least she had those to tell her that her memories were right and he hadn't always been the thing that he had become. She picked up a sweatshirt from the floor and sniffed at it, catching a hint of his scent.

"Come home, Jamal," she whispered.

In the kitchen she put away the dishes and put the kettle on. She checked her 'phone for missed calls and messages. There were none. Carole sighed and waited for the dawn.

The doorbell rang just after nine and Carole scrambled out of her chair. The daylight made it hard to discern the shape beyond the frosted glass. She couldn't keep the smile off her face as she moved towards the door. Silly boy had lost his key again. There was bacon and eggs in the fridge; she'd make him a nice breakfast. Let him have a bath while she cooked it, he'd like that. Carole's mind raced. She pulled the door open and her smile faltered. The man who stood on the landing outside her door was not Jamal; he had the same golden skin her son had once had but his hair was crisply faded, his eyes light where Jamal's were dark, his clothes were clean and expensive, gold glittered at his neck and on his fingers.

"Jamal home?"

Carole shook her head.

The young man shrugged and then barged past her into the

flat.

"He's not here. Get out!"

He turned and looked at her with cold grey eyes. He held her gaze until she looked down at her slippered feet and then put his finger to his lips.

"Hush yourself."

He walked through the flat going room to room and even looking in the wardrobes and under the bed. When he walked back out to Carole in the hallway she found the strength to look at him.

"What do you want?"

He leaned in close and looked her in the eye. He turned his head from side to side as if considering something and then cuffed her across the face with the back of his hand, rings striking the bone of her cheek.

"Your boy owes me money, been ducking me. Best you tell him to come see Two Tone else t'ing ain't gonna be nice, get me? For him or you. I don't see him then I come see you."

Carole nodded, cheek throbbing. The man stepped back over the threshold and walked calmly away down the landing. When he was gone Carole slid down the wall of the hallway and sat down on the thin carpet with a hand clasped to her burning face.

*

Want my mum. Too cold here, need her to hug the warmth back into me. How did it come to this? How did I get here? Hard to remember anything. Remember mum's face and the warmth of her love and that makes me think of things I did to her, put her through – like spitting in her face while she loved me all the time. That makes the cold come back worse. Shaking like I ain't had gear in a week. Why's it so dark? Where am I? Want to go home. Try to scream to god but nothing comes. Nothing but the dark that clings to me like an unwanted lover.

*

All through the bus ride down Jamaica Road Carole felt as though her face bore a throbbing red hand print, marking her to all the other passengers. But every time she checked it with the

51

mirror from her handbag she could see that there was barely a mark there.

Carole stepped off the bus just before The Surrey Docks Tavern and she saw the first of the morning drinkers shuffling towards the doors. She walked down Lower Road past the Osprey Estate and remembered what the place had been like before; Angelo's chip shop was gone, replaced now by a fried chicken shop, the bank that had stood on the corner was now a pawn shop with hoardings that screamed – WE WANT YOUR GOLD! She carried on down the road to where new houses had replaced the grim blocks of grey flats that had once stood there.

She walked up to a white two story house with a green door. She could hear the kids through the door. Before she could ring the bell the door opened and Carole found herself looking into the face of her daughter.

"You alright, mum?"

A wide smile. Carole forced one in return.

"Hello, babes."

Shay stepped out and carried a sack of rubbish to the bins.

"Go on in. I'll get the kettle on."

"Have you heard from your brother?"

"Why would I have?"

"Don't be like that, Shay. Have you heard anything?"

"I'm not being like anything, mum. No. I haven't seen Jamal, I haven't spoken to him and I haven't heard anything about him. No one gives a shit."

"Shay!"

"What, ma? They don't. He's got his little gear head friends and they ain't anyone that I want to know. You're better off without him there. He'll just do the same things he's a done a million times before."

Carole swayed.

"Oh, mum."

Shay put a hand on her mother's elbow and led her through to the kitchen.

"Sit down and I'll get the kettle on. Tea?"

Carole nodded and looked around the tidy, clean kitchen. Why couldn't Jamal be more like his sister?

"Nana."

Carole looked down at her granddaughter Millie who had

toddled into the kitchen and now stood in front of her with arms outstretched. She sighed and pushed thoughts of Jamal from her mind. This was family. This was what it was meant to be – not jewellery stolen and pawned, not being ashamed of your own, not being scared.

*

Still dark. Feels like I've been here forever or maybe it's only hours. Don't know. Losing track. Trying to remember. Remember any-thing. Losing mum's face, can't remember the details and can barely keep the shape of it in my mind. Can't see her anymore. Can't move. Can't feel. Try to remember my own name. I have it and then lose it again. Have to concentrate. Have to remember.

Half thoughts hit me. A shout. Boot on my neck, batons hammering down on me. Blood on the pavement. Being dragged, kicked some more. Spit and piss on me. A dark hole. No. Think about mum. Think of the good things. Try to remember the good things.

*

The Lord Nelson hadn't changed much since Carole had last been in several years ago; the same smell of spilt lager, worn maroon covered sofas and sticky carpet. The barmaids were different, but still young and blonde with low cut vest tops and a lot of hairspray, and the landlord looked the same, sat at the end of the bar with a soda water and lime and the *Racing Post*.

It wasn't packed but there were a few people in. Carole looked around and thought she could spot the people who'd come to see Mrs Shandy in the upstairs function room – they all seemed to be looking for something and had a sad look of loss in their eyes. Carole knew she must have the same look.

Joan came back from the bar with two vodka and cokes. She gestured around the pub.

"Looks like it'll be a decent turnout."

Carole nodded and sipped her drink watching a young man who'd come down from the function room. The double-breasted grey suit he wore seemed strange on him. Carole hadn't seen a man wearing a suit like that since the early nineties. It looked like he'd inherited it from the dead – a father or uncle who had passed, maybe. She looked to his face and, like the suit, it seemed wrong with a nose that was too thin, mouth too wide, and eyes that protruded out too far. He was carrying a purple velvetine bag. He stood by the landlord for a man and talked away in his ear. The big man sighed and put down his paper before he stood and rang the bell on the bar.

"Don't worry; it ain't last orders. Just to let youse know that if you're here to see Mrs Shandy it starts in ten minutes. Two pound to get in and no concessions. If you've got anything you want her to touch it goes in the bag with Kevin."

He thrust his thumb at the young man in the double breasted suit and then sat back down gesturing at one of the barmaids to refill his soda water and lime. Kevin held the sack open and walked around the room. The regulars gave him dirty looks but those who'd come to see Mrs Shandy stepped forward and dropped pictures and items into the sack.

"You brought anything, Caz?"

Carole shook her head. Joan pulled an old broach from her bag.

"Was my Great Aunt Marie's. Thought I'd see if Mrs Shandy could pick anything up from it."

Joan giggled and took a bite from her drink. Carole watched the man making his circuit of the room collecting objects and photos from the assembled. She reached into her bag and found her purse. Inside were pictures of Shay and her kids, Millie and Conrad, and another of Jamal from before the pipe had begun to own him. She kissed the picture and dropped it into the sack. Kevin smiled at her with his too wide mouth that seemed to have more teeth than was usual as though someone had stuffed a shark into a human skin.

The function room had chairs set out in rows in front of a small stage that usually hosted a dee jay or small band for birthday parties and christenings. Kevin took the money at the door and Carole and Joan managed to get seats in the second row. When everyone was seated Kevin carried a chair onto the stage and then hurried back to lower the lights. Carole wondered if he was related to Mrs Shandy, a son perhaps.

Silence descended on the gathered crowd as a small woman

54

emerged from behind the curtains. She was tiny, with an overly large head and thick jam-jar glasses. She wore a white blouse buttoned to the throat under an electric blue jacket with shoulder pads that was too big for her. She walked slowly to the chair in the centre of the small stage and sat down. Kevin stepped on to the stage, jacket off and white shirt sleeves rolled up, sack in his hands.

"Mrs Shandy will now perform a cold reading on the items I collected before the display."

He threw a cold smile at the crowd and thrust the bag towards Mrs Shandy.

"Not big on performance are they," whispered Joan.

Carole stared at the woman on the stage.

Mrs Shandy didn't even look at Kevin as she reached into the bag and rummaged around. Her hand came out clutching a soft toy, a pale lemon coloured rabbit. She looked at it and moved her hands over the soft fabric. Mrs Shandy's head snapped back on her neck so that she was looking straight up at the ceiling and a keening cry tore through the room eliciting gasps from the audience. After half a minute the cry ended and Mrs Shandy stared out into the crowd.

"It wasn't your fault."

Her voice was softer than Carole had expected. There was a sob from somewhere in the darkened room.

"It wasn't your fault. No one could know what would happen. Sometimes the little angels are called away too soon for us and for reasons we cannot comprehend."

The sobbing continued. Joan turned and tried to see who was crying.

"Britney loves her mummy and she loves her daddy. She doesn't like it when you fight. She wants you to know that neither of you are to blame for what happened and that she's happy now in the light."

Other cries joined the first and Carole distinctly thought she detected a man behind the tears. Kevin took the rabbit and stepped down off the stage. He walked out into the crowd to a couple at the back who were clutching at each other; the woman young and tired, the man big and broken down. He passed the rabbit to them and walked back to the stage.

Once more the bag was offered and once more Mrs Shandy

rummaged around. She came out with a locket on a long chain. She rubbed her hands over the locket faster and faster until Carole noticed a perplexed look on her face. Mrs Shandy looked out and Carole noticed a man sitting expectantly in the next row, a notebook on his knee.

"If you want to trick me it would be best to not to use a cheap piece of tat you bought this morning that has never been owned or loved."

The locket fell onto the floor of the stage.

"Perhaps you have a quote for our readers, Mrs Shandy?"

The man stood.

"Kevin…"

Kevin stepped off the stage and approached the man.

"For the readers, Mrs Shandy – nothing?"

Kevin grabbed the man by the shoulder and wrist and Carole saw his fingers dig deep. He turned the man towards the back of the room and marched him to the door. He pushed him out and then headed back to the stage.

Mrs Shandy gave the audience a small tight smile.

"One more reading before we break."

Her hand moved in the bag and Carole's breath caught in her throat when she saw her withdraw a photo. Mrs Shandy stared at the photo and then looked out into the audience.

"It's dark where he is. He's scared and he wants his mum."

Carole felt the tears begin to well up once more and bit them back with a deep slug of her drink.

"Jamal wants to come home."

The booze wasn't enough and a scream tore out of Carole, deep and primal. Joan turned around, startled. Mrs Shandy rose in her chair.

"He wants to come back to you, Carole. But you have to want it too."

Mrs Shandy slumped back in her chair and Kevin took the photo from her. He left her on the stage and came down to Carole. He handed her the photo back and with it a small business card.

*

There are other things here in the dark. They're close. I sense

56

more than feel them. Try to speak, to think at them. Anything to send a message, to maybe hear a response. But nothing. The dark is silent.

I heard it, heard someone calling to me in the dark. Tried to push towards it. Find the voice. Felt the other things move with me like the voice meant something to them. Not alone. Someone out there calling to me. Feel as though I'm wriggling like a worm but I can move! Wriggle wriggle towards the call.

*

Shay moved around the kitchen tidying, her husband Brendan out with the kids. She put away the dishes and with thoughts of her mum she quietened the blaring radio. Distracted now Shay headed up to her bedroom and rifled through the bedside cabinet until she found a leather-bound photo album. She took the album and sat on the bed, leafing through the pictures. Her and Jamal playing on the rug at their mum's feet, in a swimming pool in the Canary Islands, Jamal on his first day of school, Jamal in his football kit holding a small trophy and on his sixteenth birthday with a cheeky glint in his eye and his arm around Shay.

A tear fell onto the plastic covering the photos. When did she lose him? When did he stop being her brother? She took a deep breath and pushed the tears away. No. He wasn't her family anymore. Not since he stole the money for Millie's nursery fees, not since he borrowed Brendan's tools and sold them. Not since he spat on the memories they shared. But despite all that Shay echoed her mother as she whispered

"Just come home, Jamal."

*

Mrs Shandy sat, cup of tea in front of her, in Carole's front room. Kevin stood at her shoulder. Joan sat across the coffee table from them and Carole stood wishing that the tea in her cup was something stronger.

"He's out there and he wants to come home. This isn't an exact science, Mrs Smith."

"It's Miss not Mrs," said Carole but Mrs Shandy continued as though she had not heard.

"Especially when it comes to someone like your son. The drugs don't make it easy to reach out – I can't tell exactly where he is. All I can do is feel what he feels. If we all try then we may be like a beacon in the dark that will draw him towards us like a moth toward a flame."

"All I want is for him to come home."

"And we can help you," said Kevin.

Joan watched from her seat.

"What do we do?" asked Carole.

Kevin coughed and Mrs Shandy looked away. Carole sighed and pulled the fifty pounds he had requested from her pocket, in crumpled ten pound notes, and held it out. His toothy smile showed as he took the money and pocketed it. Mrs Shandy looked back.

"Pull the chairs in closer. I will act as the medium and we will call out into the darkness together."

"A medium, like what speaks to the dead?"

Mrs Shandy shook her head.

"It simply means that I reach out through the realm of spirits to find Jamal and nudge him home wherever he may be. He's in a dark place, but as I said it's hard to tell with people who have your son's condition. He could simply be sleeping it off in a stupor."

Carole looked down at her hand and saw the tremors in it and then she sat.

"Okay."

Mrs Shandy nodded and Kevin pulled up a chair, they all shuffled their chairs closer to the coffee table and reached out to join hands.

"Jamal? Jamal?"

Her voice was soft as she called. Carole risked a glance and saw that the woman's eyes were shut and her forehead wrinkled with effort.

*

There it is again. I can hear, I can feel the call. Wriggle. Move away from the things that are all around me now – clinging to me like drowning men to an able swimmer. The promise of the light on my face makes me try to move faster. Anything to be free of this dark. I can see it! I can see the light. Just need to drag myself towards it.

*

"He can hear us! I can feel him coming out of the dark."

Carole felt her heart jump in her chest and she could not help but shout.

"Come home, Jamal. Please come home."

"Be quiet."

Fire blazed in Mrs Shandy's eyes.

"Jamal, if you can her us then come towards us, come back."

*

Mum. I heard her. Drag myself to the light. Almost there. No. Get off me! What are you doing? No they're calling me – not you. Get away. She's my mum, she's calling me not you.

*

Mrs Shandy yanked her hands free and pulled them in close to her as though suffering from the cold. Her calm demeanour changed now.

"What is it?" asked Carole.

"Nothing. You've got what you wanted. Jamal is coming home."

Carole couldn't keep the smile off her face.

"Really?"

"Yes. Kevin, give them back the money."

"But…"

"Kevin, give them back the fucking money."

Kevin stared at Mrs Shandy who sat with her hands tight in to her body and then took the fifty from his pocket and held it towards Carole. Carole's eyes went from the money to Mrs Shandy who refused to meet her gaze and then she took the proffered notes.

"Come on, Kevin. We're leaving."

*

Still in the dark. No light. No sounds. Mum, help me. Find me again. I can remember it all now and can see it all so clearly. Me and Robby jacking up the old dear, snatching her purse and leaving her on the pavement. Bad magic, that. But we were hurting. Eighty nine pence in her purse. Robby cut out left to try and pick up from a bloke he thought he could get tick off.

Blue lights. Two coppers; one young, one old. Turn around to hold my hands up and get a night in the cells. Bit of brekkie. *Bang*. Baton hits me in the mouth, kick in the guts has me retching and then the old cop stands on my neck while young one works me over. Fuck, it hurt. Dragged to the car and tossed in the back like a sack of puppies that needs to go to the canal.

They take me to a dark place. From what they say in the car I work out the old dear has died. These two have had enough of people like me, want to teach me a lesson and get themselves some real justice. The hits come quick and fast until they are breathless and I am broken. Old cop stands over me and I look at him with one eye open. See the sole of his boot come down. And again. And again. All the King's horses, all the King's men...

*

Kevin put the keys in the ignition of the Corsa but then stopped before turning it.

"Why did you give them the money back? We needed that."

Mrs Shandy turned to look at him, eyes cold and mouth fixed.

"Do you have any idea what I've helped to bring through?"

Kevin shook his head and Mrs Shandy's hand cracked across his face like a flicked wet towel.

"Then don't ask me why we had to give the money back. We can always make more. Get me away from here. Take me home, Kevin."

*

Light on my face. I haven't felt that in a long time. A body, mine, drags itself up and walks. I haven't walked in a hundred years – just crawled on my belly in the dark like a worm. Push through a metal fence and stare at the neon lights. Everything so bright.

New to me. Walk as if following siren song. Smell women on the air. Not had a woman in a thousand years. A man knocks into my shoulder and I snarl. He runs. Continue on. Look at my feet – so strange the way they guide me onwards.

Look at the sky. Same stars I've seen before but in different places. No matter. Take lungfulls of air in and cough. Not far now. I can feel how close it is.

*

Joan made them another drink and Carole sparked a cigarette.

"You think she was right?"

Joan shrugged.

"I think she was. I got a good feeling, Joanie. Feel like my boy's going home."

"She's not wrong. That's what I heard. Always spot on."

Carole smiled and took a drink; plenty of money on the electric meter so he could have a shower, frozen pizza so he could eat and fresh sheets on his bed so he could sleep. In his own home, in his own bed. Jamal was coming home. A smile stole onto her face and she took another drink.

The bang at the door made them both turn. A shadow stood beyond the door.

"Silly boy forgot his key," said Carole as she got up.

The dark shape beyond the frosted glass smelt the woman's approach and waited, hungry now after so long in the dark.

WAITING
Kate Farrell

Mrs Wilson said typical. You make an appointment and when you get there they say the doctor's out on an emergency, an elderly patient. And not a word of an apology. She was right of course. Still it can't be helped. She'd given me a lift and was going to come back after she'd been shopping. I don't like to put people out so I said, no, the bus is fine.

"It's just as well my friend's not really sick," she said. "Where would she be then?"

I had a little smile to myself. The doctors told me angina could be very serious if not *monitored* - that was the word they used. Yes, monitored.

"And after she went to the trouble of phoning. Right, Edna, I'll see you later."

The door shook when she left.

"She doesn't mean anything," I said to the receptionist, "it's just her way."

I heard myself start. My husband said I went on too much. People weren't interested, that I didn't always have to explain everything, so I'd tell him, "Well, Len, I like to clear things up. I don't want to feel there's ever been any misunderstandings."

"Bloody hell, woman," he'd say, "you should go and work for the United Nations, go and sort out them Arabs and Israelis, clear up their misunderstandings. *Ha!*"

"Take a seat in the waiting room, Mrs Gould. I'll tell you when the doctor's back," said the girl.

I don't like fusses or atmospheres. They can set me off; they make me nervous. I can feel my heart beating faster and my face gets red. It's this blessed angina. Doctor Cavanaugh saw me twice a year but this new doctor says I need an examination every three months. Very insistent, he was. He looked at my notes from Doctor Cavanaugh and said, "I see you've been referred from Leeds. I was a student there."

I said, "Yes, we lived in Leeds, in Chapeltown. My husband Len worked for the Gas Board and we moved there thirty years past, nineteen sixty-three, or was it sixty-four? Going from Lancashire to Yorkshire, he said that Geoffrey Boycott had better watch out. You see he loved his cricket, and he enjoyed a joke, did Len. Anyway, he died nearly three years ago, it'll be three years come November. I'm coming back to my roots I suppose you'd call it. Manchester born and bred, that's me."

Go on, Len would have said, tell him your life history why don't you? Mine too while you're at it.

The doctor didn't seem to mind. He stroked his beard and he listened. Not many people do that any more. And he looked at me, really looked at me, like I was a person and not just a patient.

Funny, this waiting room reminds me of the front room at our home in Leeds. I daresay it's because the surgery's in a house. It's got a tiled fireplace and hearth. A picture rail. That's nice. I like a picture rail, it saves the walls. And the windows, with the metal frames I never cared much for; ours were always running in the winter months when it was cold outside. Every morning I'd have to wipe away all the water that had collected in the bottom of the panes, or they'd rust up and Len would have the painting of them in the spring. I wanted double-glazing, but Len wasn't so keen. He said it were a waste of money. He wanted to keep his nice little nest egg for when he retired, though he didn't get to spend that much of it. Always very cautious with his money, my Len. Anyway I've got double glazing now in my new flat, that and central heating. "Welcome to the twentieth century," our Carole said.

I thought I'd see more of her and Jamie when I moved back to these parts. Especially with Jamie being my only grandchild. Still, she's got that big house to look after, and Jamie. And Edward of course. I said to Len, "Fancy, our little Carole married to a bank manager!" Then there's the twins from Edward's first marriage, she sometimes has them to stay. I've not seen them since he and Carole were wed, twelve years ago. The twins were very little then, about four, running around, getting under everyone's feet at the reception. Len wanted to take his hand to them, but I told him that they were just excited, what with being bridesmaids, and getting to wear those lovely powder pink dresses and patent shoes. I think they were wearing nail polish, and they had pierced ears too. At four! I had my work cut out keeping them away from Len.

63

I said to him afterwards, "They were double trouble and no mistake! They kept me on my toes, I'll give them that."

"You need your head looking at, running round after them like a blue-arsed fly."

We were in our hotel after the wedding. I'd been a bit breathless, and started having twinges in my arm, then this tight band round my chest. The next thing you know, I was in an ambulance going to the Royal Infirmary. All wired up I was, and there were such a fuss. I don't like to make a fuss, I don't like to put people out, but all the doctors and nurses were ever so good. It's my own fault; I've always carried too much weight. I should have done something about it when I were young so I've only myself to blame.

Len were livid. He'd spent good money on the room, and we had to stay the night in a hospital. They let me go next morning, although I had to go for tests when I got home. I said the hotel might give him a refund as we'd not slept over, and he said I shouldn't be so stupid, they didn't operate like that. We'd unpacked, and used the soap and towels when we freshened up after we arrived, so there was no way we were going to get any money back.

I didn't want Carole told because it would have spoiled her special day. She and Edward left early the next morning for the honeymoon in Mauritius. She sent a postcard, signed 'Mrs Edward Lloyd!' with a big exclamation mark which I thought was ever so funny. Len wasn't that amused. He were never that keen on the name 'Edward', thought it sounded way too plummy.

When we first met Carole's intended, Len said,

"Welcome to the family then, Ted, or should we call you Ed?"

"Neither if it's all the same. I prefer Edward."

"Well, that's telling us," said Len.

I went to put the kettle on.

I wouldn't mind a cup of tea right now. My mouth gets dry when I have to wait and see the doctor. I can't always remember everything I'm supposed to tell him, and something is always bound to come back to me when I'm at home. Mrs Wilson said I should write things down, and I said I'd feel silly reading from a list about all the times I had a little twinge, or got a bit out of breath. Besides, you don't want to trouble the doctor with every last thing, not when there are seriously sick people out there. I was lucky to get an appointment, and I wouldn't want to think I was taking up his time unfairly. No, that wouldn't be right.

A cup of tea would be nice though, maybe with a slice of Battenberg, then I could relax and read one of these magazines. I wonder who brings them in. I wonder if the doctor's wife reads them, or the other patients? I used to get *People's Friend*, and *Woman's Weekly*. Len liked the *Daily Express*. We had the papers delivered, until he decided he'd walk down to the newsagent for them. Why pay a delivery charge when you've got the use of your limbs, he said. And it saved on a Christmas box for the paperboy.

Not that he was able to get out much the last year. He was hardly eating, fighting for every breath, and the oxygen cylinder was never far from reach. It wasn't much of an end for him. They were very kind at the respite care place, and offered to have him stay so I could get a little break, but it didn't somehow seem right to leave him in there, and I don't think he was all that keen. He said it were noisy and there were always someone coming or going, always people standing over him, checking if he wanted anything, when all he really needed was to be left in peace. So I kept him at home.

Carole visited, and our Steve came up from London but it was just as well they didn't stay long. They would have got on his nerves. I'd have liked the company, mind; it's hard being on your own watching someone die, someone you've been with for forty-five years.

It might have been nice if Carole had brought Jamie to see his granddad one last time. She said she didn't want the boy upset, and she wanted to remember her dad like he had been. I thought, and do you suppose I don't? Don't you think I don't want to remember him on our wedding day, so big and strong and handsome as he was then? At the end he were only seventy-two but he looked ten years older, his skin was too big for him, it were grey, and his eyes looked cloudy all the time. I know it's not a nice thing to say, but his eyes reminded me of a fish's on a slab, when it's not very fresh.

Steve drove up from London with his friend. The friend went off to do some shopping while Steve stayed an hour or so. He'd grown his hair and pulled into a ponytail. Len said, "What on earth do you look like? You look like a bloody girl, that's what."

"Good to see you too, dad," said Steve. He had on this scarf, it was made of some silky material, and he kept tying it and untying it, fussing with it like an old woman. His real name was Stephen, with a 'ph'. When he started on his hairdressing course, he told us he wanted to be called Stefan. Len didn't like that.

"We gave you a perfectly good name. What do you want to go and change it for? Stephen, now that's a man's name. Stefan? Sounds like a bloody poof."

We didn't hear from Steve much after that, though sometimes he sent pictures of his hairstyles cut from magazines. He won an award once for doing somebody's hair in a contest at the Albert Hall, I think. He's been very successful. One of my neighbours saw a photo of him in the *Daily Mirror*, he were with one of the girls from *East Enders*, or perhaps it was someone from *Coronation Street*, and the caption referred to him as 'celebrity crimper' whatever that's supposed to mean. It's a different world.

I could almost be in our old front room again. This is about the same size. We had a three piece suite instead of these hard seats. Len's chair was opposite the television, right by the fire. We only used one bar, but when he were sick we'd leave another bar on as he was feeling the cold more then. Mine was near the window, and the sofa was against the wall behind the door where they've got a fish tank here. Len had his chair and I had mine, and the sofa was for visitors. Funny isn't it, how people end up with his and her chairs; I mean a chair is just a chair really, though after a while one of them takes you on, sort of shapes itself to you without you realising it. Like shoes. Yes, it's funny that.

Len died in his chair. He'd been really poorly for a while, and we had the nurses in. They even stayed overnight so I could get my head down for a few hours. I needed to keep my strength up they said.

Mrs Harris next door, she lost her husband some years before. Her son came over to see her every week. He'd take her out, or do any odd jobs.

She had him help me make the front room into a bedroom

for Len when the stairs became too much for him. He got himself up and dressed most days, with some help from me or one of the nurses. He was a proud man my Len, he didn't like people to think he couldn't do anything for himself any more. The doctor arranged for a commode, so he'd have a bit of a wash in the kitchen and do his business without me or the nurses watching his every move. A man needs his dignity.

We'd had the six o'clock news on and I was waiting for the weather forecast to be over before I went out to make us some tea. We always watched the weather forecast, I don't know why as it never really made that much difference to us, we weren't keen gardeners or anything like that. We only had a small back yard and it didn't get much sun which were a shame. I think I might like to give gardening a go now; there's a little patio just outside the lounge in my new flat, and it gets lots of sun. Len hadn't made his usual comments on the news or the newsreader. "What has she done to her hair? She looks like the wreck of the Hesperus." That was one of his favourites. He was clawing at the arms on his chair, as if he was trying to hang on.

I knew then.

"Len, love. You let go if you want to. If you're ready. It's alright," I said.

He nodded. He was agreeing with me, the first time in forty-five years, and then he sighed like he was very, very tired.

And that was it.

I stayed with him and I held his cold, old hand. If you'd given me a hundred pounds I couldn't tell you when that last happened. We weren't given to displays. We'd taken our vows, and didn't feel the need to let everyone know how it was between us.

We waited until the nurse came. It was Hazel that night. She sat me in the kitchen with a pot of tea and some biscuits from last Christmas; they were in a blue tin with a snow scene on the lid. Then she went into the hall to make some phone calls, closing the door between us.

I can remember everything: the picture on the biscuit tin, the knock on the door when Doctor Cavanaugh arrived, and then the police – Hazel told me they had to come – then another knock

67

when the men came to take Len. She closed the kitchen door, she wouldn't let me see, but I heard one of them, it was quite a young voice, say,

"He weighs nothing this one, just a bag of bones."

Someone told him to shush.

She thought somebody should come and stay with me and wanted to phone our Carole. I didn't want anyone, I said, and besides Mrs Harris was only next door if I felt a need. So she washed and dried the cups and put everything away, then she went too.

It was about ten o'clock. I put out the lights and went to bed.

Downstairs next morning I went into the front room. I looked at Len's chair, and there was a dent where his head had been. I put my hand on it expecting it to be warm and of course it wasn't. It smelled of his hair. That smell and the hollow in the headrest; that's all that was left of him.

You're a silly old girl, Edna Gould, bringing all that up again. You should know better at your age. It's this room, isn't it, because it's like your old house, that's all it is. And because you're sitting in here on your own. If there were other patients it wouldn't be so bad, not that you'd talk to them. No, that wouldn't be right. When people are waiting to go and see the doctor, they don't want some stupid old woman chattering to them about this and that. They're not interested, they've got their own problems, that's why they're here. Len would tell me I should go and see someone about my head, not my body, carrying on like that, living in the past. He'd say it weren't healthy and he'd be right. Next visit, I'll come and wait with the others. I mean, what's so special about me?

And besides, the doctor's a busy man, I don't want to waste his time. It's good of him to see me outside surgery hours, and all because I'd had a little turn last week.

Mrs Wilson insisted.

"Get on that phone. If you don't, I will. You've paid your stamps all your life. It's your due."

That's the kind of thing Len would have said. I wonder if they would have got on? Len would probably have thought she had rather a lot to say for herself, he never really cared for that. I don't know what Mrs Wilson would have made of him; I haven't told her much, and she's hardly talked about her husband, but she's been widowed a lot longer than me. We're not like the young folk today though; we aren't always talking about feelings and emotions. Some things are private and should stay that way.

She means well. She was very kind when I moved in. It was a raw day, late January and she had tea and biscuits for me and the removal men.

She kept her front door open just in case I needed anything. Carole was going to lend a hand, but she and Edward had to go away, a week-end break in London. A hotel and a show.

They say that you want to return to your roots as you get older. Nearly two years after Len passed, I went to an estate agent and told them that I'd decided to move back to Manchester, to Hyde. They spoke to their Manchester office and they told me they had a lovely ground floor flat for sale. Mrs Harris knew about my plans. She said she'd get her son to take me over to see it and I think she liked the idea of me doing something without telling Carole. She had a heart of gold Mrs Harris but wasn't backward about speaking her mind and she told me once she thought Carole could do a lot more for me than she did. I hope I never gave the wrong impression about Carole, it's just that she's always got a lot on.

Anyway, Mrs Harris got her Andy to drive me over. The flat was perfect, and everything the old house wasn't; it had big windows, and central heating, a built in oven in the kitchen and a patio off the lounge.

The For Sale sign went up outside mine and Len's in Chapeltown and I bought number eight, Cedar Gardens, Hyde. I was well provided for, what with the sale of the house, and Len's pension. Funny, last visit the doctor asked me if I had any money worries. He said it was often a concern for some of his older patients and he seemed relieved when I told him I was comfortable. It was nice of him to ask, wasn't it?

I bought new furniture, new curtains, new pots and pans, new everything. I even bought a continental quilt. Mrs Harris had one and said it put paid to bed making. We still talk. I told her I were thinking about taking a holiday abroad, a short break somewhere with Mrs Wilson. I must look out my passport. The last time I used it, Len and I went to Holland for the tulips. That was nineteen eighty-seven, our fortieth anniversary. I loved all the purples and yellows and reds and pinks, all mixed up. Len said we could have stood outside the local florist and saved him the money.

I'll get some bulbs for the patio, something to look forward to next spring. Moving back here is the best thing I could have done. I've got a nice modern flat, good neighbours, and Carole and Jamie not that far off. I'm feeling much better. I am really.

Was that the door? Yes, it was. It must be Doctor Shipman back from his emergency.

Good.

Soon it'll be over, then I can go home and get that cup of tea.

LILLY FINDS A PLACE TO STAY
Charles Black

Lilly dressed quickly. She pulled on her clothes – panties, bra, tights, skirt, all black – aware she was under the scrutiny of Greg Haldane, who remained in bed smoking. She found the way he gazed at her unnerving, even though he'd just been intimate with every inch of her naked body. Her T-shirt was also black, apart from the white skull with blood-red blazing eyes on its front. Finally, she put on her trainers – Converse All Stars – and hurriedly tied the laces.

"Got somewhere important to go?"

"No."

"You seem to be in a hurry." Greg blew out a cloud of smoke. "Don't you like me?"

"Not really," Lilly muttered. Her answer could have applied to either of Greg's questions. The seventeen-year-old didn't particularly like him. Nor did she have anywhere specific to go, apart from anywhere that wasn't the squat. She was anxious to get away before any of the others returned. Other lads, that was.

"What was that?" Greg said sharply.

"Nothing."

"Sure." Greg's lip curled in a sneer. He didn't care whether Lilly liked him or not. He could have her whenever he wanted.

Any girls who lived in the house on Bird Hill Road were expected to have sex with any and all of the squat's male occupants. Not that they were told of this condition when they first moved in. However, it was soon made clear to them. That was bad enough. Worse was to follow, when they were made to work the streets.

This wasn't what Lilly had expected when she'd run away with her boyfriend. Her relationship with her parents had been going downhill for some time. The first bone of contention was that they didn't like the music she listened to, or the volume that

71

she played it at. Then it was her taste in clothes, the makeup she wore and the colours that she'd had her hair dyed: in turn black, purple, and then red. Her announcement that in future everyone had to call her Lilith hadn't been well received either. Finally, they didn't like the friends she'd started hanging around with. Especially Jase, who was five years older than she was. Far too old for a sixteen-year-old girl in the opinion of her parents. The arguments had grown more and more frequent, and Lilly hadn't needed much persuading when Jase had said she should come to London with him.

Everything had been great at first. Until Jase had met someone else, dumped her and kicked her out of the flat that they shared.

She moved in with Beth, a friend she'd made on Twitter some time before she'd left home. But things continued to spiral downwards. She lost her bar job after refusing to give the landlord a blowjob, and her money had soon run out. Beth proved to be not much of a friend when Lilly could no longer contribute to the rent.

Lilly should have gone home then. But stubbornly she didn't.

She'd met Greg at a gig. He'd said she could come and live in the Bird Hill Road squat. And she had.

Greg had got her into drugs. Sure, she'd smoked a joint every now and then, but Greg had got her onto the harder stuff. He'd started hitting her harder then too.

Greg suddenly jumped out of bed and grabbed Lilly's arm, squeezing tightly. "Make sure you bring some money home with you."

Lilly nodded meekly, and he let her go.

A few minutes later, she left the squat, walked down Bird Hill Road and onto Tanner Street. She didn't want to go to 'work'. She was sick of selling herself to the kerb crawlers who frequented Duckett Lane at any hour of day or night. She thought back to the argument when her father had said, "If she dressed like a slut, she'd be treated like a slut." She couldn't believe he'd said that at the time. "I'm a Goth," she'd angrily yelled back at him.

And now she was working as a prostitute.

Away from the squat, Lilly paused to light a cigarette. Instead of turning left, she went right, towards the shops.

Perhaps she could get away with some shoplifting or pickpocketing.

Lilly's luck wasn't in. No sooner had she entered the shopping mall than she had attracted the attention of a security guard. Even though he was trying not to be obvious about it, it was clear that he was following her. She hadn't done anything suspicious, so Lilly supposed he must fancy her. Yes, he was definitely eyeing her up, paying close attention to her legs. She bent over, pretending to tie her shoelace. Looking between her legs, she could see he was enjoying the view of her bum in the tight black skirt. What a pervert!

If Greg had been with her, she could have acted as a decoy, distracting the guard, while he stole something.

She wandered around a bit more, went into HMV. There was a new CD she wanted, but the guard was still tailing her.

Frustrated, Lilly flounced out of the store and out of the mall. She ignored the shops on Tanner Street, and moved onto Sherton Street. It was starting to rain and rather than entering one of the shops she went into the library.

"Can I help you, dear?" The woman who sat behind the desk spoke with an Irish accent. The badge she wore indicated that her name was Mrs Margaret O'Riorden.

"Um, can I use a computer?"

"Are you a member?"

Lilly hadn't been in the library before, never mind filled in a membership card. She shook her head. "No."

"I see." Mrs O'Riorden consulted her computer screen. "Sorry, dear. They're all booked up."

"Oh." Lilly stood for a moment thinking. "Got any books on serial killers?" She wasn't much of a reader, but this was a subject that interested her.

This caused the librarian to raise an eyebrow. "Serial killers?"

"Yeah."

The librarian smiled, and got up. "We have. I'll show you."

Lilly followed her deeper into the library.

"Here we are." The librarian indicated a shelf.

"Thanks."

Mrs O'Riorden smiled again and returned to her desk.

Lilly scanned the shelf. There weren't many, but there were enough to pass the time. Most were about Jack the Ripper, but there were also books covering Peter Sutcliffe: the Yorkshire Ripper, John Christie, Fred and Rosemary West, and Dennis Nilsen.

She pulled the books from the shelf and found a table in a quiet corner. The teenager quickly grew engrossed reading about some of the country's most notorious murderers and the victims of their grisly crimes. Most of whom were young women.

"Excuse me."

The librarian's voice made Lilly jump.

"What?"

"We're closing up in ten minutes, dear."

"Oh. But it's just for the lunch hour, right? You open again at two though, don't you?"

Mrs O'Riorden shook her head. "No, sorry. It's half-day closing today."

"Oh. Right."

"Do you want to borrow any of those?" Mrs O'Riorden nodded at the pile of books on the table.

"Oh, um. No. Probably not a good idea."

The librarian frowned, then moved on to the computer room.

Lilly wondered if she dared hide somewhere in the library. She was in no rush to go back to the squat. But she was hungry, so she got up, returned the books to their shelf, and left the building.

It was still raining and she waited in the porch considering her options. She lit a cigarette and thought. She could get something to eat, but that would leave her with very little money and if she went back to the squat without any cash, Greg would hit her. She would have to go down Duckett Lane and pick up a punter. She wouldn't have any trouble getting one; there were always plenty of dirty old men who liked their girls young.

Lilly was still in the porch when the librarian emerged from the library.

"Oh, hello, dear." Mrs O'Riorden locked the door and put the keys in her handbag.

Lilly caught a glimpse of a purse.

The Irishwoman tutted. "What dreadful weather." She looked Lilly up and down. "No coat?"

"No." Lilly shrugged. "I left it at the squat."

Mrs O'Riorden peered at the cloud-filled sky. "Doesn't look

74

like easing off. You're going to get soaked."

Lilly sighed. "Yeah."

"Tell you what, dear, why not come back to mine? It's not far. And my brolly is big enough to shelter the both of us from the worst of the rain. I can lend you a coat."

"Um." Lilly frowned. The offer was unexpected, and she hesitated before answering, scrutinising the librarian. The woman had long brown hair, she wore "sensible" shoes, and the clothes that Lilly knew she wore beneath her coat weren't what she would call fashionable, even for a woman of the librarian's age. And as for her age, she must be at least ten years older than her parents who were in their early forties. In Lilly's book that made her ancient. Ancient and not really a threat.

Mrs O'Riorden was speaking again. "My son's also interested in serial killers. He's got quite the collection of books about them. Certainly a lot better than the library's. You could take a look at them if you like."

"Well." Lilly came to a decision. "Okay." She was suspicious of the woman's motives, but going with her was better than the alternative. With a bit of luck she'd be able to pocket something valuable. The contents of the Irishwoman's purse perhaps. Or maybe there'd be some cash lying around the house somewhere.

"Good." Mrs O'Riorden smiled and put up her umbrella. "It's this way. Come on."

Mrs O'Riorden was right: it wasn't far to her house, and they walked quickly and soon arrived there.

"Round here." She went to the back door and unlocked it. "Go on in."

Lilly stepped inside. Mrs O'Riorden shook her umbrella and followed the teenager into the kitchen.

"Now then. Tea? Coffee?" Mrs O'Riorden asked, once she had taken off her coat and hung it up alongside her handbag.

"Tea. Please."

"Sit yourself down then and I'll make us a pot."

Lilly sat at the kitchen table. As Mrs O'Riorden filled the electric kettle, Lilly's gaze went round the room. The kitchen was small and to her surprise, somewhat untidy. The shelves and worktops like the table were cluttered with all sorts of things: containers of various sizes interspersed with ornaments and trinkets. None of which appeared to be valuable. Perhaps there would be some money in one of the many pots. Or maybe the other rooms would provide better pickings.

Mrs O'Riorden rummaged in a cupboard and found a tin of biscuits. Lilly gratefully accepted when the librarian told her to tuck in to them.

"Milk? Sugar?"

Lilly nodded to both, her mouth full of chocolate digestive.

"Mmm, these biscuits are delicious."

"Glad you like them, dear." Mrs O'Riorden smiled proudly. "I baked them myself. My own recipe. Made with my special secret ingredient."

The tea was good too, made just the way Lilly liked it.

"So, you're living in a squat?"

"Yeah." Lilly took another biscuit. "I intend to move out as soon as I can find somewhere better."

"How did you end up there? If you don't mind me asking."

Normally, Lilly would have minded, but for some reason, this time she didn't. "Long story. Ran away from home is the short version." She wasn't going to go into details though.

"And do your parents know where you are?"

Lilly shook her head. "We don't get on."

"Ah. I had my share of troubles with mine."

"What about your son?"

"Oh, when Sean was living here we had plenty of rows. Never causes me any trouble now though."

"This tea is the best I've had in a long time."

"Well, have some more then." Mrs O'Riorden refilled Lilly's cup.

Lilly sipped her drink. "And your son's interested in serial killers?"

"Oh, yes." Mrs O'Riorden laughed. "I can't think why. But the subject fascinated him. And so many books about them."

"Why didn't he take his books with him when he left?"

Mrs O'Riorden frowned. "I didn't say he'd left, did I?"

"Oh, sorry." Lilly was puzzled. She must've misunderstood the woman's Irish accent. "He still lives here?"

Mrs O'Riorden nodded. "He's still here."

"Oh." Lilly bit into another biscuit. This might make robbery more tricky, she thought. "Is he in?"

"Yes."

"Oh."

"You'll meet him in a bit."

"Right. What about your husband?"

Mrs O'Riorden's expression twisted into a scowl. "He did leave. The bastard."

"Oh. Sorry."

The woman sighed. "It was a long time ago. Unfortunately, these things happen." She composed her features, her lips forming a smile again. "Now, you've had enough tea?"

"Yes. Thanks."

Mrs O'Riorden got up. "Well, come on through to the sitting room then." She started to lead the way, but paused and retrieved her handbag.

Lilly smothered a curse. She'd hoped the Irishwoman had forgotten that it hung within easy reach.

Lilly rose and followed Mrs O'Riorden. The hallway was narrow and made narrower by the cardboard boxes that were stacked the length of one wall. She suddenly felt a bit dizzy and staggered, steadying herself against the boxes. She wondered what might be inside them. She had her suspicions that it would just be junk.

"Is it that squat on Bird Hill Road where you are living?"

"Yeah."

"Aw, I've heard some terrible stories about what goes on in that place. It's no place for a girl like you to be living."

"I'm going to move out." Lilly reiterated her earlier statement. "Just as soon as I find somewhere better to stay."

For the second time that day, Mrs O'Riorden made an unexpected offer. "You should move in here. I've plenty of space for a little one like you."

Lilly wasn't so sure of that. The sitting room like the hallway was cluttered, not only with more cardboard boxes, but also plastic bags, both carrier and black bin ones. It was as she had suspected – Mrs O'Riorden was a hoarder.

"I've given a home to plenty of waifs and strays like you before."

Lilly was sceptical, though she didn't say anything.

"Sit yourself down and I'll go and fetch Sean down. You'd like that wouldn't you?"

Lilly smiled and gave the barest of nods. She was still feeling dizzy; sitting down would be a good idea. However, she didn't really want to meet Sean.

There was only one free seat though, and Lilly sat in it. The other armchair and the settee were both buried under a pile of stuff.

"I shan't be a minute." Mrs O'Riorden left the room, taking her handbag with her.

As soon as she heard her host going up the stairs, Lilly got up. She felt strange, unsteady on her feet, but she knew that this was her chance. If she was going to find anything worth stealing, she had to find it now. She picked a box at random and opened it.

"Oh my God!" She gasped in astonishment at what she saw inside. It was a skull. A human skull that sat on top of a pile of bones. In an almost mesmerised state, she opened another box. Another skull stared back at her.

There were dozens of boxes; did they all contain bones? Lilly didn't care; she wasn't going to look in any more. She knew that it was time to leave. The problem was that she was having trouble moving properly. Her legs felt funny and her head was spinning.

Lilly lurched towards the door, reaching for the handle. She pulled it open.

Mrs O'Riorden stood in her way. "Oh, thank you, dear."

Lilly retreated unsteadily. Her mouth tried unsuccessfully to form words,

"Here she is, Sean." Mrs O'Riorden was alone. She was carrying a cardboard box. She entered the room and put the box down.

Lilly had backed up against the armchair. She swayed and collapsed into it. The special ingredient that her host had put in the biscuits was rapidly taking full effect. Soon, she would be unable to move at all.

"Sean." Mrs O'Riorden smiled and stroked the box. "This is Lilly. She's going to be staying here with us."

THE MUTANT'S CRY
David A. Sutton

Freddie turned up around midnight in early September, begging for a place to stay. Stan's bedsit was too small and cramped for two, but he could hardly refuse the boy a night's stay at least; he was only sixteen. Stan turned to look behind him, as if the flat might suddenly sprout an extra bedroom, then opened the door wider to allow Freddie in—he didn't need to stoop under Stan's arm.

As Stan followed him into the seedy living space, he was thinking carefully about exactly how to phrase his first words in a nice way, as Freddie looked just about done in, but they came out brutally anyway. "You can stay tonight, but that's it."

His visitor collapsed onto the room's only piece of comfortable furniture, a bulky settee upholstered in green vinyl, cracked and worn almost bare on the arm rests. His eyes closed and he sat unmoving for at least a minute. Stan thought he had fallen asleep and he peered closely at his caller's face. For a sixteen year old his features bore the appearance of an old man: protuberant nose and lips, wrinkles around his overlarge eyes, a permanent frown; a dribble of saliva on his chin. There were some spots of what looked like dried blood on the collar of his Terylene shirt. The significance, or otherwise, of that sat uneasily in Stan's thoughts.

Okay, so Freddie was in trouble maybe. But he had form; this was not the first time he had run away from home. Stan was determined he wouldn't be left "holding the baby" this time. Well, it was the only time… so far.

"Dad's kicked me out." Freddie croaked in a whisper, his eyes still closed, but it was as if he sensed that Stan was examining him at close quarters.

Stan sighed. It was a familiar story. Freddie had exhausted all his relatives… and friends. Stan did not regard himself as a friend, just an acquaintance. He had met Freddie in the local library where they'd both been reaching for the same book on an upper shelf of the film section. Stan got there first, as Freddie was a short-arse. The book was… well he couldn't recall what the title was, except that the subject was cinema, but he'd allowed Freddie to borrow it first anyway. They'd got chatting and discovered, not unexpectedly, a mutual interest in films. Since then he'd accompanied Freddie to the picture house a couple of times, mainly to vouch for his age in order so he could get in to see the "X" certificate pictures. Freddie was just too short to convince the bint in the box office at the Kingsway cinema that he was old enough. Stan hadn't known for sure that Freddie was sixteen, but what he did get to know about was his father's violent rages and the rows with his wife that ended up on the street outside their council house. He guessed Freddie was old enough to leave home, which no doubt is what his father wanted.

"It's bad this time, Stan."

It always is, Stan thought. He had left home himself at eighteen, five years ago, but not for the same reasons; he'd kicked himself out. His excuse was a drunken mother who wouldn't cook or clean. And a father who showed no affection, except for his work, seven sodding days a week.

"He beat up mum and told me it was my fault. I—" he hesitated, opened his eyes, looked up at Stan with malignant fierceness. "I punched him. Punched him and punched him!" An odd gleam came into his moist eyes. "He didn't fight back."

A bully by any other name, Stan thought, although he'd not met Freddie's dad.

"Then he cowered in the corner," Freddie added, amazed that his father had metamorphosed from pugilist to grovelling wimp. "And told me, and he was crying like a baby, told me to get out and never come back." Freddie was replaying the altercation as if he was describing a scene in a film, almost relishing the details, yet at the same time terrified at being a central character in the story. "Dad said, 'if I ever see you again I'll burn all your books and filthy magazines'. And then—"

Stan speculated for a moment… had the kid killed his dad? Was that why this was so bad, this time? The answer, when it came wasn't that awful, but the scenario was about as cruel as you could get.

"—Mum had been screamin' all the time I'd laid into dad.

Now she was screamin' again, only this time she was blaring at me. 'You little shit, get out-get out. How could you hurt your father like that?' She was saying that to me when it was dad who was always thumping mum. I thought she'd like the fact that he was getting some of his own medicine. But, she was taking his side!"

This didn't make sense, but Stan had enough experience of life and other friends' family relationships to know that often wives did not apply logic in such matters. Like an abused pet dog, which nevertheless still loves its vicious owner, and will defend him, despite the kickings and whippings.

Freddie curled up on the settee, his two-tone brown winkle pickers pointing outwards like a pixie's shoes and shortly he had fallen asleep, as if his mind and body could no longer cope with the evening's ordeal and had shut down, a light switch turned off to allow darkness to blanket him and obscure the heartlessness meted out to him at home.

The stipulation that Freddie's overnight stay be limited to just one night was out the window now, Stan decided. He stood for a moment longer, and then went down the corridor into the shared kitchen to put the kettle on for a cuppa. Mug in hand he stood by the fireplace, contemplating. He didn't own much. The settee, a small table and two chairs, the table with a plate and the remains of that night's fish and chips, plus an ashtray overflowing with nub ends. A chest of drawers on which rested a couple of framed photographs and a tarnished school cup, awarded for his athletic skills; an athleticism Freddie would never aspire to. In one recess a record player, its plastic lid raised and a seventy-eight waiting to be played. A bunch of records in brown paper sleeves leaning against the skirting board. On the floor nearby that day's *Daily Sketch*. The bedsit was too small for even another small body. And in any case, he didn't want his simple existence complicated by someone likely to go off the rails.

He was about to switch off the light and take his tea into the alcove where his bed was positioned when he noticed something rolled up, sticking out from Freddie's half-zipped bomber jacket. Stan put his mug down and carefully slid out a dog eared magazine. The reason it had caught his eye immediately became apparent—as he unfolded it a pin-up picture revealed itself on the front cover. It was a shot of an actress—vaguely familiar, but he couldn't put a name to her—chained up, provocatively posed, but with big black rectangles, one each across her boobs and snatch.

Stan picked up his tea and retired to his bed space, switching off the main light on the way. He lay on the bed, trying for a moment to forget about Freddie's problems, which had now also become his. A bedside lamp illuminated the front cover of the magazine, which he intended to have a little read of before going to sleep. He'd never seen this one in the newspaper shop. *Shock Films*. In fact, he doubted it was available in your average newsagent's.

Well, Stan thought, Freddie is into mucky mags! He took a sip of tea and turned the cover. Surprisingly the contents page did not reveal it to be a magazine about dirty movies, but something rather different, as he read the contents list. 'The Freudian messages in Paulo Antonini's *Night Gaunts*' and 'The Mutants of The Black Sleep'. Stan leafed through the pages and realised this was an intellectual magazine, a serious magazine about horror films. There were articles on film themes and reviews of several recent flicks, *The Bad Seed*, *Lust for the Vampire*, *The Gamma People* and a number of others. The whole rag contained masses of film stills and publicity shots. In the news section one of the entries had been circled in blotchy ink, he presumed by Freddie.

Director Harold Marshall turns his back on romance

Marshall, better known for his lightweight romantic comedies, *Kindest Heart* and *Love by Mail*, has changed direction with his new film, the X rated *The Mutant's Cry*. Early reports suggest that the film intends to deeply shock, horrify and affect its audience long after they leave the cinema. Marshall's Producer Aaron Shellack is quoted as saying that 'This film is like no other horror or scienti-fiction movie. Without using 3D or special effects, Harold has crafted a motion picture that will truly get under your skin'. A review will appear in a future issue of this magazine.

As drowsiness crept over him, the magazine slipped from Stan's fingers to the floor and he mulled over Freddie's obsession with creepy films. Something, and Stan thought he knew what, drew the sixteen year old to horror pictures. It was because of his, well, deformity. He was already an outsider in his teens and macabre movies were outsiders too. Not conventional, different, dodgy. They didn't fit in.

Without getting up to undress, he threw the quilt over himself and lay back on the pillow. Reaching across to the bedside lamp he felt for the switch and darkness swathed him. In his dreams a magazine flapped its pages like a bird's wings and flopped over his face, the paper feeling not like feathers but something else. When he woke in the early hours, worrying about getting up in time for work, he thought he could recall the pages having a texture of roughness, like papery bark, or coarse workman's hands.

Stan was employed as a counter clerk at the Post Office. He would be expected to be in by eight-thirty, his cash and stock put in the drawer, date stamp changed to the correct date, and his job tomorrow, now today, also included filing away the day's arrival of pension books, Premium Bond winning bank drafts and stocks of savings certificates. The office he worked at was a twenty minute bus ride away too, and he was anxious about that. He didn't want to switch on the lamp, although that was the only way he'd be able to check the time on his alarm clock and make sure the magazine had never really animated itself.

Raising his head Stan noticed that there was a light of sorts coming from near the table. Muzzily it took him a moment to comprehend that the red glow was a cigarette. Hearing a sound he realised that Freddie must have woken up and found his packet of Woodbine's. He didn't begrudge the boy a fag, but hoped he didn't chain-smoke the whole packet before breakfast.

He dreamily watched the red tip lumber around his room, disembodied from the smoker, then the ghost of a face appeared as Freddie took a long drag and the cigarette's tip flared. The lines on Freddie's face were more pronounced, lit up by the dull glow, before a disembodied hand reached across and removed the fag from his lips. Then Stan heard a quiet, muffled sobbing.

The emotion of the day's events had finally caught up with him. Freddie was still a boy, and he must be feeling utterly abandoned.

*

By the weekend Stan's flat looked like a doss house. Freddie had moved in. It was all completely unsuitable, but Stan didn't have the heart to throw him out onto the street, well not yet. The settee was now a bed, with an overcoat for a blanket. In the alcove to the right of the fireplace—in which Stan had intended eventually to put up some shelves—there now tottered two piles of magazines. Freddie had been either allowed back home to pick up his belongings, or had sneaked in while his folks were out. Mostly he'd ended up bringing the magazines, but he had over three trips on the bus managed to include a few clothes, which now were piled in two cardboard boxes.

It was Stan's day off on the Saturday, so in the morning he put Cornflakes into two bowls; usually he'd be off to work before Freddie woke. Stan wondered how his salary would cover two mouths worth of shopping as he returned from the kitchen.

Freddie emerged from under his coat fully dressed and slouched over to the little Formica table. Stan could smell his clothing, or him, or both. He returned to the fridge to fetch the milk and lit up a ciggy on the way back. Through a haze of exhaled blue smoke he noticed that Freddie was as withdrawn as ever. Stan had no experience of parenthood to draw on, so felt helpless to rally him round. His own family experiences had been either confrontational, or the opposite, of being sent to Coventry.

"What about work, then?" Stan snapped as he sloshed milk onto the flakes.

"It's Saturday."

"You know what I mean. What did you do before your parents kicked you out?"

Freddie played his spoon around in the milk and flakes, but didn't eat any. "Started an apprenticeship at Dowding and Mills. But I got sacked because of being late."

Stan liked the boy's honesty. He didn't like his lack of ambition. "You'll have to get a job soon, if you're going to stay

84

here any longer. And put in your share of the housekeeping." Just then the ceiling light went out. Stan firked around in his trouser pocket, opened the front door and started pushing coins into the electric meter in the hall. After the light came on he added, "See what I mean? There's the electric to pay for as well."

"All right. I'll start looking for a job on Monday. Can you lend me a few bob till then?"

"*Buggerin'hell*, Freddie, what for?" Stan could not suppress his exasperation or the resentment he was also attempting to subdue. He was a young man, he should have been out with his date, except he hadn't got a girl at the moment. Or he should be thinking about a night down the pub with his mates, which is what he had intended this weekend. What he shouldn't be doing at twenty-three, was babysitting. Babysitting a boy who wasn't even family.

"I want to go to the Flicks tonight. I'll pay you back when somebody gives me a job."

Stan sighed, picked up his wallet from the window sill and took out five shillings. "Where're you going, the Kingsway?" The local flea pit was only ten minutes' walk away.

"Er no," Freddie answered. "Thought I'd pop into town, there's a film I want to see on at the Jacey."

"A cartoon?" Stan knew that all the Jacey ran was cartoons and old American serials.

"No Stan, it's changed. It shows adult films now."

Stan knew what he meant. "Mucky stuff." The clientele would be dirty old men and drunks.

"No, all sorts. I want to see *The Mutant's Cry*." Stan recognized the title from the magazine Freddie had had the night he arrived.

"Then you'll need me along, otherwise a titch like you won't get past the ticket office without someone to tell 'em you're old enough." What was he saying! Stan realised that he'd booked himself an evening out babysitting and therefore wouldn't be in the pub having a decent night with his mates.

"Anyway, what's so special about this mutant film?" he asked irritably, annoyed with himself for being so soft-hearted.

"It's special. Like… like *The Tingler*, you know."

"Er no. I've never heard of it."

"It had this thing, this thing that affected you while you were watching. Made it real."

"What thing?" Stan was at a loss to understand what the boy was talking about.

"I can't remember what it's called, but it wasn't on the film, it was outside the film... you know."

Stan looked unconvinced, doubting that Freddie had ever seen such a flick. "Freddie, have you ever seen this *Tingler* film?"

"Well—"

"I knew it. You've just read about it. Same as with the film tonight. It'll probably be rubbish." He paused. "Now eat your breakfast. I don't think I've seen you eat hardly anything decent since you've stayed here, except fish, chips and dandelion and burdock." God, he thought, he sounded like his own mum, at least on the odd occasion she had been sober and maternal.

*

At lunchtime Stan went round the corner to William Hill's and placed a bet on the three o'clock at Worcester. He hoped 'The Tickler'—since it had a suggestion about it of that film of Freddie's—at five-to-one might bring in a few extra quid to ease the financial shortfall he could see coming. He'd studied the form in the paper and was now reading the news while he downed a pint in The Cross Guns.

The chance to relax away from the flat and its extra occupant had given him an idea. He thought it might be worth a visit to Freddie's parents' house. See if there couldn't be some sort of reconciliation. He'd even help Freddie take that damned pile of magazines back. The bus stop was handily positioned just outside the pub and he jumped on the next one along, paid the conductor and sat near the front, opposite the driver's cab so he could see where to get off.

Freddie's house was in the middle of a row of terraces, built on both sides of a narrow street, with two properties next door but one to Freddie's just piles of bricks. Stan thought they'd probably caught a stray bomb in the war and were still waiting re-building. There was an air of bleakness about the place, even more so than the building he rented his bedsit in, as if the whole street remained weary and worn by time and a war that had ended ten and more summer's ago, yet which still lingered in the dusty air. Number twenty three had a rusty iron knocker on a dark maroon door of flaky paint, which chipped more paint off the wood as he rapped. He waited silently, lighting a Woodbine from a box of England's Glory. Dropping the spent match he noticed a wet yellow splatter on the worn red-painted front step, as if someone had drooled or spat.

A minute seemed to pass, but it may have been only a few seconds, but in any case, Stan knocked again. Instead of being answered, the neighbour's door opened and an old man wearing trousers with braces over a worn vest poked himself out.

"After the Wilcocks?" the neighbour growled.

"Yes—"

"Gone, the both of them."

"Gone?" Stan feared something terrible had happened, but couldn't believe that Freddie had anything to do with it. "Gone where?" he asked, hoping that perhaps they'd just done a bunk, but wondering if they'd been arrested or something.

"'Ospital. Both 'f 'em."

Stan tried to take stock for a few seconds, pondering. "What happened?"

The man from next door coughed and spat of gobbet of phlegm into his front yard, and expertly managed a trajectory that sent it on an arc almost to the leaning picket fence. "Fair gimme the heebie jeebies, Tom banging on the wall the other night. I went round there, 'course and found 'em both on the floo-er, like they was havin' a fit."

"Are they—"

"Went up t'the phone box and called the amb'lance. It took 'em orf. Don't know nothin' else." The Wilcocks's neighbour disappeared inside and his door slammed shut.

Stan began to walk away when the Wilcocks's door slowly opened and a young woman peered out. "Who're you?"

"Stan Gibbons. I'm a friend—I know Freddie."

"Waster 'e is." Then she thought to submit further information. "I'm Pamela's sister. I come round to help out. They're in Selly Oak, if you want to know. I'm going 'round tonight. Don't bother tellin' Freddie to visit, he's not wanted."

"Your neighbour said they'd been taken to hospital. But… but what's happened?" Stan was by now standing on the other side of the garden gate.

Freddie's aunt shrugged and cocked her head to one side as if she was unsure, then said, "Don't know. They don't. They're not sure." She frowned. "They're keepin' them in for a few days. Doin' tests. It might be an infection."

Stan hesitated, then asked, "What ward are they in? Freddie should really be told."

The young woman looked at the doorstep, her eyes refusing to meet Stan's. She screwed up her lips and opened them, about to say something, but then hesitated. "'E's not their kid, not really. How could he be, the crip!"

"Look," Stan said, "I'm just giving Freddie a roof over his head for a day or two. I was just hoping his parents might, well, take him back?"

She sighed. "I told ya, Tom and Pam are not his mum and dad. He's some kind of mistake. I mean, look at 'im, he looks nothing like us. They thought he was just a small bab, but he's a midget. They ought to've told 'em he wasn't normal."

*

When he returned to the flat Freddie was gone, which was a good thing since it gave Stan time to think. He'd have to tell Freddie about his mum and dad, eventually, or at least tell him to go and see his aunt for a fuller explanation, since he'd not received one.

Stan wondered what he was doing, in fact what Freddie did all day while he was at work. Did he go out? Or did he just muck around in the flat? This afternoon, while Stan had been out, Freddie had obviously been poking around in his stuff. And there was a smell in the air he couldn't immediately identify. A box of his magic tricks was scattered on the linoleum. Stan used to perform little conjuring shows for his school friends ages ago, when he was in first year, and his nostalgic fondness for the craft meant he hadn't been able to get rid of his box of illusions. Stan knelt down to see that Freddie had spread out a pack of playing cards, face down, on the floor. It was Stan's 'Mocker' pack, which he'd bought by post from Ellisdons Magic & Joke firm with a one-and-thruppence postal order. From the back of any card you could tell the suit and denomination by tiny markings printed in the top left rosette of the cards' detailed floral patterned backs.

He couldn't imagine that Freddie had figured out the trick, but if he had been playing with the deck, why had he left the pack face down, except for the two jokers? Then Stan spotted the pool of vomit, a curdled fried egg-sized puddle on the lino near the foot of the bed.

The smell was disgusting, but Stan was starting to feel too tired and queasy to do anything, even scoop up the cards and put them away. Having Freddie living here was sapping his energy. Sapping his will to get on and do things. As he stood, a wave of nausea made him reach for the bed frame for support. Seconds later he found himself collapsed on the settee. Next to him was a copy of *Shock Films*, not the same issue as the one Freddie had arrived at the flat with. Picking it up desultorily he looked through it as the queasiness faded. And there was a panel down one side of the contents page about the film they were going to see tonight.

Gimmicks not the order of the day in Marshall's horror picture

If you think you've seen it all with *The House of Wax* in 3D, or William Castle's 'Percepto' gimmick in *The Tingler* think again. *The Mutant's Cry* is former comedy film director Harold Marshall's stab at making his first (unique) foray in the horror film field. This reviewer was definitely unsettled by the way in which the scriptwriter and the director managed to insinuate certain rather unpleasant thoughts... For the script, writer Llewellyn Upham says he went back to his rural Welsh roots and folklore... Read the full review and interviews on page 33.

Stan put down the magazine. He didn't want to read any more about the film, he'd be going to see it soon enough. At that moment Freddie chose to return and he looked worn out.

"You all right, lad? You've been sick, haven't you?"

"Mmm. Just need to rest a bit. Tired." His breath was raspy and laboured. "Was going to the paper shop for a magazine." He'd obviously not made it that far as he was empty handed.

"You look like you've been on a cross country run," Stan

said, trying a bit of humour. Then, "You've looked peaky all week. Maybe you should see the doctor. Your face is wrinkled up and pasty as an old man's." Not only that, Stan thought, he looked more hunched up than usual, as if the weight of the world was bearing down on his knobbly shoulders.

"No, I'm okay, maybe it's just a cold comin' on. I just want to have a rest before we go and see the film. I watched the trailer the other week and it looks great."

Stan doubted that. "Not enough fresh air, boy, that's what it is. Stuck indoors all the time. In fact, you probably caught the flu last week in the picture house." Stan lit up a gasper and then realised he probably wasn't helping too much with the provision of fresh air either.

On the bus into town they sat upstairs as Stan wanted a smoke. He was beginning to become a little shaky again and wondered if he really had caught the flu from his lodger. The cigarette settled things down and they were soon in town and at the entrance to the Jacey. Stan needn't have worried about having to vouch for Freddie's age, the lady in the ticket booth hardly glanced at him when Stan paid for two seats.

Inside the darkened auditorium, once his eyes had got used to the lack of illumination, he saw there were very few punters. Those few who had paid to see the film were scattered far and wide, the backs of their dark heads propped up like occasional coconuts at the shy. Freddie had picked seats on the back row and, since it was otherwise unoccupied, and he could get a clear view, Stan was happy to sit there.

The B feature was a cowboy film called *The Range Busters*, an old black and white film that Stan thought he'd maybe seen some years ago. He lit up and smoked a couple of Woodbine's to try to stay awake, he'd become so drowsy again, meanwhile noting that Freddie had fallen asleep. He was definitely coming down with something. They both were.

Pearl & Dean came on and Stan nudged Freddie awake. "Wake up, it'll be on in a minute." Freddie grunted and shuffled in his seat.

The curtains closed as the adverts faded and opened again a few seconds later, the screen filling with the black BBFC 'X' certificate notice. Stan noticed something odd straight away. The film's title, handwritten on the certificate by the president of the censor's board, said "The Mutant Cries", yet a minute later when the main title appeared on screen, Freddie's magazine review agreed that it was called –

THE MUTANT'S CRY

Figures in a darkened monochrome landscape darted across the screen, humped shapes dashing in a flowing mist behind the credits as they scrolled up. Then —

~ The Producers Of This Film ~
~ Would Like To Stress That ~
~ People Of A Nervous Disposition May Suffer ~
~ Delusions & Nightmares ~
~ After Watching What Is About To Happen…~

*

Afterwards, Freddie was very quiet as they walked from the cinema to the bus stop. In Stan's experience most kids were fired up by a film, enacting, in conversation at least, the salient moments of the plot. Instead Freddie was timidly holding close to his part-time landlord. As if he had been terrified by the film, which Stan could definitely relate to.

Stan felt uneasy too. The flick had been pretty powerful. "Those things, those creatures in the film, don't try to relate to them—they're just acting." While he spoke he wondered where they'd found actors with such… such horrible features, unless the makeup department was much better than he expected from a cheap horror film. Well it was difficult to remember it all, the film had had a tranquillising effect; Stan remembered being put off by the plot, which didn't make much sense, and his mind was on other things.

"I know what the director meant. I know what the scriptwriter researched. Don't worry about me, Stan. I'm okay as long as I'm with you." Stan wondered whether he was trying to convince himself that the plot of the film bore no relationship with reality.

Stan was beginning to feel sorry for him, but also frustrated. Frustrated that Freddie had been disowned by his so-called parents and that he, a relative stranger, was picking up the pieces. He needed his freedom, his space, he needed Freddie out,

91

he wasn't his responsibility and never had been. He felt trapped. When he eventually found a moment to tell Freddie that his folks were in the hospital, that might be the catalyst for a return back home, if he chose the right time.

Or perhaps make the situation worse. Freddie might think his bit of snooping detective work on his parents was merely in order to turf him out, which wouldn't have been too far from the truth. Either way, he couldn't leave it much longer before he told Freddie what he knew, even though Freddie was undoubtedly still burning with hatred for two adults who should have loved him.

At the bus stop, several people who had also just come out of the Jacey were waiting in line. There was no shelter and a shower of cold rain was soon soaking everyone. The erstwhile passengers hunched into their raincoats, turning their backs on the downpour. Stan gathered himself next to Freddie, noticing how bow-backed he was. He would never have called him a dwarf or a midget, as his aunt had described him, but Freddie was, for his age, small and that just emphasized his deformity.

The rain began to pelt down and everyone appeared to sink into themselves more than was possible. Conversely, Stan got the impression that he himself was stretching, he felt a little like Alice after she had sipped the strange drink and eaten the cake; taller than he was, smaller than he should be. His proportions felt all wrong. He really was coming down with the flu... if those peculiar sensations were some of the symptoms.

When they got off the bus, Stan could sense the remnants of the wet huddle at the bus stop shuffling to get off behind him. He needed a drink with some company, he knew, but he doubted if he could get Freddie into the Cross Guns. In the end he dragged his companion into the Outdoor adjacent and bought a bottle of whisky; he only just had enough money on him. But it was going to be worth it to temper the creeping wooziness.

"Not joinin' you-er mates?" the woman behind the counter asked as she reached for the bottle of Johnny Walker.

"Nah. My... my... friend's over," he nodded towards his diminutive companion. "Y'know how it is..."

"'E's a one, isn't 'e?" She paused. "That'll be... 'ere, is 'e all right?"

Freddie was almost kneeling and appeared half his normal

height. Rain was dripping from his Mac. He was breathing heavily, a worm of snot squirming its way from his nostrils to the floor.

Stan began to get flustered. "Freddie, behave yourself, boy." Then to the barmaid, "He's a joker all right. He's coming down with a dose of lurgy. Don't you worry about him. I'm looking after him." He threw a ten bob note on the counter and waited impatiently for his change.

Outside, through the bottle-glass windows, the rain pelted down, and distorted, diminutive shapes scuttled along, Stan's gaze caught in the moment as if a scene in tonight's film was somehow being replayed outside, releasing its inhabitants onto the street.

"Her'yare." She glanced through the window, then at Freddie. "Don't like 'im, mate. Take 'im out. 'E's not right."

On the street again, the rain had hardly let up, but the people foreshortened by the off-licence windows, who must have been running from the rain, had disappeared.

"I need a drink of this," Stan explained as they walked back to the flat. "I'm catching whatever you've got."

Freddie mumbled, bent over, avoiding the cold and the rain.

"And we need to talk." Perhaps he should tell Freddie now, let the news sink in before they arrived back at the flat. But the sky's deluge wouldn't let up. Freddie was hobbling along, bent under the weight of the weather.

"I need to tell you something."

"It's the film." Freddie managed to mumble.

"No, not that." Then "Right, right. Shouldn't have taken you. It was too horrible."

Freddie almost bent double and made a sound; it was probably a laugh, but to Stan it sounded more a cry of acquiescence; of what he wasn't at all sure.

At the bedsit, Stan put on the electric fire and steam and the smell of wet and soiled clothing soon began to permeate the room. As he began to close the flimsy curtains, down on the street below there were some people wandering about. It was madness in that downpour, but they were trying their best to fend off the rain by humping their shoulders forward and withdrawing their heads into the bulky clothing they wore. Even more oddly they didn't seem to be moving with any purpose.

You'd have thought they wanted to get out of the rain, onto a bus, anything, out of the driving rain. Instead, they shambled around aimlessly.

"They must be bollocking mad."

Freddie didn't ask who he was talking about, he just said, "I know. I know."

"You know bloody what?" He went and found a glass from the sink, swilled it in cold water and opened his bottle of whisky. "Sit down, Freddie. You need to rest and get warm."

"No, I know."

"What—"

"—Who they are." He nodded towards the window.

Stan pushed the curtain aside with his left hand and peered out, at the same time raising his right, which held the glass, to his lips. "What those nutters?" He pointed with his glass. Down below the street was awash with a flood, roiling like a river in spate. The rain was a grey misty swirl caught by the streetlamp.

With a decided grasp the spirit throttled his oesophagus, Stan's breath choking to escape in a fume of alcoholic vapour.

"I shouldn't never have stayed here. You've been a real friend, like a brother, but it can't be like that, I realise now, after seeing the film. It's too late now. Now I know."

Stan gulped another tot of whisky, flicking the curtain halfway back into place, as he watched the people outside congregating by the house gate, the rain driving them into an assembly of weirdly Freddie-like figures.

"Do you know those people, Freddie? Are they looking for you? Who the sodding hell are they?"

Freddie was now sitting with his back to Stan. Though he was moving oddly, as if he needed to cough up phlegm, he was silent and Stan's shout went unanswered. Only when there was a dull thud on the outer door at the bottom of the stairs did a sound utter from his lodger's mouth. Stan was thinking of him as an anonymous tenant now, not Freddie, who needed looking after. Whose parents were inexplicably in the hospital. A boarder who paid no rent and who had brought some disease into his flat. But then when Stan concentrated on the sounds from the hunchbacked form on the couch, it spoke no English. If it wasn't gibberish, if it was a foreign language, it was one whose rasping, gooey timbre Stan had never heard before. Except in *The*

Mutant's Cry.

But then that was simply a film. And here was reality, with his companion just play-acting a role like kids do when they've just seen a film and, in the rain-lashed street outside merely those others who had succumbed to the same delusions and nightmares.

THE SANITATION SOLUTION
Walter Gascoigne

'Garbage dump oh garbage dump
Why are you called a garbage dump
Garbage dump oh garbage dump
That sums it up, in one big lump'

Lyrics by Charles Manson 'Garbage Dump'

From my vantage point on top of this mountain of trash and maggots, I could see the rats were the size of small dogs. Just last week I saw one tearing apart what was left of a tiny infant. The rats seemed to sense a kindred spirit in myself and left me alone to my own devices. A tattered, worn out, and smelly old Lay-Z-Boy is my throne, from which I watch the fires continually burn over my Land of Oz. The filth that is beginning to fill the country started with me or perhaps you can say I just helped it along. It's a matter of opinion after all. When media services were still working properly, you may have heard about my accomplishments from news reports or the internet, for those who haven't I'll try to tell my tale as well as memory serves me.

Forgive me if I skip around, but it is my story, and I believe I have a right to tell it in any way I choose. After all it is a free country now isn't it? Let me tell you where I got my ultimate solution from. Many people to this day still think I had some grand scheme in the works for years or some secret backing by foreign governments that allowed things to get this far. Let me tell you, it isn't true. I think these things were bound to happen; I was just the catalyst that started the wheels in motion. I never would have guessed what I was capable of.

The whole thing started as a simple conversation with a co-worker about my soon to be ex-wife. I was going on my fifteenth year of being a garbage collector, picking up people's waste so the masses could stay sanitary. It started with us in the washroom, me with my coveralls and a name tag in bold letters OSCAR, and my colleague in his with the name BERT stamped in red. He and I were just getting done with our shift for the day, as a garbage collector the faster you worked and got your route done the sooner we were able to head home. Bert was a great guy; we had been working together for the better part of six years. We had always talked to each other about our problems at home and he would always say some statement that would cheer me up. He knew that my wife was trying to take my little girl away from me forever.

"How's the divorce coming Oz?" Bert asked. "Has your lawyer made any headway on getting you joint custody of Maggie?"

"My lawyer keeps taking my money and telling me everything is going to work out, I think he's full of shit," I said.

"Lawyers, politicians, and septic tanks. They all full of shit!" Bert always knew what to say.

"Thanks to my fat mother-in-law, Rose can afford the best lawyers in town, there's not a chance in hell I'm going to get Maggie back." It was getting very close to the final court date. I had thrown every penny I owned down my lawyers throat. I felt like the weight of a compactor was crushing me.

"I know this won't make things any better, but if you want to have a little fun and get some revenge, I got a real sticker for ya." A little fun Bert said, if he only would have known. "Here's what you do, you take a big smelly crap, place that in a paper bag with a dash of kerosene. Then go lay that stink bomb on Rosie's mom's porch. Light it up, ring the doorbell, and watch the fireworks!"

"Sounds very juvenile, and also very poetic, our marriage took a shit a long time ago." I finished washing up and put my uniform in my locker. "Later Bert, don't let the bedbugs bite. I'll see you in the morning." He said goodnight and I headed to the parking lot. I had no intention of taking Bert's advice at the time, although the idea brought a smile to my face as I got into my Buick.

Her lawyers were basing their case on the domestic violence incident that occurred on the last night we were together. Rose and I were married for five years, six months, and thirteen days before the divorce was finalized. She was a pretty girl, somewhat naive, average build, brown eyes, and a great set of legs. Although she was seven years younger than me we always shared the same topics of interest and liked the same shows and music. For the most part we had a good marriage, not ideal, but not bad either. We had arguments over money and relatives, but I think every relationship had that.

It was about three years into our marriage that I noticed she was becoming distant. I thought nothing of it at the time. I was working long hours and sometimes I was a little grumpy when I got home and sometimes I took it out on her. I always apologized and things would seem to be okay. For a while they were, eventually we stopped sleeping together, then we stopped eating together, and finally we hardly spoke at all. The days seemed to stretch out into a wasteland of picking up a never ending pile of trash.

Maggie was the only thing that kept us together, her beautiful smile, her laugh, her tiny little hands. On the day she was born I was the happiest man on earth. Rose was exhausted from childbirth so I went and watched the doctors clean her up and put her under a heating lamp. When they handed her back to us in a blanket we both wept and mumbled something about "I love you." I will never forget my daughter's smile, so different from the world I know now.

I didn't think anything about telling Rose that I got transferred to a different route for my job, I didn't think she would care. So when I got the same route that our house was on I never mentioned it to her. I noticed two blocks away from my house, that there was something out of place with my garbage. Because people often put their trash in with other people's receptacles, I thought very little of it. When we pulled up to the front of my house I began to unload our trash. From inside of a smaller black bag of a type we never used before, I caught something that drew my attention. I saw inside several prescription bottles with my wife's name on them for prenatal vitamins and appointments that were kept with an obstetrician. Knowing that we had not been intimate for over eight months, I knew the child was not mine. At that moment my life had become as meaningless as the clutter I deliver to the dump.

My anger boiled up and festered for weeks after that incident. I said nothing to Rose and she said nothing to me. Until one night when after a long shift of picking up dirty diapers and beer bottles, I stopped and had some drinks with Bert at the local pub. I told him what I had found out.

"Damn shame Oz, I'm sorry." We took a swig of our beers and sat in silence.

"What should I do Bert? What can I do? My life seems meaningless now."

"Let me tell ya Ozzie, having been married three times, I was never the one who had been cheated on, I was always the cheater, so I can't put myself in your shoes," Bert said as he took another gulp of his beer. "But I can tell you one thing, that if the relationship is built on lies, the only thing that can come from it is a heap of bullshit. I can tell you this because I have seen plenty of bullshit in my time, and right now, my friend, your life is pretty shitty. So the best I can say is move on and use that knowledge to build yourself a new kingdom." Bert always knew the right thing to say.

When I got home that evening, Maggie was in bed, Rose was watching C.S.I. and paid no attention to me when I walked into the living room. I stared at her in the glow of the television, I noticed her belly was getting slightly larger. At that moment I hated myself more than her, I thought what a fool I was for not having noticed before. My anger took over then and I began screaming.

"Why! Why didn't you tell me you are pregnant?" My face was flushed red and tears were streaming down. "Who is he? How long has this been going on?" She was about to deny everything, but when she saw the look in my eyes she must have known it wasn't going to work.

"Alright Ozzie, you really want to know?" Her voice began to rise. "It's been over between us for years! All you care about is that stupid job and going for drinks with your buddies." Sobbing, she flung herself off the couch and began pointing a finger directly at my face. Tears pooled up in her eyes. "If you really want to know who cares more about me than you, ask Maggie. Dan has been here for her more than you have!"

I should have known, Dan, the loser from down the street. My rage took control; I grabbed her by the arms and began shaking her, all the while screaming, "Why? Why? *Why!*" I may have hit her, I don't remember. Somehow she managed to break free and ran into our bedroom, I followed and began hammering at the door, screaming obscenities. By then Maggie was awake from all the yelling and I could hear her sobbing in her bed. I didn't realize Rose had called the police until the doorbell sounded. When she heard the doorbell she burst from the room and ran right for the front door.

Everything after that is kind of a blur. I remember being handcuffed, brought to jail, and told there was a seventy two hour temporary restraining order on me. There was to be no contact with my wife or child in that period. Bert came the next morning and bailed me out, he was even kind enough to let me stay with him for a few days. He told me Rose had moved in with her mother but it would be best just to stay with him for a bit. I tried to call Rose several times, but always got her mother's answering machine. I knew if Rose's mother had her way I would never spend time with my Maggie again, and I was right.

Not long after my conversation with Bert about the paper poo bag, my divorced was finalized. The lawyers on her side made sure to show pictures of the bruises on her arms and the mark on her face. They played me up to be a drunken father who tormented his child with threats and intimidation. My lawyer just sat there, never saying a word in my defence. All the while my fat mother-in-law was sitting there with a shit eating grin. The court awarded full custody to Rose. They also specified that until I went through the various anger management classes, I was to have no contact with my child. Even after such time all visitations were to be supervised until the court was satisfied with my conduct. That's the day I made up my mind to put a little present on my ex-wife's door. That's the day I really lost everything.

Now I'm not the one to do a job half-ass, pun intended, so I began to eat as many greasy fries and burgers that my stomach could handle. When I knew the time had come, I squatted over a large Tupperware container and did my business, the smell was atrocious. After securing the lid, I went and collected a paper bag and some kerosene from the garage and waited for dawn.

Around five A.M. I parked my car in the next subdivision, my munitions on the seat beside me. I opened the container and placed the contents into the bag, splashing on a bit of kerosene and noticing how the smell seemed even more potent. I got out of the car, paper bag in hand, lighter in my pocket, and binoculars around my neck. The sprawling houses in this subdivision looked exactly the same as my mother-in-law's. Huge two story houses with arched porches, built so close to each other that they were virtually one long house. Some porch lights were on but as it became lighter outside some began to turn off due to their timers. When I got to my intended destination their porch light was off and the sun had just crept over the first roofs in the neighbourhood. I placed the bag on the cement porch, lit it with my lighter, rang the doorbell several times, and dashed across the street. I waited in some bushes and focused in my binoculars. When Rose's mother opened the door, groggy eyed and still half asleep, she failed to notice the odour, but not the fire. She began stomping on it with her slipper, and when that caught fire began hopping around on one leg screaming bloody murder. I believe she yelled something about her feet being on fire, but I prefer to think she said my faeces were on fire. One of the funniest things I ever saw, I almost shit myself laughing.

Of course my ex suspected that it was my doing and said so in the police report, but without any witnesses they couldn't prove it was me. Turns out old fatty ended up with second degree burns and a trip to the hospital. I knew I had to let things blow over for a while before I played my next big act. But what could that be? What other weapons did I have at my disposal other than bowel movements? Then it hit me, garbage, I had lots and lots of garbage.

For the next few months I attended my anger management meetings and worked extra hours. I thought a lot about Maggie. I also started to keep some of the smelliest garbage from my route and store it in my garage. To keep my neighbours from noticing the awful smell, I enclosed all of it in large sealed plastic bins. When I arrived at mother-in-law's house one stormy evening they didn't even notice me scattering the filth a foot high in their front lawn. The next day in the newspaper there was a small article on page six about vandalism which read;

The suspect, who remains at large, left over one ton of garbage at a home in the Birch Road community. Residents are asking for anyone with information to please come forward. Estimate of the damages are in the thousands.

I knew my next plan had to be on a much larger scale. The police already suspected me, but again they had no proof that I was the perpetrator. The following week I told Bert he could head home early and I would finish off the day, dumping our load at the collection facility. He thanked me as I dropped him off and I hurried to my intended destination. I swerved into the subdivision doing about fifty miles an hour, hopping a few curbs and taking out a few bushes. When I reached the mother-in-law's I slammed on the brakes and pulled the lever that raises and releases the load. Two tons of garbage piled almost as high as the house sat on their front porch. I was still laughing when the cops cuffed me.

Bert bailed me out again and that same day a news reporter shows up at my house. He asked a lot of questions: Why did I do it? What was I trying to prove? Are you glad you did it? I answered him as best I could, he thanked me and said the article would be in the newspaper sometime this week, if his editor approved it.

Lo and behold in the Friday edition, there on the front page in big black type were the words;

One Man's Sanitation Solution

The article went on to talk about an average Joe who worked as a garbage man, and was finally fed up with the court system. He went on to extol the virtues of the trodden on labourer. How by my example others could challenge the system. Not with words or bombs but with trash. He even had several good metaphors for life and how it pertains to waste. I never really said any of those things, I just told him my story. Leave it to a writer to embellish things.

The story caught on fast, went viral as they used to say, and before long it was on every T.V. station, news network, and internet blogging site. Not even the reporter that wrote the story could have conceived of what came next. At first it was just a few small incidents, here and there, people dumping trash on the police station steps or the courthouse parking lot, disgruntled McDonald's employees throwing shakes to the floor, simple stuff. It didn't take long before more and more people joined in and the streets were beginning to fill with garbage. Union workers left their jobs and began throwing trash. The police and emergency personnel were at a loss at what to do, there was just too much garbage and not enough people picking it up. In some areas it was waist high, enough so that it began to block several major intersections. It was around that time that reports were coming in from all the major cities that it was occurring in other parts of the country as well. Communications started to break down and it was every man for himself.

It was when the last reports started coming out of L.A. that I knew I needed to get Maggie out of town. Canada was already turning back refugees and it was only a matter of time before Mexico did the same. Seeing the insanity of what was happening the first week, I had already stocked up on food, water, and ammunition for my pistol. Bert had left that same week and begged me to leave the city with him. I couldn't leave Maggie and he knew it, without another word he drove off. There was no way a car was going to make it across town so I put my supplies in my backpack and began to walk, gun in hand. Dusk was nearing and the fires from several trash heaps lead my way. In the distance I could hear gunshots and screaming, I avoided the main roads and hurried along. When I arrived at their subdivision, most of the houses were burned down, others in flames. Urgently I ran down the blocks of streets, littered with trash, until I came to where my daughter lived. The house was engulfed in flames, I tried to get close but the heat pushed me back. There was the same smell in the air as the time I lit the pile of shit on fire and I still wonder if my mother-in-law's ghost may have deliberately made that odour or if it came from the rubbish burning everywhere around me. All I could do was fall over weeping, while the smell of charred shit rose up around me.

After the flames died down and it was cool enough for me to go through the rubble, I found the remains of my daughter still clutching her mother around her neck. I wept for the last time as I began to pile mounds of garbage over their bodies. It was much easier than trying to get to the soil, which by now wasn't even visible through the debris. So I piled the refuse as high as I could get, set an old Lay-Z-Boy on top and shot anyone coming close to the tomb of my daughter. The rats leave me alone.

It was raining the morning a piece of scorched paper flying by on the wind caught my attention. I snatched it from the air and read:

"Good name in man and woman, dear my Lord,
Is the immediate jewel of their souls.
Who steals my purse steals trash; 'tis something, nothing'

103

'Twas mine, 'tis his, and has been slaved to thousands'
But he that filches from me my good name
Robs me of that which not enriches him,
And makes me poor indeed."

How right Shakespeare could be at times. I crumbled the paper, and sat in my chair as a rainbow appeared through the clouds.

UP AND OUT OF HERE
Mark Patrick Lynch

Dylan Mulch learned about flying the hard way. In one sense it was a lot like sex, in that it was something you didn't do in public. Or if you did, then you better be damn sure everyone else was doing it too. Because if you were performing out there in the open all by yourself, you could be sure as sixes people were going to get freaked by it.

—Huh? You see that guy?

—Oh my God.

—He's flying!

Like that. And maybe with some screams added in too.

Understandably, he did his best not to fly in public. But sometimes, without him realising, it just came upon him.

"Thing of it is," Dylan told his friend Buddy. "The only time I get really high is when I don't know it's happening. When I'm trying to do it, it's so hard. A couple of feet off the floor at best. Usually it's just a few inches."

"But you're still doing it," Buddy said. "That's what you've got to remember."

To do it on command, Dylan would tense up his thighs, bunch them tight as he could. Then, when he felt he couldn't squeeze anymore, he'd make that extra effort and go at it a little farther, and then a little farther, holding his breath and straining his ears so it sounded like boulders were rolling in his head. He'd hold his breath and clench his legs until he was sure his veins were going to burst, start worrying his feet would shrivel up through lack of blood and his shoes fall off.

And he'd fly.

Which was a helluva thing.

Or so you'd think. For most people.

*

Jade-Louise Fletcher wasn't impressed that Dylan could fly.

"Dylan, how many times? It means nothing to me."

It'd got so he was wondering what would impress her. If flying wasn't the ticket, something he could do, then that left the impossible. And even the impossible... well, he knew enough about Jade-Louise to understand parting the sea would be a washout as far as she was concerned.

There didn't seem any easy answer.

The thing about Jade-Louise, she blew gum, big bubbles. It wasn't a profession, but if it had then she'd've been a leading figure in the field. Gum. Big gum. At times bigger than any Dylan had seen in his life. The size of snowmen. She thought that was a more useful skill than flying.

As she sat taking up the sofa and watching non-stop junk TV, Dylan could see what she was thinking as he told her once more about the flying and how he was an amazing guy to be able to do such a thing. Her face told him a story he didn't want to hear: gum had a hundred uses; flying a couple of inches, well where could you go with that?

"So?" she'd said when again Dylan floated above a dull carpet that hadn't been vacuumed in weeks.

Jade-Louise Fletcher was a hard girl to impress.

Deflated, Dylan was coming to realise he'd need to put in some extra effort if she was going to smile at him with anything but indifference each time he came around the terraced cottage she shared with her brother.

"Well, it's not everyone can fly, Jade-Louise," he said, kind of hating the pleading tone that crept into his voice.

"But that's hardly flying, is it? A couple of inches. If that." Finding a put-down of no originality, she said,"Typical man – exaggerating everything."

"It's not exaggerating, not if I'm off the ground."

"You're not off the ground now."

"That's because I breathed out. It happens like that. I can't breathe and fly at the same time. It's too hard."

He reckoned it was part of the reason he couldn't as yet will himself higher than a foot or two: because he'd not learned how to do both at once. The second he thought about it, it went wrong. This visit, well it must've been the umpteenth time he'd flown for Jade-Louise. Or, as Buddy insisted, levitated. He'd gone up higher than usual too. Made a real attempt, busting his gut, craning his head forward so he didn't bump the ceiling as he ascended. But he'd only managed half a foot. Still, it brought no reaction worth talking about.

So?

Maybe if Jade-Louise saw it happen to him when he wasn't trying… He'd been up higher than a house in the past, sending people running screaming, especially when he fell out of the air without control. Talk about bruises. If he'd had the language, Dylan could recount an epic narrative about them. But the thing about height was that it had always come to him unintentionally. Intending to fly, that was different; it took energy, concentration. And the best he ever did was – okay, yeah, as Buddy pointed out – a bit of levitation. It saved in bruises but was far less impressive.

"It's still flying," Dylan said, aware the levitation had tired him and he was soaking with sweat. He hoped he didn't smell. "It is," he insisted, "it's flying."

Jade-Louise snorted.

And God help him, but he found that attractive too.

"Aw, Jade…"

"I'm not impressed, Dylan. I don't know what you want me to say. I'm sorry, love."

When it escaped him, the sound of his sigh was pitiful. He was glad the sudden loud whoops and applause from the TV meant she didn't catch it.

"What's this you're watching, then?" he said.

"Jeremy Kyle."

"Oh right. He's good, him."

"He's okay."

Dylan nodded. His head was buzzing, but with nothing he could drag out to keep up the conversation.

He'd sit next to Jade-Louise on the sofa if he could, but she was a big girl and there was a spread of magazines and bags of open sweets beside her. If he did try, chances were he'd put himself on something she wanted, cause the Liquorice Alsorts to tumble out of their bag and slip down between the cushions. Maybe he'd get a humbug stuck to his trouser seat too. No hearing the end of that, and probably how disgusting he was if it did happen. Especially if he then lifted his arms and she keeled over at the smell of his BO.

So because he couldn't sit beside her Dylan stayed standing, legs aching after his efforts so that he worried he might collapse.

Flying. It freaked some, did nothing for Jade-Louise, and tired the crap out of him. What was the point?

Even Reacher, the German Shepard who'd watch with interest each time Dylan levitated, was curled up in the armchair, snoring softly.

Or he was for a moment.

"Buddy!" Jade-Louise shouted at the beamed ceiling, causing the dog's head to jerk up and Dylan to jump almost as high as he'd levitated. A commercial break had interrupted her show, and now Jade-Louise had time for other things. "Dylan's still here, you know. Get yer arse in gear." Then to Dylan, not unkindly, "He'll be on his way."

"It's okay," Dylan said. "I'm not rushed."

Truth was, even when she was ignoring him, Dylan liked being around Jade-Louise. She was big, sure, and not everyone would like that; but she was attractive on it. Had nice hair and eyes the colour of a warm sky. He'd got his job as much for her as himself, gainful employment to impress her. Getting off the doss at last and with money for a proper haircut. But she never seemed to notice.

"I can wait all day today," he added.

Jade-Louise didn't say anything, but he got the impression she was counting time out with her tongue on the roof of her mouth. Hopefully the irritation was only at Buddy.

There were some sounds from upstairs. Dylan heard footsteps moving about, the ceiling creaking. There was only one bedroom and a walk-in closet space up there, a small bathroom with a shower unit but no bath, a square yard of landing.

Brother and sister shared the house.

Dylan didn't know how that worked, if they slept in the same bed, Buddy and Jade-Louise. He'd never asked, didn't like to, though he'd often wondered about it, and how it'd been when their mother was still alive, how they'd gone on then. All together in one tiny terraced cottage.

"He's on his way," Jade-Louise said.

Dylan nodded. The toilet had flushed, the concertina vinyl door protesting as it was squashed open. Dylan heard footsteps descending the stairs, a curse and the sound of magazines spilling down them, a frantic grab for the handrail to prevent Buddy going head over arse, heavy cursing.

His voice came through the thin wall after the heel of a fist thumped it about halfway down. His voice through the wall, slightly muffled, "Bloody hell, Jade, trying to kill me with these fuckin things?"

Jade-Louise rolled her eyes. "No luck yet," she told Dylan with a quick-fire laugh like a run of hiccups.

Still cursing, Buddy pushed through the door from the narrow, standing room-only hall, the top of his boots flapping untied. You could see Buddy today. He wasn't invisible. Dylan was grateful for that. One time, still unsure how he did it, Buddy had wound up invisible all day. Now it was most mornings, some afternoons too. Invisibility: if flying had no uses in Jade-Louise's eyes, then invisibility had even fewer. Hard to see what good it could do anyone. Even Buddy was troubled by its impracticalities.

Buddy grinned at Dylan as he clomped toward the kitchen bar.

"Dylan."

"Buddy."

"How goes?"

"Okay. You?"

"Uh huh." Buddy nodded, took a carton of orange juice from the fridge and gulped mouthfuls down until it was empty. His untied boots jangled and thumped, slipping off his foot with each step so it looked like he was stumbling all the time. He dug under clothes on the kitchen counter till he found a carrier bag leaking old frozen food packages, into which he dumped his litter. He made a show of turning his attentions to Jade-Louise, shook his head at what he saw lolling on the couch, passed a glance to Dylan, as if inviting him to comment. Look at her. A joke between two men of the world, right?

Dylan averted his eyes.

"What?" Jade-Louise said, having caught the look. "Because if it's something you wanna start, then you better tell me now. I'm not playing your games, Buddy. I'm not in the mood."

Shrugging, Buddy took out his cigarettes and patted his pockets for his lighter. When he couldn't find it, he hit the gas on the oven, ducked his face with a James Dean sneer to the flame, cigarette twitching in his lips. Pulled back quickly when his hair fell forward. But the cigarette was lit, and his hair didn't go up, which Dylan had seen happen once.

"Buddy, I'm serious," Jade-Louise was saying.

"Never said anything, did I?" Buddy gave a big pantomime what've-I-done-? shrug.

Jade-Louise ignored him, turned her eyes back to the television set, a widescreen science fiction device plugged into the cable network, a hundred channels of nothing on and extras if you paid more. Jeremy Kyle set to repeat, because you couldn't believe it the first time you saw it.

She wired it for sound with the remote now the ads were done.

Music and studio applause, a dramatic moment of silence while Kyle pulled out the results of a lie detector test his guests – a thin rat-faced guy and a sullen woman with a heavy jaw and cow eyes – had undertaken to confirm their stupidity. As if being on TV to talk about it wasn't proof enough.

"We on our way?" Buddy said.

Dylan nodded. "Yeah, if you want." He tried to keep his eyes on Buddy. But Jade-Louise, it was like she was magnetic or something, you had to look.

Buddy slapped him on the arm. "C'mon, I'm ready. Showered, shaved, and shat. Except for the shower and the shave."

"Take a key," Jade-Louise said, as close as she'd come to saying goodbye. "I'm out to the shops later."

Before he went after Buddy, Dylan took a last look at Jade-Louise, tried to think of something to say. She was blowing a new ball of gum, somehow shaping it so it looked like a crescent moon, making sure there was a space she could see through to the TV. He felt his heart do a special beat, like a scat-man was playing with it, and he floated up off the floor a couple of inches without knowing he was doing so.

She didn't answer his, "See you later, Jade-Louise."

*

They made for the rec, still quiet this late in the afternoon. Buddy had been thinking about invisibility and was keen to share his thoughts. He'd already been through the merits and failings of flying with Dylan, now he was cogitating on his own predicament.

"In the wrong conditions, like early in the mornings when no one can see me and I can't do anything about it, it's going to be a curse," Buddy said as they approached the deserted play area. Kids stayed away from here. Dealers were supposed to hang around the grounds, or so Dylan had heard. Two scruffy guys. But he and Buddy had never seen them in all the times they'd sat smoking on the end of the slide. And they were here every other day. Went to show, you couldn't believe all the rumours.

"Like, say I turn now," Buddy was saying. "You know, phase out like I can without realising it, the way you suddenly take off. No one sees me, right, and so I've got to remember to get out of their way if they're coming at me. Like with that woman over there with the pram. If I was walking in front of her."

Buddy shook his head, stretched out his legs and crossed his boots on the strips of shredded rubber making up the safety patch for kids to fall into when they slid off the slide.

"But you can forget. Because how often do you stop during the day, remind yourself people can see you? It's the same with being invisible when it happens. You got to remember to remind yourself no one can see you. Otherwise, you're gonna walk out in front of a car one day, and it's gonna speed up, not knowing you're there, run you down." Buddy nodded sagely at this, as if impressed with his own thoughts. He fixed his eyes sightlessly on the string of grey council housing that squared in the slope of the long recreation field.

"So anyway that's what I've been thinking," he told Dylan. "It's got hazardous potential written all over it. Invisibility is dangerous. No use to anyone."

"But we can do these things, and no one else can," Dylan said. "We're like superheroes. So there's gotta be a good side to it."

"It's finding how to use it to our advantage, to our…" Buddy sifted his vocabulary for an impressive enough word… "Our betterment. See, so far it's not helped you make better money. Look at you, still earning the usual. What's your job?"

Buddy already knew he worked the bin round, so Dylan figured it for one of those rhetorical questions Buddy kept bringing up. Dylan didn't have to answer when he got asked one of those. For instance: is it a good idea to stick your fingers in an electrical socket? The answer's so obvious it doesn't need saying.

"See, you being able to levitate…"

"Fly," Dylan said. "I can fly. It's what I do."

Buddy inclined his head, not wanting to debate the point. "… it hasn't got you a better job than emptying people's rubbish. And you could do that even if you couldn't fly." Buddy blew smoke from the remainder of his cigarette, shook his head. "It's not right, my friend. Not right at all."

Dylan couldn't argue. But his reasons for taking that job weren't anything to do with flying, or hiding out under a secret identity like Spider-Man taking photographs for a living. For a smart guy, Buddy sometimes missed the obvious. Whether he knew Dylan felt for Jade-Louise, Dylan didn't know. But he must have a clue Dylan was interested.

"Super heroes manage okay," he said so low Buddy didn't hear.

He leaned back, caught the pale moon out early in the late afternoon light. It was kind of romantic, in a dreary council estate way. Some romance you could make on the rec under afternoon moonlight, though; it was hardly a South Pacific beach with native girls singing in the background. Jade-Louise, he thought, what would it take to pull a smile out of her? What would Spider-Man do? Kiss her from a web, hanging upside down in the rain.

"Special powers, huh?" Buddy said, still on with that. He held out his hand to his friend. He'd bunched a fist with the little finger hanging crooked out of it. "Pull on that?"

"I've seen it," Dylan said. "My granddad had the same thing." Tug on it and he'd rip a fart. Dylan didn't think, in the grand scheme of things, that was much of a super power.

"See, what we've got to do," Buddy said, pulling his hand back and lifting an arse cheek to let a long slow trumpet out, "we've got to decide how we use these things, our abilities. We know we can't just show them off in the street. But there's gotta be something. Invisibility, it's useless, unless you're a pervert or a thief. So there has to be something. We need to think it through."

He flicked the end of his cigarette into the pieces of churned safety rubber.

"I mean, the worst super hero ever, it's the Invisible Woman from Fantastic Four, right? What's she going to do, make you stop looking at her, so don't take over the world, evil guy. You're okay, flying's got something to it."

Dylan said, "But people don't like it when I fly, not even when I only do it a little bit. And for sure not where I'm suddenly twenty feet up in the air and then I fall out of the sky."

They were quiet for a moment, and then Buddy said, "There's always the circus."

But they'd already had this conversation. They couldn't join the circus. For one, it had been fifteen years since anyone Dylan knew had even seen a circus in these parts; and for two, what kind of half-arsed act could they put on: a guy who could levitate a couple of feet wouldn't be seen from the back row of the Big Top – and the invisible man, they wouldn't even be able to see him from the front row.

"Forget the circus," Dylan said. "It's no good. We know."

"Yeah, but…"

Feeling a sudden sense of propulsion, the need to act and change things, Dylan said, "Do you think Jade-Louise likes me?"

Buddy shrugged. "She's never said she doesn't. You're always around, she hasn't said anything about it being a problem. Would've done if she didn't like you, didn't want you in the house."

"No, I meant – well, you know, likes me."

Buddy fastened Dylan with a new look, like he was only seeing him for the first time and wasn't certain he liked what he saw, noticing he'd got a ski-jump nose with a strand of snot hanging out of a nostril or something. "Likes you?" he said. "My sister? Likes you? You gone crazy or something? How many fingers am I holding up?"

Dylan looked, but Buddy had phased his hand into invisibility.

"Huh? How many, Dylan?"

"Funny," Dylan said. "If you don't want to talk about it, forget I asked, okay. I just wondered, that's all."

It went quiet for a moment, felt awkward, and then Dylan sighed. "Aw, what the hell. You could always ask her."

"Maybe I will."

"You will, yeah?"

"Yeah."

"Straight away?"

"I guess."

"Okay." Buddy stood up. He was completely visible now. For a moment Dylan had worried his friend was going to vanish completely, so that Dylan wouldn't have a clue where he was, if he was sitting there by himself or not, a washed out moon above looking down on one person or two. "Hey, Jade," Buddy called, "come over here a minute."

"Yeah, funny." Dylan looked around, half expecting this to be one of Dylan's attempts at comedy, but a little scared it wasn't.

And wouldn't you know, it wasn't.

Jade-Louise's familiar figure, holding onto an extendable blue leash as thick as a rope, was over the other end of the rec, Reacher taking a crap near a sign threatening a fifty pound fine for just that. Jade-Louise stood still a moment, and Dylan thought she wasn't going to come, hoped so anyway, because right now his stomach had knotted up. Her brother was shouting her up the steep slope, an act that was as likely to summon her as was a guy in a flashing mac telling her to come and check out this really great surprise he's got for her.

Sure enough, she gave Buddy her middle finger, turned back to Reacher.

"I don't think she's in the mood for it," Dylan said. He pulled his jacket tight around his middle. Getting cold now, a cruel turn on the thin wind. Soon be the thick of November. The moon was getting brighter, turning a neat cream colour. There were flickers of TV screens in the mean windows of some of the council houses.

"Nah, she'll come," Buddy said. Then he shouted: "Jade! Come on! Please!"

The please carried, gave her cause for thought. Dylan watched, his stomach full of nerves, as she tugged on Reacher's leash and started toward them, all the way up the slope of the rec playing field. He had a feeling, the way she was coming, she wouldn't be in too good a mood when she got here.

"How come we can't be superheroes?" he said, thinking maybe he could turn the conversation into that by the time Jade-

Louise and Reacher arrived. Maybe she'd be impressed with the thought of the two of them using their powers for good.

Buddy didn't quite sneer, but you could tell he didn't think much to the idea. "What? And you'd get all the glory? 'The Invisible Man, we didn't see him stopping the guys holding up the Post Office.' And anyway, how many robberies have we ever come across? We'd just be standing there, waiting in the hope someone came around with a shotgun. And then what? They fire a warning shot at nothing, only I'm standing there, they didn't see me. I'm dead, bleeding invisible blood on the floor. You don't know about it till you trip over me when you land."

"Okay," Dylan said. "Then no to the superhero thing. I was just wondering."

Actually, what he was really wondering was how he could get out of here without Jade-Louise reaping the same sort of carnage on him you'd see in a train wreck. But if he went now, Buddy was sure to tell her Dylan was interested in her, and Buddy, he'd frame it in the crudest way he could. Like,

Hey, Jade, Dylan was wondering if he could get a squirt or two up you. What do you think?

Maybe he'd add, It's okay by me, long as you don't wet my side of the bed.

Dylan had to stay and face it.

Buddy turned to him as Jade-Louise got closer. "Another thing. What kind of superheroes would we be? We don't have costumes."

"If you're invisible, you wouldn't need one."

Buddy grunted. "Here comes Bubble-Girl."

Actually, it was Reacher who was first, sniffing around the playground, recognising Buddy and Dylan before moving on. Jade-Louise was hanging onto his leash, had let him pull her part the way up. She looked flustered, well out of breath.

"There's dealers hang around here," she said, voice heavy from climbing the incline. "You want to be careful. People'll think it's you. The police'll be asking about you."

She had some gum on the go, and now she was on level ground it inflated and sank with her breath. Dylan knew if she tried she could make it into a massive ball. Do it quickly too. You'd be surprised.

He smiled, couldn't help it, thinking on what Buddy had

called her. Bubble-Girl. Because she did fit the part. And the way Buddy was talking, though he'd been dismissive about it all at first, maybe this was something they could get together on. Dylan would be Sky Boy or something, Buddy would of course be the Invisible Man and leader, and Jade-Louise was good for go as Bubble-Girl. Maybe Reacher could get involved too. Hero Dog or something. Dylan would think on it later.

"We've never seen any dealers," Buddy said. "Not once, all the time we've been here."

Jade-Louise was still getting her breath back. A lot of it was escaping her mouth, showing on the air, another sign how cold it was getting, while the rest gave her gum a frosty effect, which was kind of enchanting.

"So," she said, chewing it back inside. "What is it you're wanting? It's not him again, is it, going to fly? I've said, the flying doesn't matter to me."

"Depends on your answer, I reckon," Buddy said.

"Answer to what?"

"Well, he wants—"

Dylan cut in, before any form of crudity crossed Buddy's lips. "I wanted to ask if you'll go out with me."

There, gone and said it. He felt something in his throat, a big bulge of emotion, which he reckoned would make it hard for him to speak whatever Jade-Louise said next. When he summoned the courage to look at her, she was nodding, actually had a smile on her face, a genuine one, not cruel.

"Okay. Take me to the pictures tomorrow night, then across to Frankie and Benny's after."

Dylan couldn't speak. She didn't care he could fly, but she was still going to go out with him? He stammered something like, "Yeah. That's good."

Then after smiling at an astonished Buddy, who you could suddenly see straight through like he was painted on glass, he closed his eyes feeling great, a whoosh of happiness rising through him, carrying him high, full of dizziness.

He thought he heard warning shouts, Buddy telling him to watch out, but he didn't care, he felt too good to let anything spoil this.

When he opened his eyes, he found he was a long way off the ground, heading to the moon and no stopping. For a while he didn't question it, just let it happen, enjoying himself, the way he was feeling. But that'd change, he knew; it always did. The second he thought about how he was doing this, it'd all give. He'd take a breath and fall back to Earth.

Before he reached that point of maximum height and plummeted from the sky, he had time to hope Jade-Louise was blowing a big enough bubble out of her gum to catch him with.

She'd save him. She'd have to.

Because the Invisible Man, he was no use at all.

LATE SHIFT
Adrian Cole

Been working the late shift now for near enough ten years. Started part time, taking on a bit of night work, then about five years ago went full time at it. Never looked back. I met Rod two years ago when my workload got too big for me to handle alone and he's been with me ever since. Rod's a good lad, twenty five to my fifty. Introduced to me by a mate of mine who works as a guard in a prison.

Rod had been in and out of institutions since he was a kid, always nicking things until he got mixed up with a bad lot. Bit off more than he could chew. It got him two years in the slammer and he was in danger of being screwed up for life. Except that he was brilliant at mechanics. He admitted he'd never done much with it. Buggered about at school and not much better when he left. It was only when he was inside he started to use his talent and maybe his brain with it.

My mate had a word with me in our local one day, and told me about this kid who was about to be released. "You're looking for someone to work with you, Mac," he said. "Give the kid a try out. He needs someone like you."

"You think I'm a father figure? Shit, I'm not much cop at that, mate. I hardly ever see my two boys these days. Or men, more like. One in Australia, the other at sea." I'd split with my wife when they'd been youngsters. She found some white collar bloke who earned a lot more than me and who she said was less temperamental and fucked off with him. I rarely see her any more. I regret it some days, not having a woman, but mostly I reckon it's an arrangement that suits us both. Last I heard, she's got some other bloke now. Good luck to him.

Anyway, I did give Rod a try and it worked out from the word go. He was a natural. Just needed someone to tease it out of him. Give him a machine – any damn machine – and he'd dismantle it, put it back together and have it running like clockwork. He lived for his work – well, we both did, so that was near perfect in our little world. He was a loner, but I thought

118

more than once he could have done with more of his own age for company, seeing as how we don't meet that many in our line of work. And as for girls, well, we joked about them, but the kid was human, with the usual urges. Needed that sort of thing in his life. He didn't say so, but it must have chafed at him. More so than me.

I said about the late shift. I worked for a big garage, here in the city. Did my apprenticeship years ago, a combination of professional training, a bit of night school, and as many hard knocks as a young bloke takes working with the lot I was teamed with. I did okay. They knew I was good and I worked hard.

When I started on the night work, I loved it. I'd be sent off with a small crew to somewhere that had to work through the day – like a big bus depot – and where all the repairs and maintenance had to be done at night. So we kept all the vehicles on the road and none of the daytime transport schedules were lost. The other guys in the gang did shifts. Most of them didn't like sleeping in the day and working at night. With me, it was the other way round.

I didn't sleep all day, just took what sleep I needed. Worked from ten at night through until about six in the morning. My body got used to it and whenever there was a call for a late shift, they put me down for it. The company got greedy and started hiring some of us out. The bosses did okay out of us, though they didn't give much of a shit for us, as long as we did the work. Typical. That's when I twigged that I could do a whole lot better if I worked for myself. I wasn't too hot at paperwork, but I had a couple of good contacts, guys whose vehicles I looked after. Prestige service. They helped me start up my own business. I waved two fingers at the bosses and did pretty good.

Like I said, I got too busy to manage alone and that's where Rod came in. The two of us did very nicely once we got going. It wasn't just the work, it was the way of life. The late shift. We travelled around to most of the major cities and we had a network of places where we stayed, with landlords and landladies who were used to us booking in, having a day time nap and then going out all night to work. Some said nothing about it, keeping to themselves, others had a laugh with us. I must have heard all the vampire jokes going.

Rod was a dead loss at paperwork, so I looked after that for him. We had a flat, a bit of a dump, which we used as a base, but there weren't many days a year when we stayed there. We were too busy. We paid our rates and stuff and we kept to ourselves.

In our line of work, you get to meet people, even though the hours are what they call 'unsocial.' It's always surprised me how many people there are like me and Rod, who live the late shift and don't bother much with the day. We were a kind of alternative society. I don't mean like hippies, or tramps, though we met a few of them along the way. We were no different from ordinary day people. It's just that the connections with them were more limited. And there's a kind of code, not laws exactly, but things that are common to all of us.

There's not a lot of contact from city to city, or town to town, except through a few travelling guys like me and Rod. Most of the late shift groups are self-centred. They don't have problems with the day people – okay, I daresay they do have differences from time to time – but generally they don't have a lot to do with each other, apart from where the job calls for it. Like night porters, or the stockers working in the big superstores. They all have superiors to deal with and someone who sorts out their pay and employment stuff.

It's impossible to be totally independent, mind. You try and shut yourself off from the day world altogether, and it can get rough, if the chips are down. I'll tell you what I mean.

*

Our landlady liked to gossip. We'd stayed with her a few times and were used to it when we arrived. She'd moan about the Government, the local Council and her old man. We hardly ever saw him. He was a day worker, but once he'd had his grub, he was off out. It seemed to suit the woman, whose own life was centred around the TV, mostly soaps. People she said she felt she knew. What she called, real people. Me and Rod always agreed, but we never saw any of that crap. Another fucking world, not ours.

"So this time you're working at the Tube Factory?" she said as we were dumping our stuff in the cramped bedroom. She knew the place, a huge concern where the company turned out steel tubes like endless sausages, and she reckoned some of her mates had sons and daughters working the machines there. Day workers.

"Yeah," I said. "The factory has a fleet of vehicles they like to keep busy from dawn till dusk. Rod and me are going in to do all the inspections and keep them ticking over. About a week's work."

"You don't mind working all night?"

She always asked the same question, like we were a bit weird and should have said how much we hated it and wished we could work normal hours.

I always said the same thing back. "Someone has to do it."

She seemed a bit agitated. "It's none of my business, but my friend Maisey – she works in the canteen up there – she says there's a lot of talk about something going on at night. It's a bit odd." She was waiting for me to take the bait and tell her whatever I knew.

"Odd?"

"Like a ghost, or something."

I laughed. It wasn't the first time I'd been told a place was haunted. Some people believe in all that stuff. I reckon believing in it is what makes it work – for the believer, anyway. "I'll take my crucifix and holy water."

She grimaced. "You can laugh. But Maisey said some of them aren't very happy about it."

Rod and I didn't think any more of it. We had a bite to eat and drove up to the Tube Factory in our van. The security guard on the gate, Rick, let us in with the usual wave. We left the van in the almost deserted car park and headed for the door into the caretaker's area. I noticed a strange smell drifting on the night air from beyond the car park boundary - like animals, a rich farm smell, meaty and pungent. Seemed unlikely there'd be a farm nearby.

Len, the night caretaker, let us in. He was a tall, wiry guy, about sixty, bald as a coot, his face a mass of freckles. He'd sorted out a deal with the other main caretaker, Arthur, and now Len worked exclusively at night. Arthur was a family man and liked day work. Len was a loner. Like me, he'd been married, but his old lady had died of cancer about four years ago. He'd let his old life die out along with her passing. He reckoned night work suited him now.

In Len's base, a big room piled high with crates and tools and with a desk buried under paperwork – Len hated it – we found ourselves a couple of battered chairs and sat down while Len brewed up on the cooker. In a moment a few of the cleaners came in. They were all night workers, mostly women, but some men. Some husband and wife teams. Len introduced those we hadn't met last time, telling them we were night workers, part of the family, as he put it.

"So how's things?" I asked, breaking the silence as we all sipped our hot drinks. "Everything ticking over?"

I could tell they were uneasy about something. The usual good humour was missing. But no one said anything about ghosts and the like. If they knew anything, they weren't going to spill it. One of the security guards came in, another all night man, Boone, who was not much older than Rod. Don't reckon he ever said more than a handful of words, but he was always respectful to us. He'd been out of the factory to a nearby all-night supermarket and he dumped some piles of shopping – food and stuff – on a table. A lot of the night staff lived in these days – there were good facilities for washing and enough rooms to fix up bedding. Rod and I had seen a lot of this on our travels. People who never left their work places.

"Go up and see Davey," said Len. "New computer man. Does all the night work on the system. In charge of the closed circuit stuff. He'll give you guys access to the vehicle compound. Take him some grub. He's got his own coffee."

Rod and I finished up and left. We saw a few more cleaners on the way to the computer mainframe rooms, swabbing the floors or wiping things down. Out on the factory floor we could see other shapes as the machine specialists were busy re-greasing and polishing. We climbed up a back stairway to the IT area, pressing a coded pad to get the technician's attention.

Davey let us in and waved us to some chairs in his cramped central room. Banks of computers loomed over us, little lights winking on and off, the whole place buzzing like a quiet beehive. It would have driven me nuts to work in such a claustrophobic den, but the IT people were like that. They kind of hooked into the machines like they were bolted on.

"You're the regular vehicle men," said Davey. There were a

whole lot of computer screens at his end of the room and he was watching all of them at once, ignoring us. His pale face was lit by the screens. He looked like someone piloting a spaceship. Rod was fascinated by all the hardware. His thing was vehicles, but I knew that computers and the like intrigued him. We never had a lot of time for it.

"That's right," I said to Davey. "You're new here. Like it?"

He nodded. "Sure. Suits me. I've got my own office out the back. I can shut myself off in the day and get a good kip. I've got a good understanding with the day techies."

"Where do you want us to start?"

"I would have said Block Five and the big transits, but there's a problem." His eyes were still on the screens. He tapped at a keyboard and changed the images on one screen, bringing an area of the factory into focus. It was the huge underground section where the vehicle fleet, some fifty strong, were parked up in rows, sectioned off in Blocks.

"Block Five," said Davey. He leaned forward as if he was trying to find something among the transits. Rod and I looked over his shoulder. Davey had put some lights on down there – he could control them all from his console. He drew back. "Did you see anything?"

I would have said not, but Rod had. "Shadow," he said. "Someone there. Moved behind the vans when you changed the lights."

"The others are talking about a ghost," Davey said bluntly. "Some of them are superstitious. The older ones."

"So what do you reckon it is?" I said.

"Intruder. Someone's got in. Maybe hid on a van. They've been here for a week. I've never seen them, but I've come close, like just now. I've looked through every screen we have. Just caught enough to know that someone's down there."

"What about Boone, the security guard? Has he looked?"

"Hasn't found anything. He's seen things on the screens, but nothing he can place. So the word's gone round that it's a ghost."

"Only one way to deal with them. Find the bastard and heave him out. Is it a tramp?"

"No, they'd leave a trace. Most people would."

"Why Block Five?" said Rod. "You said that was where the problem was."

"That's where it always shows up."

"Right," I said. "You open up that area, Davey, mate. Rod and I will start right there. If there is an intruder, we'll find him and grab him by the bollocks. No, come on. No point wasting time. We've got a lot to do. Can't be fucked about by some twat from outside."

Rod and me went down among the vehicles and Davey made sure Block Five was fully lit. We had our tool bags with us and singled out the first of the transits for its inspection. We dumped our bags and took out a couple of big spanners, just in case. We had a good look around, but there was no one there and no fag ends, or food wrappings, the kind of stuff you'd expect an intruder to leave. The concrete floor was smooth, oily in places, but there were no footprints or even smears to suggest them.

"Shall I get started?" Rod asked me.

"Okay. Don't like leaving it unsorted, though. If someone is in here, they're taking the piss. Why be secretive about it? If they were open, Len and his people might be willing to put up with it. Like at that bus plant we did last month. The two old boys who just wanted a place to hole up. They asked if it was okay." They'd been accepted in by the night shift because they agreed to abide by the rules and had offered to be the go-betweens to get food and stuff. They claimed State benefits, so they paid for their keep.

This was different. This sounded like some sod trying to sneak a ride without paying. If they'd been open, maybe Len would've okayed it. Rod and me were part of this group, even though we weren't permanently on site, and we had our duty to the group. You had to have that, or it wouldn't work.

"Keep your ears open," I told Rod. He was already at work on the first transit engine. I knew it would be his world until he'd finished the job.

I was restless. Like I said, I don't believe in ghosts. Or God, or any of that shit. Seems to me that people use God, or their version of it, to do what the fuck they like. I kept away from it. I think the night shift workers were the same. Didn't want it interfering in their world. Another reason why this intruder had to be sorted out. Disruption. No need for it.

I had finished my first vehicle, switching off the engine and re-locking the doors. Nice machine, set to run smoothly for a good few years yet. I heard something. Between another two transits. It was a scraping, metallic sound. Not a fucking ghost, that was for sure. I picked up the big spanner and eased my way towards the place where I'd heard the sound.

Got it! There was a manhole cover, a circular metal disc over two foot across, set into the floor. I checked out the rim and yeah, there were scrape marks, faint but they were there. This thing had been moved. I took out my mobile and called up Boone.

"You see me on the screen?"

He said he could.

"I've found something. What's under this manhole?"

"Main service duct. Runs right under the buildings."

I got him to join me. He and Rod both checked the manhole cover. Neither of them looked very happy.

"Someone moved it," I said. "How big is the service duct?"

Boone scowled. "You can walk or drive a buggy through it. All the main pipes and electrical feeds are in there."

"That's not all that's in there. Can you light it?"

"You want to go down?"

"That's where your intruder is," I told him. "If we want to get the fucker out, we've got to go fetch."

Boone was shaking his head. "No one could lift that manhole on their own, not from below. And only one bloke could stand on the ladder under it. Much too heavy. It'll take two of us to get it open."

"Does the CCTV circuit include the duct?" asked Rod.

Boone shook his head again. "No need. It's always securely shut down. Lights when we need them. Waste of time putting CCTV down there."

"Good place to hide then," I said. "Look, it may be a fucking mystery, mate, but we need to look."

By the time Boone had gone and fetched the lifting bars for the manhole, Len had joined us. He and Boone used the bars to prize up the cover. I could see it was hard work, and not something one person could have managed.

"Seems like there may be more than one person."

"That, or it's a fucking gorilla," said Len.

We were laughing, but we were all pretty uneasy. No one wanted to be the first down the manhole, even though the lights in the wide duct below were now fully on, bright as daylight. I didn't want them to think I was chicken so I took the plunge, still gripping my spanner. This was no ghost. Ghosts walked through walls and floors and didn't need to shift fucking great manhole covers.

Down in the duct there was no sign of anything, no footprints in the thin dust, although it might have been disturbed. Possibly someone had brushed any signs away: we wouldn't have known. We split up, me and Rod going up the slope of the duct, Len and Boone going down it. Above us there were a load of pipes of all sizes, one as fat as a sewer, as well as scores of wires, all colours. They ran the whole length of the duct, some going up into the ceiling, others into the walls.

There were a couple of narrower ducts branching off. Rod stopped at one. He was sniffing the air. "You smell petrol?" he said.

I went into the side duct. He was right. There was a faint trace.

"That van I was working on," he said. "It was very low on petrol."

"Mine, too," I nodded. "Is that what these bastards were after?"

The side duct wasn't lit, but there was a switch. We threw it and went on. All the pipes and wires gradually disappeared into the superstructure and the duct reached a dead end. Except that it wasn't. There was a long vertical crack in the concrete and it had been worked at, widened. Enough for a body to get through. To where? There was only earth beyond. The factory was built into a sloping hill.

Rod had been smart enough to bring a torch. He used its wide beam to probe the crack. He turned back to me. "This is where they get in. There's a tunnel."

I checked it out, amazed. He was right. There was a tunnel winding off into the dark earth, just about big enough for someone to bend double along it. You'd have to be bloody mad to risk it. That earth could collapse at any time.

I called up Len and Boone on my mobile and Rod and me waited for them to join us. Like me, Len was shocked. "I don't get it," he said. "Must be a hell of a long tunnel to get here from the surface. Fucking dangerous. Someone must be desperate."

He called up Davey. "We're going to have to monitor these

ducts," he told him. "Fix the cameras so that all the manholes are watched. How hard would it be to run one off the system to monitor this side duct?"

"I'd need more wire, but easy enough. You say it's a tunnel?"

"So what?"

We were all listening to Davey's voice on Len's mobile. "At my last place, a big warehouse in the north of the city, they had intruders. They found a tunnel. They were going to plug it with concrete. I left before it was done."

"Who were the intruders?"

"Never saw them. But we lost chemical supplies. And petrol. Some of the company vans had all the petrol syphoned off."

"That's what they're after," I told Len. ""Me and Rod thought we could smell petrol. You have to stop this, Len. I reckon you've got druggies at work. Won't be just one. If you don't cut it short, they'll be swarming like flies."

Rod was scowling like he'd just thought of something else. "You know that public service garage we were at a few weeks back? I had a feeling something was wrong. Didn't say anything. Wasn't sure. One of their drivers reckoned someone was nicking petrol."

"Jeeze," I said. "This could be a network. It's not just an intruder, it's a fucking invasion."

"Get out of it," said Len. "This is just a gang or two."

"You reckon? That's how these things start. Small, then they grow. Before you know it, you'll be overrun. Like rats. They get a hold, you've got a big problem."

"He's right," said Boone, who was usually quiet. "We can't have these people running around down here. This is our territory."

"You want to involve the police?" I asked Len.

"Not yet. They're Authority. Work for their bosses, not us." He was right. Where there were police around the country who did a lot of night shift work, they couldn't really be said to fit into the night community. They couldn't be independent, like us. Most of them were okay. They knew about us and our ways, but they were tied to their masters. The best they could do was turn a blind eye.

"May have to let the Administrator know," Len went on. "I reckon he'll want us to deal with this ourselves, though. No need to bother Management. If it's a bigger network, like you said, Mac, we'll need help. That's okay. I can bring people in. Night people."

We decided to get the tunnel monitored and wait until someone came out. Then we'd jump them and twist their arms to find out what was going on. Meanwhile Rod and me went back to our work with the vehicles. We found a lot of them with very little petrol. Len sent one of the cleaners to get the wire Davey needed from an all-night supplier and it wasn't long before Davey patched up the kit he needed to have the side duct and its tunnel watched. He did a good job hiding the camera.

Nothing more happened that night. Rod and I were on schedule by the time we finished and went back to our digs. We slipped in just after dawn and crashed out. Slept until mid-afternoon, when our landlady fed us a huge roast, all we could eat, and a thick chunk of apple pie. Even Rod, who's a skinny bugger, ate a plateful. She made us a couple of big flasks of coffee to take with us for the night's work. I don't think it would have taken much to have brought her over to the night workers. Her old man wouldn't have noticed.

Back at work on the next lot of vehicles, we got a call on my mobile from Davey. There was panic in his voice.

"Something's in the side duct. I can see movement, sort of glow. Came out of the hole. Moving towards the main duct. You guys better get out of there."

"No way," I told him. I called Rod over. "We'll be ready for them. Cheeky fuckers. Where's Len and Boone? Send them to us. We'll have a reception party waiting, mate. We'll sort this out right now."

"They're in the main duct – now. Christ, the first one's a girl. Teenager. There's two, no three others. They're all dressed in rags, filthy. They're making for the nearest steel ladder up to a manhole. Jeeze, they're so thin." He could see us on another screen and directed us to the manhole and Rod and me got behind the nearest vehicle to it, a big truck, and waited.

The silence was broken by footsteps that made us jump, but it was Len and Boone, and two more of the caretakers, Dom and Cal. They were all carrying makeshift weapons, crowbars, spanners, an axe. They didn't look very happy. Weren't used to a fight. Nor were Rod and me, not like this. Just had to hope we could use threats to get what we wanted. Couldn't see us using the weapons.

"How they going to open the manhole?" I said quietly into my mobile.

"Two of them are up the ladder. Can't see their faces for the shadow. They don't look strong enough –" Davey's voice cut off and I knew why. I could hear the manhole cover shifting, grinding against the concrete.

The intruders were pushing it open. They may have been skinny, but they were strong. Abnormally strong.

The cover slid to one side and the first figure climbed out. It was the girl. Like Davey had said, she was a teenager, slight, frail, with the weirdest white skin I'd ever seen. Not pale – white. I'd never seen a corpse, but that's how white she must have been. She was wearing a dress down to her knees and her legs below it were spindly and that dreadful white. She had a pinched face, narrow and gaunt, but her eyes were alive. Her hair was brownish, lank and greasy.

Behind her, three young men came up out of the manhole. Like her, they were gaunt and dressed in rags, splotched with earth and torn in places. None of the group looked like they'd been made up. This was for real.

All of us watched them from our hiding places. They paused together and started to sniff the air, like dogs. They must have smelled us, because they all turned to look in our direction.

I motioned for Len and the caretakers to circle around the back of them and I stepped out from the truck's shadow. The girl drew back when she saw me, but the three men behind her – none of them much more than kids – made no move. Their faces were the same deathly white as hers, but otherwise they looked no different to anyone else. They were scowling, menacing. They weren't going to turn and scarper down the manhole.

"You're in the wrong place," I said, my voice a bit thin. I was gripping the big spanner tightly, but realised my hand was shaking. "The best thing you can do is beat it back up that tunnel and stay there. Your little game is rumbled. Go on, get the fuck out of here before the police arrive."

None of them spoke, or moved. The girl looked like she would say something, her eyes turning to Rod. There was something in her expression, a sort of pleading look I suppose you might call it. I could see Rod had noticed it. He didn't see the girl as a threat, or even an enemy. Maybe he was drawn to her, that awkward strangeness.

We all stood like that for what must have been a few minutes, waiting for someone to move. Len and the others were behind the young men. Impasse. I felt a bit of a jerk. What was I supposed to do now? Threaten them with violence?

Davey's voice came to me from my mobile, which I still clutched in my left hand. "Be careful," he was saying. "They lifted the manhole cover. Don't ask me how."

He was right. Abnormal. If they were that strong, and we attacked them, Christ knows what they would do.

Then, very gently, the girl was reaching out slowly towards Rod. Her incredibly white hand, with its bony fingers, inched across the space towards him. Instead of drawing back, he inched forward, the spanner he was holding down at his side, not a threat. He reached out and let the girl hold his own hand. We were all mesmerised, but the three youths just glared, waiting.

"It's okay," said Rod to the girl. "No one's going to get hurt. But you can't go on stealing petrol. Not from here."

She was holding his hand to her side as if she was glad of his protection. Her lips were slightly open but she didn't say a word. Her expression was odd, like she was so glad Rod was here, like she was his girl, or something. She waited.

I was getting impatient. We had to do something. Before I could move, the first of the three men turned aside, ignoring us all, and went towards one of the big trucks. I knew what he was going to do – syphon the petrol. Right in front of us! He was just going to go ahead and do it, as if we weren't there. The girl gently tugged Rod aside and he watched, like he didn't give a damn about the petrol.

The youth reached for the petrol cap.

"What the fuck do you think you're doing?" said Boone, stepping over to the guy, a long cold chisel raised. The youth reacted in a blur, sweeping his arm out and catching Boone a blow on his forearm that must have hurt. Boone yelped with pain and the chisel spun away, clattering on the concrete. Boone bent over double, he was in that much pain. The youth ignored him and started to unscrew the petrol cap.

I moved in on him, but I was wary. He'd struck so fast. Abnormally fast. And strong, like Davey had said. Who the fuck were these people? I was reluctant to attack. I wanted to hit the guy, but now that it came to it, I wasn't used to violence. It was all right talking tough, but doing it, hitting someone – with a fucking spanner for Christ's sake – was a different thing. If I had hit him, I'd have broken a bone or two, even killed him. I hadn't got that in me. Maybe it's what soldiers did. Trained for it.

I could only watch as the youth stretched up on the balls of his feet and put his mouth to the circular opening that led to the vehicle's petrol tank below. I couldn't see clearly, but it looked as if the kid's tongue stretched out and into the hole. For Christ's sake, he was drinking the petrol, sucking it up. I was expecting him to pull a length of rubber pipe out of his pocket and drop it into the tank, but he didn't. Besides, he didn't have a small tin or anything to collect the petrol in. He just went on drinking it.

I knew the others were horrified. They each chose another vehicle and none of us had the guts to step in and deter them. It was too bizarre. This was how they stole the petrol. How the hell did it not kill them? Don't ask me. What I saw should have been impossible.

Rod just waited, like he was indifferent. He was still holding the girl's hand and she had moved tight to his side. It wasn't a sexual thing, more like a kid snuggling up to her old man, being protected. From what? The three weirdoes? Did she want help? Rescuing from them?

The youths finished, licked their lips with those long, slick tongues and turned slowly away towards the manhole. Like animals who'd visited a water hole, going back to their lair. We were all too dumbstruck to do anything. The girl was still holding Rod's hand and she tugged him gently. It was obvious she wanted him to go with her. He took a step or two.

"Rod," I called. "What are you doing?"

"She wants me to go with her."

"Don't be so fucking stupid!"

"No, it's okay."

He was only a kid. Never had a girlfriend. Easy prey, but here, in this situation? This was crazy.

Two of the youths had climbed back down the manhole and still no one made a move to stop them. The girl led Rod to it. He looked at me a last time, an awkward kind of smile on his face.

I started forward, but the last of the youths bristled like a dog, although he didn't make a sound. That was one of the weirdest things about these kids.

"When are you coming back? Six? Six o'clock?" I said. I tried to keep the desperation out of my voice.

Rod nodded as he started to climb down. "Yeah, that's okay," he called. "I'll see you at six."

Minutes later they were all gone, the last of them tugging the heavy manhole cover across the hole and guiding it into place, so that it sealed tight. Len and I gaped at each other. One of them had moved it on his own.

A groan from Boone, who had slipped to his knees, drew our attention and we went to him.

"Fucking broken," he said, nursing his forearm.

"I'll get him to casualty," said Dom, relieved to have something to do that would get him away. I knew there was a hospital nearby.

Davey's voice buzzed from my mobile. "Hello, hello? What's happening? I can see three guys and a girl in the duct, and Rod is with them. Does he know them? They seem okay."

I didn't know what to say. "We're coming back up."

"What are we going to do?" said Len. He looked totally lost.

"You heard Rod. He'll come back at six. No reason why he shouldn't."

"What the hell were they?"

"Druggies are my guess. See how white they were? Hard drugs."

"All that petrol they drank. I almost puked watching them."

"We wait till six," I said. "If he's not back by then, we go after him. I've got a couple of things we can take with us." I went over to my tool bag and pulled out the small blow-torch for stripping paint. It had a powerful burner.

"You'd use that?" said Len, knowing none of us would have had the guts to use the other tools we'd had.

"It's that or we call the police. You want to risk that? Don't know what they'll make of it. What would you tell them? What we saw? Rod going off with a bunch of dope heads? Think the cops would believe us if we said they'd been drinking petrol? They'd think we were idiots."

Len shook his head.

I gazed around at the vehicle fleet. "I've lost most of tonight's work –"

"I'll help you with that. Cal here's a good mechanic. We'll get you up to speed. Be finished by six."

I nodded, and we were all glad to have the work to occupy us. I guess it glossed over our feelings of inadequacy. We got on with it, making more noise than usual, constantly looking at the manholes. Davey gave us reports from time to time, but there were no further signs of the people from below. Or of Rod.

Six o'clock came and went. No Rod.

We put it off as long as we could, all of us more than a bit scared. The more we thought about it we wondered why the hell we'd let Rod go in the first place. Then Len and the two other caretakers and me went down into the duct and beyond it to the hole in the end of the side duct. I led the way in. It was cramped and smelled of damp earth. The big worry was a cave in, but I couldn't back down now.

As I went along, torch pointing out the slightly curved way, all sounds were blotted out and I felt the weight of the ground overhead. Whoever had dug this out had got rid of all the soil, so it must have been a lot of work. Maybe there'd been more people involved than just the ones we'd seen. I could feel my heart thudding, uncomfortable as hell.

I don't know how far in we'd gone when the tunnel forked. Both branches had become taller, so at least we could straighten up. I didn't say anything to Len, but we were both thinking the same thing – what were we really up against here? This must have been going on for years. Our own little community of night workers had a real rival outfit.

The left fork sloped upward. There was a stench coming from it that made me turn my head. It was a bit like the rich fetor of a rubbish dump, acrid as a sewer. And something else. I couldn't face going that way.

Len agreed. "You know where that tunnel leads to – what's behind the factory on top of the embankment. It's an abattoir."

His revelation felt like a kick in the balls. I remembered that stink outside. For a minute it was all I could do to call this off and get the fuck out of there. Why the hell would they want to bury their way up to a slaughterhouse? It was obvious, though.

A source of food. I shone my torch up the slope and I could see something jutting out of the earth wall. A curved bone. Beyond it another. I didn't want to think about it, not down here in this suffocating hole.

The right hand branch was more level. "This way must lead to the church," said Len. It was a relief to go that way. The air was hot and musty, but nothing like as rank as it had been at the fork. The tunnel rose more sharply, its floor cut into rough steps, flattened by the passage of feet over a long period of time.

"The crypts must be right up ahead," said Len. "Never been in them, but it's a big church."

We got to a wooden door, caked in mud and fungus that I reckoned would rot it soon enough. There was a rusted handle, so I turned it slowly and pushed. The door resisted, but not much, so we were quickly through. We'd come to a walled crypt, its rows of fat stone columns like grey trees in the semi-dark. There were a load of old stone coffins, like oversized baths, with thick lids.

The four of us kept very close together and I was careful with the torch. We moved through the crypt very slowly. There were stone basins – old fonts? – on one side of us and I could smell petrol in them. That and something sour, a mixed stench. I almost gagged. And there were more bones scattered about, splintered and opened up. Brought from that slaughterhouse?

Len heard something to our left and pointed. Through a couple of the pillars we could see light. Not much of it, but something was over there. We moved toward it, our weapons gripped as though this time we meant business. Scared shitless, the lot of us.

The crypt wall was beyond, an old oil lamp hanging from it. By its glow we saw the girl, standing perfectly still, like she'd been waiting for us. Rod moved out of the shadows and stood next to her. They were like a couple of ghosts and to me Rod's face seemed more pale than usual.

"Hell, Mac, you didn't have to come," he said. "I'm okay."

He was holding hands with the girl. "What are you doing here?" I asked him. "You can't stay here. What about the job?"

"I'll get by."

I realised he meant it. Shit, he was going to give up his job with me and live with these people, here in this dump? That

134

couldn't be right. What had they done to him? They must have trapped him, done something to him.

"You can't do it, Rod. I don't care if you've got yourself a girl. Bring her back with you, but you can't stay here. What will you live on?"

"We've got all we need," he said, wiping a hand across his mouth. It was then I noticed the bits of meat spattered on his neck and upper shirt. My mind swung back to that fork in the tunnel, the path up to the abattoir. Christ, that couldn't be right.

Len nudged me and I realised that there were several shapes gathering about us, emerging from the pillars. Maybe as many of a dozen of these druggies. A whole fucking clan of them. They stayed silent.

I reached out for Rod. He was still the youth I'd taken under my wing and I couldn't bear the thought of just walking out on him. Maybe he was too scared to say what he really thought, maybe inside he was as terrified as me and the others. As I moved, one of the figures moved with me, an emaciated hand reaching for mine before I could get to Rod. I brushed it aside with the blow-torch I was holding and I heard the youth growl, a sound like a dog makes when you try to take a bone off it.

I sensed an attack and instinctively ignited the blow-torch. Its blue flame roared in the confined space. Two figures converged on me and I swung the blow-torch, more to scare them off than strike them. Rod must have lunged forward – I heard him shout something. In the light I could see that his shirt front was wet, and I could smell the fumes coming off it. He was trying to thrust one of the other youths aside and in the confusion, my blow-torch flame hit Rod's chest.

It caught fire instantly and in seconds Rod staggered backwards into the girl, who screamed as flames licked up from Rod's shirt to his face. Petrol! It was petrol. He'd…what, been drinking it? Like these freaks?

He collapsed and three of the youths fell on him immediately. I stood helplessly by, holding out the blow-torch defensively, Len and the others behind me, appalled but helpless. I didn't know what the fuck to do, but the youths were scooping earth over Rod, trying to douse the flames. It took them a while, but they smothered them, all the time Rod shrieking with pain, the girl howling like an animal.

135

They got him still, the flames out, and the girl knelt down and cradled his head. We couldn't see the effect of the flames, but we knew it must have been bad. He was sobbing. The youths turned to us and even though I swung the blow-torch around, they seemed hell-bent on making us pay for what had happened. Sounds around us made it clear we were surrounded by God knew how many. Everything had happened so quickly.

I thought I was going to have to try and ignite another of them – and I would have this time, goaded by the sheer terror of the situation – but I heard a strong voice. At last someone had spoken. Their leader maybe.

They parted and I saw a different figure. It was dressed in black robes. It would have been even more disturbing, but it was wearing a crucifix on a chain around its neck. It was the priest, or vicar, or whoever was in charge of the church.

"There's no need for violence," he said to me.

I lowered the blow-torch. The youths had backed right off, as if they were afraid of the priest.

"What's happened?" he said. I tried to explain, make him understand what kind of nightmare he was harbouring here under his church. He listened patiently, then bent down to Rod. "Let me see that." I knew then that he knew all about these people.

The girl let him turn Rod's face to the light. I almost retched at the mess I'd made of it. His eyes – would the poor bastard be able to see again?

"He needs medical treatment," said the priest. "You understand?" he asked the girl.

She nodded but wouldn't let go of Rod's hand.

"I have to take him," the priest said, as though apologising to her and the shapes around her. He turned to me. "Help me get him up."

I was in a kind of daze, but I did as he asked me and we had to prize the girl off him. Rod was too much in shock to resist. Now and then he emitted a low moan. The youths watched, but none of them lifted a finger to help, or interfere. And still they were silent.

Step by step the priest and I got Rod through the crypt to the stair that led up into the church. At its foot, the priest turned to the girl. "You can come, but the boy won't be returning. He has

136

to go back now. It's the only chance he has."

Her eyes had filled with tears as she slowly let him go. She dropped to her knees, pathetic in her grief. I felt a sudden stab of pity and I wanted to put an arm around her and tell her it was going to be okay. I knew she wouldn't come with us. Much as she cared about Rod, her place was below. She just watched us climb the steps, her tiny body shaking with sobs.

It was daylight and the church was filled with sunlight. It was like emerging from a bad dream, but it didn't make me feel any cleaner. I just wanted the night to return and swallow me up.

"Who are those people?" Len asked the priest. "They're not…"

"No, they're not what they seem. Just different. God's children, like all of us," he said. "They survive as they must. And they will. They're strong, united."

We got Rod to hospital and they did all they could for him.

He didn't make a complete recovery but he's not blind, though his eyesight is poor. He can't work anymore. I do what I can for him. He's not said a word since the accident. I don't talk about it either. I'm back on day work now, working for a firm of roofers. I do all the high level stuff. I like heights. But I don't sleep well, I don't sleep well at all.

THE GREAT ESTATE
Shaun Avery

Dave Holland was dead.

There were just no two ways about it.

As soon as he dropped the little bombshell that he had been carrying around with him since Connie's unexpected phone call, his parents were going to kill him.

His dad especially.

Pregnant, he thought.

How in the hell could she be pregnant?

Well, no, wait a minute… that was an easy one to answer, right? He knew all too well both how and why she was pregnant, up the duff, with child – though the copious amount of Extra-Strength but Ultra-Cheap lager they'd both consumed at the party where it had happened made some of the actual specifics kind of hard to recall. He wondered if he'd been good. He hoped he'd made her cum.

But now he had more important things to worry about.

I wore a condom, he said to himself.

Didn't I?

He wasn't sure. But he knew now that he would tell his dad that he had, that the contraceptive device must have failed. The old guy might fly into less of a rage that way. And if Connie contradicted him later, he would say that she was remembering it wrong. Or lying. That would probably work.

Sighing, he stopped and looked up at the unappealing building that was the local Social Club. Where his father had said to meet him.

He took a deep breath and then he stepped inside.

The interior of the place was loud and raucous, and smelled of stale sweat and cheap beer – once upon a time it would have stank of smoke, too, but the indoor smoking ban, a Government intervention much derided by his dad and his friends, had made that a thing of the past.

He walked through the crowded bar area, numerous people that he sort of recognised slapping him on the shoulder and asking how he'd been, and into the pool table area, where his dad could normally be found.

And there he was.

Jack Holland.

"Son!" he cried, seeing Dave. "Come on over!"

Dave did so.

He took a seat beside his dad and then leant in closer to the man, speaking into his ear in an effort to be heard over the hubbub of the Club.

"Dad," he said. "I've got something I need to tell you."

His father mimed raising a pint to his lips, despite having several of them on the table in front of him. "Drink first?"

Yep, a small part of Dave would have liked to have a drink very much – a little Dutch courage would have come in handy right about now. But a greater part of him wanted to get this ordeal over and done with, so he said, "No, I have to tell you now, Dad."

"Tell me what, son?"

Dave had dreaded this moment, been so terrified of speaking the words, had built this up to a ridiculous level inside his head. But now that it was here, he found the words coming out of his mouth in a rush, unstoppable.

"It's Connie, dad. I've got her pregnant."

At which point the smile slid from Jack's lips, and his face turned a peculiar shade of red.

He stood.

"Follow me, lad," he said.

Noticing the change from "son" to "lad," Dave groaned.

He knew that this could not be good.

But still he obeyed and followed his father towards the Function Room at the back of the Club.

He caught glimpses of Jack's face along the way.

Terror surged through Dave as he imagined what the old guy would do to him when they were in private.

But when Jack pushed open the huge double doors of the Function Room…

Dave saw that they were not, in fact, in private.

The room had been done out as if for a party, with balloons all around, and tables piled high with buffet-style food. There were at least forty people standing around the area, all men roughly the same age as his father, all with drinks in their hands, which they raised to Dave as he entered. And hanging above the small stage that usually played host to racist comedians and mediocre cover bands was a banner with the words CONGRATULATIONS DAVE! written on it.

"Yeah," said Jack, shrugging slightly, pointing to the banner. "We never got a chance to put that one up." He looked back to his son. "Sorry."

The apology was lost on Dave, as he was momentarily speechless, bewildered by what he was seeing.

"Dad," he said a few seconds later. "What's this all about?"

"We all just wanted to welcome you, son."

"Welcome me to what?"

There was glee in Jack's voice as he replied:

"To the Shitty Fathers Society, son!"

Dave was half-convinced this was some sort of prank, that at any minute now his father was going to bend him over and unleash his belt.

But the old guy looked so happy . . .

"You mean you already knew?" Dave asked. "How?"

"Could tell it in your voice when you called me earlier, son," he said, placing an arm around Dave's shoulders.

"Then why did you look so angry back when I first told you?"

"All part of the act, son," Jack said. "You'll get it soon enough."

Dave was about to inquire further, still curious. But then his dad called out:

"Someone get my boy here a drink!"

Someone did.

In fact, several someones did.

Which was why he woke up the next morning with an agonising hangover.

Groaning, he rolled over in his bed.

Which dislodged a dozen empty lager cans, scattering them onto the floor.

He reached down past them, nudging aside the half-empty kebab box, and grabbed his phone.

And sat bolt upright, suddenly completely awake.

He had twelve missed calls from Connie.

Worried that it had to be something with the baby, he called her back.

"Dave!" she said, answering on the very first ring as if she'd had the phone right there in her hand just waiting for him. "Where've you been?"

"I was…" He looked around the debris of his room, uncertain of how to describe whatever it was that he'd been up to last night. "Asleep."

"Ha!" she said. She often said this instead of laughing, the word somehow making her sound more amused than a fit of raucous laughter would have done. "Must have been some party."

"What makes you say that?"

"Well…" She paused. "You told him, right?"

Even through the throb and pulse of his hangover, two whirling, writhing snakes within his head, he knew who she meant.

"Yeah," he said. "I told him."

"That's great!" she said. "I was worried you'd…"

She didn't complete the sentence, but he knew what she meant. She was worried he'd wimp out of telling his dad. He couldn't find it in himself to be offended by this, as he'd thought the same thing too.

"So then what happened?" she asked.

Often when he drank, Dave completely forgot the events of the night before. Now, though, he just wished that were the case. It was too weird to really think about the stuff that had happened at the Club, to remember the… what had his father called it? The Shitty Fathers Society. Yes, that. How could he try to explain all of that to Connie, a girl that, if he did not quite love, he at least liked enough to not do a runner when she'd told him she was pregnant with his child?

As he wondered, he heard a voice calling out his name.

He thought, at first, that it was Connie. But then he realised two things: one, the voice was coming not from his phone but from the garden, and two, it belonged to a man.

"We had a bit of a drink." Which was the understatement of the century. "Hold on a minute."

He walked over to the bedroom window, successfully navigating the mess on his floor with a skill borne of years of experience.

And saw his friend Skunk standing down in the garden, waiting for him.

"Will I see you later?" Connie was asking.

"Maybe," Dave said into the phone. "I'll call you later." Then ended with something he had never said to her before: "Take care."

The two extra words made him feel quite heroic about himself as he headed back out in last night's clothes.

And he never once wondered how she'd known there was a party.

Every street on their estate had a resident called Skunk – someone who'd tried to dye their hair and made a mess of it, leaving a single streak of their original colour behind. The one who now walked beside Dave had pretty much become Skunk over the years – the days where anyone called him by his actual birth-given name, Mark, were long in the past.

"So," he said now, "I heard you got that lass you've been seeing pregnant."

Dave looked at him. "Where'd you hear that?"

"My dad was at your party last night."

"He was?"

Skunk nodded.

Dave thought back, but he still drew a blank.

"Bet she did it just to trap you," Skunk said, grinning. "That's what my dad says my mother did to him."

Skunk had three brothers and two sisters, so how any man could be caught in the same trap six times was a mystery to Dave. That said, having seen Skunk's mother – a woman who looked like a giant pile of dough, only less sexy, and whose skin had to be made up of at least ninety-five per cent stretchmark – it

142

was kind of hard to believe that any man would have sex with her that many times. Or once.

"I heard it was a good party, though."

"Yeah." Dave rubbed his aching head. "Hair of the dog to sort me out?"

"Maybe later," said Skunk. "I've got something to show you first."

His friend led him towards a dingy shed in the middle of the dodgy "allotment" area – a place where you were more likely to see drugs passing hands than vegetables pushing through muck.

"Dad was so mortal when he got in this morning," Skunk was saying. "He slept in and missed his appointment at the Job Office."

"Won't they dock his pay?" Dave asked.

"Probably," Skunk replied. "The bastards."

"Yeah," Dave said. "So why weren't you at my party last night?"

"Dads and going-to-be dads only," Skunk told him. "I wasn't allowed at this one."

Then he knocked on the door of the shed.

A few seconds later the door creaked open, and an old-looking man with bad skin and a bulbous drinker's nose stared out at them.

"Skunk!" the man said, sounding cheerful, his mouth cracking into a smile that was completely devoid of any teeth.

Living on this estate, Dave was kind of used to that sight. But still he ran his tongue over his own teeth, completely terrified of ever losing them.

"Morning Craig," Skunk said. "This is my friend Dave."

Craig tipped him a wink. "All right, Dave?"

Dave flashed him a weak smile by way of reply.

"Well," Craig said, speaking now to them both. "Come in."

They did so.

Though Dave was slightly hesitant to follow Skunk inside.

He wasn't sure why.

He'd spent a lot of time hanging around this allotment – getting underage drunk on a night-time or playing truant from school during the day. He'd even broken into a few derelict ones – in fact, he'd lost his virginity in one. So why did Craig's place

143

feel so different?

Perhaps it was the three other guys sitting in there on uncomfortable-looking wooden chairs.

Perhaps it was the large, unmarked crate on which Craig now sat.

The couch on which he bade Dave and Skunk sit was old and tatty, clearly sixth-hand and probably stolen, not to mention stained with numerous crusty white marks that Dave most fervently hoped came just from milk. He tried to perch as close to the edge of a threadbare cushion as possible. And as far away from those stains as was polite.

That was when he took a closer look at Craig's trio of companions.

And frowned at what he saw.

All three men were drooling.

Dementia? Dave wondered.

But they weren't old enough for that.

Were they?

"That's my friends Bernie, Frank and Lou," Craig explained. "Say hello to our visitors, boys."

They drooled some more.

The one in the middle muttered something that could have been "hello."

Crept out by what he was seeing, Dave was just about ready to vault for the door.

But then Skunk laid a reassuring hand on his wrist.

"Relax," he said. "Craig's cool."

As if to prove this point, Craig stood and pulled the top off the crate, reached down into it.

Came back up with two joints and a lighter.

Dave grinned.

"Give them both to him," Skunk said, smiling himself. "Dave's celebrating."

Craig raised an eyebrow. "Oh?"

"Well, I guess I am," Dave admitted. He felt slightly embarrassed, being the centre of attention this way, not just Craig's gaze upon him but that of the three drooling men, whose eyes suddenly seemed to be gleaming, looking at him raptly. "My, uh... well, I'm going to have a baby."

"Shit," Craig said. "You'll be needing these."

144

He handed over both joints and lighter.

Dave lit up one of them, inhaled.

And slowly felt himself mellow, sank back into the couch, thinking fuck the milk stains.

"This your first?" asked one of the three men on the wooden chairs – Frank, Dave thought.

"Course it is," he said. "I'm only twenty-two."

"I had four kids by then," Craig said. "No, five." He smiled, rubbed a hand over his crotch. "Five different women, of course." He licked his lips. "Cousins."

"He always was a stud," said Bernie, second of the drooling men.

The third of them, the one in the middle, made a vague noise in Dave's general direction.

Dave looked to Skunk. "What'd he say?"

"He asked you how the party was," Skunk told him.

"What?" Dave looked around them all. "How's everyone know about that already?"

Craig shrugged. "It was a pretty big party."

Dave met his eyes. "You were there, too?"

"All us Shitty Fathers were," Craig told him.

Dave shook his head. Which made him wince, the hangover still playing havoc with his senses.

Noticing this, Craig told Skunk, "You should bring Dave back around tomorrow." Then added, "He looks a little... delicate today."

"But aren't we going to...?"

Skunk pointed at the crate.

Craig's voice was much firmer this time.

"Tomorrow," he said.

As it turned out, though, "tomorrow" took Dave elsewhere.

They forgot to make arrangements for a re-visit to Craig's shed, and by the time Skunk called the next morning he had already made plans to spend the day shopping with Connie.

"Puff," Skunk said when he heard this news.

The insult might have made Dave change his mind about his plans.

But Connie was already at the door.

And in those tight jeans and that low-cut top, she looked pretty good.

Dave thought about that later, as he walked hand-in-hand with her into the Shopping Centre. She didn't look any different, not really, and it was kind of hard for him to believe that she was carrying something so life-changing around inside of her. Harder still to believe that he would stick around for what came after. God knew his own dad hadn't, leaving his mother and starting the first of several unsuccessful new relationships with various other women around the estate when Dave was barely out of the womb.

They never lasted, of course. And he always came crawling back to the life and home of his actual, long-suffering wife. And good old Mavis Holland always took him back.

He stopped mulling over his past and took a look around.

And saw that Connie had taken them into a DVD store.

She had mentioned earlier that she wanted to get a film for them to watch later tonight – "Date Night," she called it. Her parents were going out, so they would have her place to themselves. Which meant they could –

Dave frowned.

Could they?

He wasn't sure if you could still have sex with someone when they were pregnant.

Skunk would know, having seen his mother with child so many times. But Dave was that rarest of things around here: an only child. He had never been intimate friends with anyone who was pregnant before.

He sighed.

He should have paid more attention in Biology back at school. Not spent all of his time staring with lust-filled eyes at the teacher's tight-clad feet as she flicked her high-heeled shoes on and off . . .

Ah, memories.

He came back to the present as Connie waved a romantic comedy DVD in his face and said, "This one?"

"Sure," he told her.

But the question that was suddenly on his mind was:

Should we pay for it?

It had been a popular concern, back when he was a kid,

shoplifting… "knocking some shops over," they had called it. As forms of entertainment went, it was right up there with making bomb threats. And Dave had been pretty good at it, too. In fact, when the Careers Advice Officer, some twat whose sole talent seemed to be letting his beard take over his own face, had asked him where he thought his skills lay, he'd often wished he could tell the guy about the growing stash of CDs and VHS cassettes (this being the days long before DVDs) underneath his bed. But even as a naïve teenager he had sensed that this would not go over too well.

And right now, in the present, he wasn't too sure that Connie would approve either.

He had always thought that she had an honest streak about her – a character trait that made her not only different but in fact unique amongst people he had known. That was why she had never really got to know Skunk, why she was just "that lass you've been seeing" to him. Dave got the feeling that she kind of disapproved of him.

He looked at her, admiring her, wondering what she was thinking.

She caught him watching her, smiled.

"What?" she said.

"Oh, nothing," he replied.

But Dave saw the glint that appeared in her eye, and he knew she was thinking of something.

He was right.

Because after buying the DVD, Connie took him by the hand and led him into one of the Shopping Centre's public toilets.

And showed him that yes, you could indeed have sex whilst pregnant.

A few hours later they headed back to her house. They were laden down with bags – Connie had got a little carried away with her shopping.

Still, Dave thought, at least we paid for it all.

"I can't wait to show Suzanne this," she said, hoisting up a carrier bag that contained a sparkly new top.

"Yeah." Suzanne was Connie's older sister, whom Dave had met only a few times but whom he harboured something of a guilty crush on. "Cool."

Then he followed her into her home.

Her parents were ready and waiting for their night out, and rose from the living room couch when Dave and Connie entered.

"Hello, Mr Williams," Dave said, standing in the doorway, looking at them. "Mrs Williams." He flashed what he hoped was a winning smile at the latter. "You look nice."

She smiled back. "Such a charmer."

"That's why I'm with him," Connie said, nudging him aside slightly with a hip and coming over to kiss her parents goodbye.

Dave watched her do so with a slight touch of regret.

She seemed so much closer to her parents than he had ever been to his.

Then they were gone, and Dave was at last alone with Connie.

"Load up the DVD player," she said. "I'll get us sorted with some popcorn."

He did so.

And soon they sat watching the romantic comedy she had bought, her bare feet up on his lap, the two of them sprawled out on the couch, the popcorn on the glass coffee table that laid before it.

It didn't take long for Dave to get bored, and feel the need to start talking.

"So where is it your parents are going?" he asked.

"The Social."

"Oh," he said. "My dad's there tonight."

He wasn't sure why he felt the need to say this, considering that his dad drank at the Social Club pretty much every night.

"Yes," she said. "I know."

"They seemed quite friendly tonight," he said.

She looked at him, then rolled her eyes. "I told you, Dave," she said. "My parents don't have a problem with you."

"I just thought..." He pointed at her belly. "How'd they take it, anyway?"

"They were fine," she said. "I think they were expecting it. My Suzanne was about this age, too."

She looked straight ahead as she spoke, not taking her eyes off the screen.

"That's good, "Dave said. "I –"

148

"Shush," she said, pointing at the TV. "The film."

And because he knew that she was boss, Dave went ahead and shushed.

"Enjoy it when you can, mate," Skunk said.

Dave looked over at him. "What do you mean?"

"She won't fit in a toilet, when she gets much bigger." Skunk scratched his chin, where a little bit of facial hair, colloquially known as "bum-fluff", was starting to grow. "Our ma was massive when she had our Kimberley."

Your ma's massive now, Dave thought but did not say.

They were heading towards Craig's shed on the allotment again. Dave hadn't been too keen on a re-visit at first, remembering the odd atmosphere and the three drooling men. But his friend had talked him into it. Plus, you know, the weed had been some pretty good stuff. He didn't mind giving that another try.

"So," Skunk said, "is it any different?"

"What?"

"Fucking her. Now she's pregnant, I mean."

"I don't know," Dave said.

He really didn't. Yesterday was the first time they'd had sex since she told him she was pregnant, and he had been too caught up in the illicit thrill of outdoor (albeit inside a toilet) shenanigans to really pay much attention to the ins and outs of the actual physical experience. It seemed, looking back and dissecting things, that she might have felt slightly heavier, straddling him on the toilet seat like that, her shoes removed and in her hands behind his ears so that no passing security guard could see them and wonder why a pair of woman's heels were in a male cubicle. But that had to be his imagination, right? Surely she wasn't far enough along for it to be really noticeable?

He kind of wished he had the kind of relationship with his father where he could ask him all of this stuff. But the time for forging such a bond was long in the past – decimated probably the first parent's evening that Jack was too drunk to show up for. The last one, not coincidentally, where Dave had a full attendance record.

"I bet it did," Skunk said. "I bet it felt great."

149

"Why the sudden interest?" Dave asked, starting to feel a little uncomfortable with where this conversation seeming to be going.

"I just haven't fucked a pregnant girl," Skunk told him. "Yet."

Dave was just about to question that last word when the door to Craig's shed swung open.

And Lou, Frank and Bernie stepped out with hammers in their hands.

Elsewhere, in the kitchen of the Holland household . . .

Jack put down the tabloid newspaper and licked his lips.

The woman on Page Three was giving him a raging stork-on, and he fancied having a right good tug over her perky little tits.

But sadly his on-off-on-again wife Mavis was looking at him with a petulant look on her face.

He tried to win her over with a smile. It used to be easy to do so. Of course, he'd had a lot more teeth then. And had a lot less affairs.

Still, he needed his release. He was an important man around this estate. As he was sure his wife was about to tell him.

He was right.

"You need to talk to him, you know," she said. "You need to tell him what's going to happen."

"I'll get round to it," he said. "I'll take the lad for a pint."

That said, thinking the matter was settled, he reached out for his paper.

But Mavis grabbed his wrist.

Had any other woman done that, he'd have blacked their eye. But Mavis was the one he always came back to. The one who he felt closest to. So now he looked up at her as she said, "I mean it, Jack."

"I know you do, love," he said.

And flashed a smile at her that came close to genuine warmth.

She smiled back.

Then said, "Do you think the girl understands?"

"Course she does." Jack stood up, headed over to the kettle to make them both a cup of tea. "Her dad was at the show last night." He grinned, remembering the comedian's banter back at the Club: immigrants and puffs and dykes, and that was just the opening line. "Her mother, too. They know the score."

Mavis raised an eyebrow. "I thought you said it was men only at the show."

Shit! Jack thought. He had indeed said that, but that was only because he was meeting his newest bit on the side, Melody, there.

"She, ah, came to pick him up," Jack said, improvising. "They were getting a curry on the way home."

"Nice for them," Mavis said, happy to perform this well-practiced dance with her husband because she'd had her own lover, Corky, over when Jack was at the show.

"Anyway, don't worry," Jack went on, trying to get this whole conversation over with before the cutlery started flying. "They've been through it before with her sister, when she was pregnant."

"Okay," she said. "It's just…"

"It'll be fine," Jack reassured her. "Our Dave was a one off."

Then started pouring out their tea.

"Christ," said Skunk, practically convulsing with laughter. "Your fucking face!"

"Yeah, yeah," Dave replied, hoping he didn't sound as embarrassed as he felt. "What do you expect when they come out waving fucking hammers at me?"

They were back in Craig's shed, sitting on his threadbare couch. Craig was on his crate, looking strangely serious now that his own laughing fit had subsided. And Craig's three companions were on their wooden chairs, hammers hanging limply from their hands.

Dave cast a suspicious eye at the items in question.

"What were you doing with those things anyway?" he asked.

"Good question," Craig said. He looked to the three men. "Bernie, Frank – why don't you show Dave here what you use those hammers for?"

Something about those words made Dave feel nervous.

He cast an eye towards the door, wondering how quickly he could make it there were he to bolt suddenly from this couch.

But why would he need to bolt?

There was nothing strange going on here.

Was there?

As he wondered, he watched Bernie and Frank stand up.

"Watch this," Skunk said behind him. "It's great."

Bernie grinned at them both.

Then swung his hammer savagely and hit Frank on the temple.

"Jesus Christ!" Dave exclaimed, leaping up from his chair.

"Will you relax?" Craig said, and reached down into his crate. He came back with a four pack of lager, which he tossed to Skunk. "Here, have a drink."

But for possibly the first time since he was a kid, Dave had no interest in drinking.

He merely stared on as Bernie staggered backwards a little, shook his head, and then swung with his own weapon, hitting Frank atop the head.

Then both men were smiling, and wrapping arms around each other's shoulders.

"What the hell is this?" Dave said, looking back to Skunk, slack-jawed.

Skunk cracked open a can.

"Tell him, Craig," he said.

"I will," Craig replied. His voice was cold as he added, "Just tell him to sit down first. Guy's making me nervous, standing there like that."

"Sit down, man," Skunk said, his own voice friendly, calm. "Get one of these down you."

He opened up another can, held it out to Dave.

Sitting, shaking slightly as he did so, Dave took the can.

He raised it to his lips, looking at Craig over the top of it.

"Relax, Dave," Craig said. "They're just making themselves stupid. That's all."

"What?"

"That's the only defence they've got now," Craig explained. "Job Office has signed them all off healthy enough to work now. Even Lou there, with his gammy liver."

Lou, who had not yet risen from his chair, looked around them all shyly.

"I mean, of course, none of them can read," Craig went on. "That's obvious. But those Job Office bastards thought of that, too. They keep sending them on courses so they can learn. And if they look like they're not trying…"

"Fuckers sanction 'em," Skunk put in.

"Well said," Craig commented. "That's why we come up with this. If we can't be too ill to work, we'll get too dumb to work."

"By hitting yourselves with hammers?" Dave said, not quite believing that those words had just emerged from his lips.

"Well, not just hammers," Craig said, and stood up from the crate. "Come on, take a look."

Dave walked over and did so, taking his can of lager with him.

He peered down.

And looked back up at Craig, wide-eyed.

"Drills?" he said. "You can't use those!"

"Why not?"

"They'll kill themselves!"

"Not these," Craig said, and pulled one out. "They're Pound Store drills."

Dave shook his head.

Then looked to Lou.

"So what about him?" he asked. "Who does him?"

By way of reply, Lou stood up, and smashed the hammer into the middle of his own forehead.

"I had to ask," Dave said.

He glanced back at Skunk.

And saw his friend was grinning.

"Hey," Connie said, looking down and back at him, "we'll not be able to do this much longer, will we?"

He smiled at her, at the mischievous smile in her eyes.

"We'll get a few more months out of it yet," he told her.

Then stepped aside as the swing came back towards him, Connie kicking her legs to go higher so hard that one of her shoes was starting to slip off.

The sight reminded him of her taking them off the other day, back whilst having some fun in the public toilet.

Most of his erotic memories were tied up with feet, he was starting to realise.

He wondered why that was.

But he was starting to wonder about some other things, too.

He sat in the swing next to her and put his hands in his pockets.

"Something wrong?" Connie asked, looking over at him.

He looked back at her, met her eyes, felt some emotion for her swelling up inside whose name he could only guess at.

He wanted to tell her.

About everything.

About the strange party at the Social Club, about the odd goings-on in Craig's shed.

But he was scared.

And what scared him the most was not that she would not believe him but that she would simply shrug and say, "So what?" when he told her. That she would be like Skunk and his dad and think that these events were nothing out of the ordinary.

He didn't want to risk that.

So instead he asked:

"Do you want a girl or a boy?"

There was no hesitation. "A girl."

She brought the swing to a stop.

He was surprised by her response.

"I thought you'd have to think about it," Dave said.

"I have thought about it," she said, and there was an edge to her voice that made him think he'd better drop the subject.

She started swinging again.

But she did not ask him to push her.

Oh no, Dave thought, and groaned inside.

Had he just blown it?

Had he offended her?

He wasn't sure.

But in his uncertainty about things he had to go on, had to ask more of her.

"Will we have to move in together?" he wondered.

"It would help. That's what Suzanne did, when she got pregnant." She paused. "Would you want to move in together?"

But she was kicking again as she said it, and whoops there went her shoe.

She looked to him, giggled.

"I'll get it," he said, glad of the opportunity to think before replying.

154

He walked back across the park to her a few seconds later, shoe in hand.

He bent down at her feet.

She had pretty little feet. He took the chance to look at the bare one.

Then looked around to make sure they were alone.

And stuck out his tongue, licked across her toes.

"Dave!" she cried, laughing. "That tickles!"

Grinning, he stood back up, slid her shoe back on.

And returned to his swing.

She came back to a stop, turned to face him, the smile suddenly gone from her face, something serious now shining in her eyes.

"Well?" she said.

He thought about it.

It would be no hardship at all to stop living with his dad – old Jacky-boy had walked in and out of his life more times that Dave cared to remember, which he guessed explained the old guy's eminent standing at the Shitty Fathers Society. Though, curiously, Jack never really moved far – just in with other women around the estate, before always crawling back a few months later.

Dave would not miss him.

It would be strange, though, not living with his mother. Sure, she wasn't perfect, and she'd had a fair few fancy-men in her time, even when she was supposed to be with his dad, but still, living with her was all he'd really known.

But maybe it would be nice, Dave thought, to have a little change.

"Yeah," he said eventually. "I think I'd like that."

Connie started swinging again, seemingly pleased.

But Dave was not yet done.

He had to ask just one more question.

"Would you ever want to move from here?"

It was dark by the time he dropped Connie off and headed home, and Dave was hoping his mother would have something cooked, ready for his return.

But before he even made it on to his street he heard the sound of shouting coming from his house, and he knew that an argument was in full swing between his mother and father.

155

Soon, he got close enough to make out what they were saying.

"You promised me you'd take care of this!" That was his mother.

"I will." His dad, doing his best to sound repentant, as usual, but coming off just shifty. As usual.

"It's too late!" Dave heard his mother cry, and then came the sound of plates being thrown.

Another familiar noise.

Dave stepped inside the house.

Headed towards the kitchen, where his mother was sitting at the table rubbing her eyes and his father stood by the kettle, a pile of broken crockery around him.

They both turned to face Dave.

In the past, he would have skirted around the issue, tried to act like he hadn't already realised that something was up. But now – perhaps because he was going to be a father, and therefore felt more mature and responsible already – he had no patience for such game-playing, and instead looked at them both and said, "What?"

His parents glanced at each other.

Then Jack said, "Sit down."

Dave sat, his eyes sliding towards his mother as he did so.

The sight of her crying made him want to go to her, to comfort her. Just like he'd done each and every time his dad had pulled one of his usual disappearing tricks.

But he remained seated.

Too unsure of what was going on to make a move.

"So I hear," Jack said, the sound of his speech not breaking the tension in the room but instead adding to it, "that you're thinking of leaving us."

Dave held back a gasp. "What?" he said again, stalling, playing for time.

But the answer was already flashing in his mind:

Connie.

They'd talked about it at the park, and as soon as he'd dropped her off she must have got straight on the phone and grassed him up to his dad.

But why would she do that?

"Well?" said his mother. "Is that true?"

156

"We, uh... we talked about it," Dave admitted.

"Talked about it." Jack's tone was dangerously flat, his face unreadable. "Don't you think you should have talked to us about something like that, not some girl?"

"She's my girlfriend, dad," Dave said. At least, he hoped she was – they'd never really discussed it, had not put an official name on whatever it was they had between them. "And she's having my baby."

"Exactly," Mavis said, wiping away the tears from her cheek. "So why would you want to take her away from everything she knows?"

That was a very good question, and one that he couldn't really answer himself. It was just a feeling, acerbated by the sudden rush of strange things that seemed to be happening around the estate, that his child, be it boy or girl or both, would have a better start to life some place other than here.

But how could he tell his parents that, when they and their parents and even their grandparents had all spent the whole of their lives here?

He couldn't.

So he did the one thing that he had learnt from his dad:

He lied.

Or rather acted – his face relaxing into a big goofy grin and his body sinking down into the kitchen chair like a little kid's and his mouth saying, "it was just crazy talk, that's all." He met both sets of eyes, strengthening the lie with, "I couldn't leave you guys here." He grinned. "Who'd do the babysitting?"

Mavis sobbed again, but this time with happiness, and her arms stretched out for a hug.

Dave gladly gave it.

And wondered why he didn't feel like a shit for just looking at them and lying like that.

But the answer to that one was obvious, too, wasn't it?

He was just his father's son, through and through.

And as if to prove it…

"Put the lad down, love," Jack said. "I think he needs a drink with his old man."

The drink in question was not partaken of at home, of course, but rather at his father's true favourite place: the Social Club.

The comedian in the Function Room was reciting dirty limericks.

"There once was a young man called Venus..."

Dave squinted up at the person on the stage.

"Hey," he said, "I didn't think women were allowed in here."

"They are at special functions." Jack tipped him a wink. "And when they serve a special purpose."

Dave wasn't sure he wanted to know what that meant.

"There once was a girl named Regina…"

It felt kind of weird, hearing a girl tell such crude jokes. Well, a woman, really. Dave wondered what she was like in bed. Then reminded himself that he had a girlfriend. Maybe.

"There was a young man called Mike Hunt…"

The guys in the audience really liked that one.

And one or two of them were familiar, Dave saw.

He headed over to a table to say hello to some of them.

"All right, Lou?" Dave said. "I almost didn't recognise you without your hammer there."

The old man made some noise that could have been a laugh.

"No Frank and Bern today?" Dave asked.

"Nah," said the man who was sitting next to Lou, "he's just here with me."

"So I see," Dave said. "You two friends, then, Skunk?"

"You kidding?" Skunk grinned. He slid an arm around Lou's barely there shoulders, almost swallowing the man whole. "Old Lou here bought me my first lager, when I was six." He hugged the man tight to him.

Watching this, Dave was touched.

That right there was more affection than he had ever seen his friend give to his actual parents. Then again, with his beast of a mother, who could blame him?

Dave returned to sit at the bar with his dad.

Who had by now attracted company in the shape of Skunk's dad, Barry.

Used to being pushed aside whenever something more interesting appeared, Dave pointed towards an empty table in the middle of the room and said, "Should I…?"

"Not today, son," Jack said, grinning broadly. "You're one of us now – a Shitty Father!"

Smiling an uncertain smile, Dave took a seat.

And realised that both men were looking at him, as if waiting for him to do something.

So he did the only thing he could think of:

He reached for his bottled lager.

The pair roared with laughter.

Dave looked to his dad, helpless.

"Oh, God." Jack was wiping his eyes now, tears of glee running down his cheeks. "That's my boy."

"What?" Dave wiped his lips. "What did I do?"

"That's one of the best things you can do," said Jack, pointing towards the bottle, "when your kids are trying to get your attention."

"Or hit them," said Barry. "That helps, too."

Which explains, Dave thought, why your son is sitting over there with someone else.

Jack was nodding. "That's right."

"But why would you want to do that?" Dave said.

Jack shrugged. "That's what makes you a Shitty Father."

"Yeah, but why do you want to be… one of those?"

"That's just the way we do things around here, son," Jack told him. "You'll understand soon enough."

Then he finished his own bottle and motioned to the bartender, Stan, for another.

But Stan was shaking his head.

"I'm out," he said.

"You what?"

"I need to re-stock."

His eyes met Jack's.

"Don't I?"

And as Dave watched, something seemed to pass between them.

Then Jack turned to face him.

"Go down to the cellar, Dave," he said. "Get us a box of those."

He indicated his empty bottle.

"I can't go down there," Dave protested. "That's staff only!"

"Not when you're in the Club," Jack replied. "Get going."

And partly because he still wanted to please his dad, partly because he fancied another bottle himself, Dave went.

The air was fresh and cool down in the cellar, and he was surrounded by so many varieties of lager and cider and alcopops, all in sealed cardboard boxes that bore their names, that it made his head want to explode just looking at them. He wondered how drunk you'd get if you consumed them all. Then suspected that Skunk's friend Lou would probably know the answer.

There were the beer kegs too.

Being dull and silver, they were less impressive to look at than the colourful boxes that held the bottles. Yet Dave knew they held the sweetest liquid of all.

He sighed.

He and his dad both preferred beer from the pumps.

But the bottled stuff was cheaper.

So that was what they drank.

Still, he could not help but think how cool it would be to just puncture one of the kegs, to spray himself with all that ale. But he suspected that Stan would frown on that, even if he was a member of the Shitty Fathers Club.

So he headed straight for the box of lager that he and Jack were drinking.

Then suddenly stopped.

Looked back at the keg he had just passed.

And frowned.

Had he heard something coming from inside the keg?

He had.

He was sure he had.

Probably gas, Dave thought. Air escaping.

But then he heard it again.

And it didn't sound like gas.

It sounded like scratching.

Nails scratching.

It came again.

Louder.

And now it came not just from one keg but from all of them.

He grabbed the case and got out of there.

But just before he reached the final step, the noise became something else.

Laughter.

Female laughter.

160

He slammed the door behind him and stepped back into the Function Room.

Where he saw that his dad had joined Skunk and Lou at their table.

And someone else, too.

He was currently tongue-volleying the female comic, one hand down inside her blouse pawing at a breast.

Skunk nudged him as Dave approached.

"It's all right," Jack said, pulling himself away from the comic and staring up at Dave. "He won't tell his mam. Will you, Dave?"

Dave, standing there with the box in his hands, shook his head.

And felt like a little kid again.

One powerless to stand up to his father, one incapable of denying him.

He turned and took the box over to the bar.

"It's just not right, is it?" Stan was saying, standing with his hands on his hips, shaking his head.

Dave placed the box down on the bar top. "What isn't?"

Stan motioned towards the box. "Lager out of bottles." He sniffed, face wrinkling up in disgust. "It just doesn't taste the same." He nodded towards the beer pumps. "I prefer it out of those."

Yeah, Dave thought. And "those" are linked up to the kegs down in the cellar. Aren't they?

He looked at Stan.

The barman was looking back at him.

Was the guy making some kind of a joke at his expense?

Did he know what had just happened in the cellar?

Had it really happened?

He was so caught up in these thoughts that when the hand fell on his shoulder he jumped.

But it was just Skunk.

"What's up with you?" his friend said. "I just came to buy you a drink."

He was a baby and he was floating within the womb of his mother and yet he knew what was going on outside of this small world and he could smell decay and he didn't know why and then his eyes squinted downwards and he saw the dead dog lying there rotting out its insides and a mist was rising from the corpse and floating towards him but it was a mist with teeth, a mist with eyes, and those eyes were searching for him, those eyes wanted him, and he wanted to run, he somehow understood that the mist wanted to harm him, and he looked to those that were standing over him for protection, but they had the mist hanging over them too, but they embraced the mist, they loved it, and his cries had become screams, his panic now morphed into outright terror, and then it was upon him, eating him, but it could not swallow him, he got only halfway down what passed for its throat, something wet and slippery and black, like a waterslide in a charnel house, before it started gagging and choking and it spat him out and –

He woke with a gasp.

Saw that his bedroom door was open.

And his mother was looking in at him.

"Mam?" he said.

Just like earlier that night, in the Function Room, he felt like a little kid again.

One who wanted nothing more than for a parent to come in and comfort him.

But he could see that her bedroom door was open, too.

He could see through into her bed.

Could see the man lying there waiting for her.

The man that was not his father.

She nodded to him, a knowing look on her face.

Then stepped into her room, closing the door behind her.

A few seconds later, Dave heard the bedsprings start to go.

He wondered what it would be like to have a normal set of parents, a normal kind of life.

And sobbed for what he had never known into the darkness of the night.

There was a picture message waiting on his phone when he awoke.

It was from Connie.

She was showing off a new dress.

Nice, he texted back. You buy that yesterday?

No, came the reply. My sister gave it to me!

He grinned, typing back, second-hand clothes?

A few seconds later she replied with, traditional clothes. For special occasions!

What special occasion? he asked.

You'll see, she told him.

Then she sent him a second photo.

One in which she was wearing nothing.

He spent a couple of minutes having some alone time with that one.

When he was done, he gave himself a quick wipe down and then got dressed and headed over to knock on Skunk.

As he tapped on the door, he remembered the first time they'd met.

Dave had had lots of friends at secondary school when he'd bothered to attend, even a few that he had considered "best" friends. But he'd drifted apart from even the closest companion when they all graduated, some of them heading off to other parts of the estate, some of them starting off on a long and painful relationship with the prison services.

So he'd been feeling pretty lonely and despondent that day outside of the Job Office, another pointless meeting with a simultaneously bored and patronising twat in a suit behind him.

That was when he saw the guy with the two-tone hair crouching down on the grimy floor and pulling out a tape measure.

Now, on this estate, you always saw crazy things – drunken midgets trying to pick up wheelie-bins and jaded kids setting fire to their own shoes to see who could go the longest without stamping out the flames were just two of the delights Dave had witnessed growing up around here – and normally you just ignored them – it was much safer that way. This time, however, Dave ignored local protocol and said to the guy, "What are you doing?"

He looked up and grinned and said, "Measuring how far my spit can go."

And from that fact a friendship had formed.

Now his friend opened up the door.

163

His hair was a scraggly mess, suggesting that he'd only just got up.

"Mate," Skunk said, "you know you look like shit, don't you?"

"Bad dream," Dave explained.

"Shouldn't have had those cheesy chips with your kebab last night." Skunk laughed. "Come in a minute when I get sorted."

Dave followed, hoping that since it was only midday his friend's mother would still be in bed.

She wasn't.

She was at her usual chair by the kitchen table, rolls of her voluminous fat dangling down from the sides of it.

"Why, it's David," she wheezed, smiling at him as Skunk headed into the bathroom.

No one else ever called Dave that. Not his parents, not even Connie when she was about to cum. Though she often called him "duck" at times like that, as in "do it to me faster, duck!" He guessed she could be a little odd sometimes.

"Come sit down by your aunty Bella when Skunk's getting ready," the large woman said, indicating an empty chair just next to her.

What sort of woman, Dave wondered, calls me something that no one else does but calls her own son by his nickname?

He wasn't sure.

But he chose to sit down across the table from her, never taking his eyes off the woman as he did so.

The woman grinned, as if amused by his slight.

As repulsive as she was, there was something strangely fascinating about watching her grin. Her mouth seemed to be some huge cavern. Especially with so few teeth in there, leaving plenty extra space.

"I hear you're going to be a daddy," she said.

Dave sighed, irritated that people always seemed to be "hearing" things recently. But this, at least, was a subject he was happy to talk about, so he said, "That's right."

"That's nice," Bella said. "I bet you'll make a lovely dad, David."

Had anyone else said that, he would have accepted it as a lovely compliment. With Bella, though, it was kind of hard to get past the memory of that time she had come on to him when her husband and son were passed out on the kitchen floor.

Still, he felt obligated to tell her, "Thanks."

"Just telling the truth as I see it," she said. "So, you hoping for a boy or a girl?"

"I don't mind," he said, and he was pleased to realise that he really didn't. "But Connie –"

"Connie?"

"My girlfriend," he explained, feeling a lot more confident about calling her that than the last time he had used those words. "The one who's pregnant."

"Oh yes," said Bella. "Of course. Lovely girl."

"You know her?" Dave said, surprised.

"Of her."

Something about those words made Dave feel nervous.

"Anyway," he went on, trying to ignore the feeling, "she'd like a girl."

"How lovely," Bella said. "And what position were you fucking her in when she got pregnant?"

Dave's mouth flapped open, his brain not quite believing what his ears were telling him.

Thankfully, that was when Skunk appeared at the kitchen door.

"Come on, man," he said to Dave.

"Skunk," Bella said, and placed a meaty finger against an equally meaty cheek.

With an embarrassed shrug towards Dave, Skunk walked over and placed a kiss on the spot she'd marked.

Then Dave followed his friend out of the front door.

He wished he could believe that he had just misheard the woman.

But he knew that he hadn't.

They had nothing to do with their day – a not uncommon occurrence in their lives – so they had decided to grab a few cans and then head to the park.

But when they reached the off licence they found Lou curled up on the ground outside of it.

"Christ," Dave said, rearing back from the smell of the man. "How much did you two drink last night?"

Skunk, shaking his head at the question, bent down over the older man. "What happened, what's wrong?"

Dave was surprised to hear that his friend sounded genuinely concerned.

Lou muttered something indecipherable.

"He says the dole just stopped his money," Skunk said to Dave. "They said he's not trying hard enough to find a job."

Lou made a few more sounds.

"He just spent the last of his money on cans," Skunk said.

"Thanks," Dave said. "I can smell that."

Lou moaned and then he started crying.

"Dave," Skunk said, now sounding angry rather than concerned. "What the fuck is wrong with you? Can't you see he's upset?"

"Sorry," Dave said, blushing at his lack of tact.

"Come on," said Skunk, ignoring his apology. "Help me get him up."

"What for?"

"So we can get him to Craig's," Skunk said.

"Doesn't Craig have a house?"

They were heading towards the shed again, supporting Lou's slender frame between them.

"Yeah," Skunk told him. "But too many people know he lives there."

Dave guessed that "people" meant debt collectors. Having been evicted to a series of increasingly depressing houses around the estate when his dad "forgot" to pay the rent over the years, he knew all too well the sound of that dreaded knock upon the door.

And speaking of doors...

"Christ," Craig said when his swung open and he saw the state that Lou was in. "What happened to him?"

Skunk explained.

Craig's anger rose as he listened.

"Fucking dole," he said. Then motioned them inside, saying, "Come in, come in."

They did so, placing Lou down in his usual chair between his two friends.

They were still drooling, blood-soaked baseball bats in their hands, multiple cuts and bruises upon their foreheads and temples.

"Don't they ever leave?" Dave asked.

"Where would they go?" Craig countered.

Touché, Dave thought.

Dave looked back at Skunk, who was sitting on the couch.

His friend was looking at Lou, with sadness in his eyes.

Dave had never seen him appear so concerned about anything before.

"I think I'd best get us all a drink," Craig said.

And reached down into the crate on which he usually sat.

But then Lou stood up.

Mumbled something that made no sense to Dave.

But clearly Craig understood it, as he said "All right," and stepped back from the crate.

Why does everyone else understand him and I don't? Dave said to himself. He looked at the barely lucid Bernie and Frank, dripping equal amounts of drool and blood down onto the floor of the shed. And why does no one else seem to think that any of this is strange?

He wondered if he should have been more courageous at the park yesterday, whether he should have told Connie what had been going on.

And just like that the decision was made:

He would tell her later.

And he would also tell her they were getting the fuck off this estate.

Them and their unborn child.

He was ready to drink to that.

But it wasn't a six-pack of lager that Lou pulled up and out of the crate.

It was instead a drill.

One of the drills that Dave had found in there earlier this week.

"No," Craig said patiently. "That's not what you were looking for, Lou."

But Dave wasn't so sure about that.

Because Lou was suddenly smiling.

Dave did not like that smile.

There was something wrong about it. Something that indicated its owner had nothing to lose.

"Lou?"

Skunk's voice, coming from behind Dave, sounded very

small, not like his usual one at all.

Lou paid no attention either way.

He just revved the drill.

Which, for a supposed Pound Store one, sounded pretty dangerous.

And now it was not just revving but was also moving.

Working its way up Lou's body until it got to his face.

"Come on, Lou," said Craig. He sounded calm, but panic was starting to show upon his face. "Just put the drill down and have a beer. We'll sort this out with the dole guys. I promise."

But Lou was shaking his head, tears forming in his eyes.

And he revved up the drill one last time and then rammed the drill bit into his eye.

Skunk yelled "No!" and leapt towards the man.

But Lou had already fallen to the ground, his legs convulsing, his body thrashing. But his grip never loosening on the drill, his finger still on the power button.

By the time they reached him he was no longer moving.

But, Dave saw…

He was still smiling.

Later that day.

"Come on, man."

Skunk just looked at him.

"You don't even know who it was he saw."

"I don't care," Skunk said.

And pulled the balaclava down over his face.

"It's not even dark yet," Dave protested.

"Look," Skunk told him. "I'm going to grab whoever comes out of that Job Office when the place closes and kick the fucking shit out of them." He tensed his hands into fists in preparation. "I don't give a fuck if you help me or not."

Dave watched his friend, torn.

God knew he'd helped his friend kick in a few faces before.

But things were different now.

Weren't they?

He closed his eyes, pictured Connie.

And decided that they were.

"I'm sorry," was all he could say. "But, it's just…" He

floundered, a drowning man. "Connie…"

"Yeah," Skunk said.

Then turned and stalked towards the Job Office where they had first met.

And as he watched him go, Dave could not help but feel that something special had just been lost.

But, he thought, I still have Connie.

He pulled out his phone and called her.

It was evening now, around five-fifteen.

"David!" she answered, and he froze.

"Something wrong?" she said a few seconds later.

"No," he said, trying to dispel the image of Skunk's mother from his mind. "It's just you… never called me that before."

"A-ha," she said, "but tonight's that special occasion I was telling you about."

"It is?"

"That's right."

He closed his eyes.

He didn't know what she was talking about, what was going on, and he was sick of feeling that way. Not just about Connie but about everything.

"I don't know what you're talking about," he said.

"I know you don't," she said, and when he heard the sympathy in her voice he realised that it really was love that he felt for this girl. "You haven't talked to your mam and dad yet." She paused. "Mine are here with me. Want to say hi to them?"

And before he could respond he heard them both shout "Hi Dave!" in the background.

It could have been just a normal greeting.

But nothing was normal around this estate of late.

Perhaps it never had been.

He flashed back to his dream.

And realised there was something else that had been bothering him.

"Connie," he said. "Did you tell my dad what we'd been talking about at the park?"

"Of course I did," she said. "I had to warn him."

He stopped walking and leant against a wall, suddenly feeling close to tears.

"Why?" he said.

"Just go home to your parents," she said. "They'll tell you everything." He heard the smile in her voice as she added, "And then I'll see you later."

"No," he said. "I'm coming to see you now."

"Don't," she said. "I won't be here."

Then she hung up on him.

Something else she'd never done before.

He put his head in his hands, despairing.

He knew there was only one thing for it.

He would have to go home.

But not yet.

He had somewhere else he wanted to go first.

Connie put down the mobile phone and looked back at her parents.

At her sister, too.

At her little niece, Rebecca.

This night was going to be beautiful.

So beautiful.

That was why she was still wearing her dress.

She'd put it back on, after taking that naughty nudie picture for Dave.

"You look good in it," Suzanne said, indicating the dress.

"Thanks," she said. "Do I look better than you did?"

Suzanne smiled. "Well…"

"Come on, love," said her dad, interrupting. "Let's get going. You don't want to be late. You know he won't be."

The thought made her giggle.

But got her a little bit excited, too.

They all headed out, Connie bringing up the rear.

She went to lock the front door.

"Don't bother," said her mother. "No one will rob us tonight. Besides…"

She pointed up the street, to where someone was walking towards them, waving.

"Oh yeah," Connie said.

She headed towards the family car, the rest of them already inside and waiting.

Then waved back to the person who was now entering their

house.

It was going to be one fun night for everybody.

Dave sat in the park, drinking.

This was what they'd originally planned to do. Before...

Lou.

In the aftermath of the suicide, Craig had ushered them out of the shed. Already looking to blame whoever had stopped Lou's money at the Job Office, Skunk had gone willingly and with haste. But Dave had been slightly more reluctant to leave, with what he thought was good reason.

"Don't worry," Craig had said, and at that moment the other two men rose from their seats at the exact same time, as if responding to some kind of demand. "We'll take care of it."

Dave had left without a word, not sure that he wanted to know just what the guy meant.

Now, though, he couldn't stop thinking about it.

And Skunk.

It was about half-seven now, and still he had not texted his friend. Probably a little worried, he had to admit, that he might be in police custody by now.

And if he wasn't? Where would their friendship go after today?

But he was sick of all these thoughts.

And alcohol, the one thing that normally took care of that, was no longer working.

Sighing, he got up and left the park.

He hoped he'd find someone to pick a fight with on the way home, just to get rid of some of the tension that was building up inside of him.

But the streets of the estate were curiously deserted.

Damn it, he thought.

And pushed open his front door.

To see Skunk standing in the kitchen.

They'd had many a fall-out before, normally alcohol-inspired, and so they had played out this reunion scene many a time in the past. But a few things set it apart this time. The first was the presence of his parents, standing solemnly behind Skunk. The second was the man bound to a chair in the middle of the room, a gag in his mouth and blood on his face.

Dave came into the room, closing the door behind him.

"What's going on?" he said.

But Dave had an inkling that he already knew the answer.

On Skunk's part, anyway.

The bound man, with his nice suit and tie, was clearly not one of them. Was obviously the person that Skunk had snatched from the Job Office.

But why were his parents involved with any of this?

Why had Skunk brought the man here?

As he wondered this, his mother took a step towards him.

"Connie called," she said.

"That's right," Jack added.

"She was worried about you," Skunk added. "That's why I came over here. Thought I could help your parents show you what's what."

Dave looked to him. "Connie called you?"

Skunk nodded.

"Thought you two didn't get along," Dave said.

"We all get along here," Mavis told him.

"We're all one big family," Jack added.

"Except you," Skunk said, sounding bitter.

"He's right, son." Jack was shaking his head. "I was disappointed you didn't help your friend with this one here." He cuffed the bound man around the ear.

"I have... Connie to think of," Dave told them.

"That right?" Skunk grinned. "Going to protect her, are you? What you going to do, get a job?"

They all laughed at that one.

Dave, blushing, swallowing what felt like a huge ball of phlegm, looked around them, trying to keep his cool.

"If I have to," he said.

"Mate," Skunk said, and now he sounded almost sad, as if the friendship between them had not been damaged, "you don't understand. Connie's one of us."

"She's nothing like you," Dave said. "She's good, and sweet, and..."

"So why isn't she here?" Mavis said.

"You know where she is, son?" Jack asked.

Dave could only shake his head.

"Help us with this," Skunk said, "and we'll tell you."

And he held out a knife towards Dave.

The bound man started to thrash around, tried to scream from behind his gag.

Mavis smashed a plate down over his head, and he sagged within the ropes.

"Thank you, darling," Jack said.

"Any time, lover," Mavis told him.

And they kissed.

Actually, they more than kissed. They were practically naked, Jack's fingers deep inside of her, when they remembered they had an audience.

"Ahem," Jack said. "To be continued."

Then looked back to his son.

"So," he said. "What's it going to be?"

Skunk took a step towards Dave, still holding out the knife.

"Whose side are you on?" Jack added.

Dave looked at the unconscious man.

"Why him?" he said. "What's he ever done?"

"Don't you remember?" Skunk said. "He killed Lou."

"Skunk," Dave said, voice now a pleading tone, "Lou killed himself."

A dark look passed across Skunk's face. "Don't say that."

"But it's true." Dave met his friend's gaze. "I was there. I saw it."

"No," Skunk said, face resolute. "Lou wouldn't do that."

And Dave suddenly saw.

He looked deep into his friend's eyes, and he saw the truth.

"My God," he said. "He…"

"Lou loved me," Skunk said. "Now take this fucking knife and kill him, or I swear to God I'll…"

But Dave was already shaking his head.

His decision made.

"You fucking traitor," Skunk said, and rushed him.

They crashed back onto the floor, Skunk atop him, and any hope Dave had held out that his parents would finally try to protect him was dashed as they ran around the thrashing pair, commenting on the moves they were making like spectators at a boxing match.

"Go on you fucker!" his dad cried.

"Get in there!" added his mother.

The knife came down towards his face and he grabbed at Skunk's wrist, his friend growling above him, drooling like his friends from the shed.

"Fuck you!" he was screaming. "Fuck you, man!"

Dave tried to see reason in his eyes.

And saw only madness and rage.

He got a grip on Skunk's wrist and pulled it downwards, jamming the blade of the knife into the floor.

Not to be denied, Skunk opened his mouth wide, trying to snap at Dave with his teeth.

Dave drove a knee up between his legs.

"Ooh!" Jack cried. "Dirty fighter!"

Skunk groaned and rolled off and to the side, cupping his wounded genitals.

Dave grabbed the knife.

"Go on," Jack said, eyes gleaming with excitement. "Kill him. Finish him off."

But Dave had a better idea.

He walked over to the man in the chair.

"Dave," Skunk said, trying to catch his breath. "Don't you fucking dare."

Dave paid him no attention.

Got busy instead cutting through the ropes that bound the suited man.

"I have to hand it to you, son," Jack said. "You're not scared of making enemies."

And Dave realised that this was the first time he had ever heard his dad sound impressed at anything he'd ever done.

Shame it had come twenty-two years too late.

He walked sideways towards the front door, pushing the still groggy man along with him.

Skunk tried to grab at them both as they headed out of the door.

Dave kicked him in the head.

"Here," he said, looking back at his parents. "Keep your

174

fucking knife."

He tossed it back at them.

Then headed out into the night.

The Job Office man didn't hang around, and ran away from him as soon as he was lucid.

Dave couldn't suppose he blamed him.

He ran back through the streets, and though they were still empty, the same could not be said of the doorways of the estate.

They were all open.

Families standing out in them.

Watching him as he ran by.

"He's coming," they all chanted. "He's coming, he's coming."

He tried to ignore them.

Just carried on running.

But when he reached his destination, he saw that the door hung open.

"Connie?" he said, hesitantly, timidly.

Of course she'd said she wouldn't be here. But he'd hoped it was just another one of her jokes.

Apparently not.

He stepped inside.

"Connie?" he said again.

He headed into the living room.

And heard a giggle.

It did not belong to the woman that he now knew he loved.

But it was a woman.

Sort of.

For Skunk's mother Bella lay on the couch.

She was completely naked, her clothes folded up on the glass coffee table.

Not the way that Connie would look naked, he saw – no luscious breasts, so eager for his hands and lips to find them, rose up from her chest, no inviting vaginal lips lay waiting for him to part them.

She was instead one big mound of rubbery flesh.

She was toying with a saucer-sized nipple when he came into the room.

"Where's Connie?" he asked.

"God," she said. "Didn't your parents tell you?"

"They didn't really get the chance," he said.

"Guess it's up to me, then," she said, and grinned that huge-mouthed grin of hers.

"So where is she?" he said. "Tell me!"

"Gone already," she said. "Went a long time ago."

"Gone where?"

She rolled her eyes. "Where do you think? To the Social Club. She's guest of honour."

"What are you talking about?"

Instead of replying, she indicated her huge, flabby feet, hanging off the arm of the couch.

"I hear you're good with feet," she said. "I hear you have a thing for them. So here's a deal: why don't you rub and lick and suck on them, and then I'll tell you." She grinned. "And it's not just your fingers I want you to rub them with."

He looked at the items in question.

They weren't at all like Connie's.

Nor even his old biology teacher's, so hot in those tights she wore.

"I don't think so," he said.

"No touch no talk," she said, and slid a finger inside herself, opening her up.

The look on his face was the only response he needed to give.

"Fuck you and your little whore, then!" she growled. "See how you look at her when she's had seven kids!"

That was when Dave lost it, and finally gave her what she wanted.

He touched her feet.

But only to pull and throw and tip her off the couch.

She fell face-first into the table and then fell through it, her vast bulk smashing it to pieces that then cut and tore her body open.

"Oh God," he said, looking down at her. "Oh God, I'm sorry!"

But then he heard her laughing.

"Stick your cock in me," she said, turning to face him with glass jutting out of her chins, "and I'll forgive you."

He bolted then, ran back out into the night.

Towards the Club.

There were dozens of men and women staggering around outside of the place when he arrived, all clearly drunk.

Dave grabbed one of them: Barry, Skunk's dad.

"What's going on?" he asked.

"Had to drink the kegs dry," he said, releasing breath that was almost toxic. "You'll see why."

He wanted to push the old man away.

But some spark of decency inside still made him say:

"Look, your wife…"

"Is a fucking dog," the man finished for him. "That's why I've been going with her."

He pointed towards an unconscious woman lying face-down in a pool of sick, her bottom up in the air and her knickers down around her ankles.

Shaking his head, Dave headed inside the Club.

The front bar was empty, but he could hear noise coming from the Function Room.

He stepped into it.

And saw the place was crowded, packed, filled with people from all over the estate.

At the forefront of the crowd were his parents.

"Hey, Dave," he said. "Glad you could make it!"

"Where's Connie, you bastard?"

Jack smirked and pointed.

The curtain slowly lifted, revealing the stage.

And Connie upon it, sitting on a threadbare throne, wearing her new dress and looking lovely.

"Hi Dave!" she cried.

He took a step towards her.

But Jack held him back, placing a restraining hand upon his chest.

"Wait," he said. "Don't you want to see what these are for?"

And he indicated the empty beer kegs scattered all around.

As Dave watched, hands emerged from inside the kegs.

Female hands.

"The other night," Dave said, remembering. "Sending me down into the cellar. That was all a set-up?"

"That's right," Jack said.

"Yep," said a voice from the crowd that Dave recognised as barman Stan's.

"But why?" Dave said. "What's in there?"

The answer was already becoming apparent, though.

Naked women were standing up from the kegs, their skin dripping with lager.

"They live in the kegs," Jack explained. "They can change their shape. And when someone gets pregnant... when it's time for him to come and feed..."

They were lying down on the floor of the function room now, spreading their shapely legs.

"But they're pregnant," Dave pointed out.

"No, son." His father put a hand on his shoulder, and despite everything that had happened he still liked the way that this felt. "That's just the form he makes them take. See, him and them... they're not from around here."

Dave could see that.

Their eyes were sheer black.

They had long and scaly tongues.

But this didn't stop the men of this great estate, who were starting to pull down their tracksuit bottoms and join the woman-things on the floor.

"I don't understand any of this," Dave said.

Then looked around.

"Where's Skunk?"

Jack pointed.

"Look at me," Skunk was screaming, pumping away atop one of the creatures. "I'm fucking a pregnant lass!"

He stopped for a second and looked up at Dave, face sweaty. "Oh, hi, mate."

Dave looked back to his dad.

"It doesn't bother him, does it?" he said, finally understanding. "We tried to kill each other, and now we're totally fine."

"That's his way," Jack told him, sounding like some kind of preacher. "That's the power we take from the Estate Father. That's what he gives us for what... we give to him."

Dave could only shake his head.

"Go," Jack said. "Join your girlfriend."

And, as if walking through a dream, he did so.

He passed through the orgy and headed for the stage where Connie was waiting, arms stretched out for him.

178

"Isn't it great?" she said when he was close enough to hear her over the sound of the rutting. "He's coming just for us. For our baby."

"What?"

"Don't worry," she said, and stroked his cheek lovingly. "It's going to be just great." She pointed to the stage just in front of her. "Sit."

He did so, placing himself down at her feet.

Then Jack shouted, "Silence!"

The revellers obeyed him.

"Connie," Jack said. "Get ready."

Smiling, she pulled down her knickers.

Dave gasped.

But not because of what his girlfriend had just done.

No.

Because of what was happening at the door to the Function Room.

Craig, Bernie and Frank were walking through it. And in their arms, cradled between them, was the dead body of Lou.

Skunk let out a sob, withdrawing from his partner as the three men walked past.

"It's all right, lad," Jack said, laying a comforting hand on his shoulder. "This is a great honour."

Then he turned and addressed the rest of the crowd.

"Normally," he said, "we'd sacrifice an animal to call up the Estate Father. But this time, one of our own has offered up his body."

That's not how it happened, Dave thought.

But he kept his silence as they placed the body down on the stage.

They laid a hammer and a baseball bat and the drill with which he'd killed himself upon the corpse.

Dave looked down at the punctured eyeball, the bloody face.

But then the body began to gag and retch.

As a black mist rose out of it.

And Dave was suddenly back in his dream, but he knew now that it was not just a dream but was instead a memory.

The mist was the *he* to which his dad had been referring all night.

The mist was the Estate Father.

It was grinning now, as it floated before him.

I remember you, it said, speaking directly into his mind. The one whose hope I couldn't take. The one I couldn't swallow.

Hope? Dave thought.

That's what I take, it told him. The emotions that will become a child's hope, a child's ambition – I suck all that out whilst they're still in the womb. That's what makes you different, boy – you were born with hope. With a desire for something more.

Dave looked around the crowd.

They were staring up at the mist, transfixed.

But it won't happen a second time, the Estate Father said, and zoomed for Connie's exposed vagina.

But Dave blocked its way.

And gasped as he found that he could actually touch it.

He wrestled with it, grasped, struggled to keep it from touching his girlfriend, his unborn child.

"Dave!" Jack cried, and for the first time Dave heard genuine panic in his voice. "Stop that! You stop that now!"

Fuck you, dad, he thought, and victory surged through him as he pushed back the mist, as he realised that he was finally going to win here today.

But then he felt something crash across the backs of his legs, and he toppled to his knees.

He looked back.

Saw Connie standing there, Lou's baseball bat in her hands.

And despair took him.

"Connie," he moaned. "No."

"Yes," she said. "Yes, Dave."

Then she fell backwards onto the throne, gasping as the Estate Father flooded into her and began to feed.

"Oh," she cried. "Oh!"

And knowing that it was too late, Dave leapt for her anyway.

But this time, the crowd was quicker.

Fists and feet fell upon him, and voices screamed in his face.

He tried to keep his eyes on Connie.

But soon his own blood was all he saw.

And then they dragged him to the edge of the estate and dumped him in the middle of the road.

The majority of them headed back towards the Social Club, chanting and leaving a trail of broken and empty beer bottles in their wake. But his parents remained, stood over him.

"I was so ashamed," Mavis told him. "All the other kids were fine. He never had any problem eating their ambition."

"There, there, love," Jack said, patting her shoulder.

"Why do you think you were an only child?" she went on. "We couldn't stand the thought of it happening again."

Dave heard all of this, and he knew now that it was true.

But still he tried to reach them, tried to reason with them.

"The Job Office man," he said, spitting out blood. "He'll tell the police what happened to him."

Jack nodded. "Probably he will, son," he said. "But we'll all alibi each other. They'll never prove a thing."

Dave closed his eyes, let out a sob.

"Oh son," Jack said, shaking his head. "You still don't get it, do you? You don't see why we can cheat on each other, why people around here can get into fights and beat each other up and mug their grannies and still be able to sleep at night, do you?"

"That's what he gives us," his mother said. "A way to do what we want without ever feeling guilt. All we have to do is give up our hope."

"That's why no one ever leaves this estate," Jack said. "We have everything we'll ever need here. We'll never have it so good anywhere else." A dark gleam fell across his face. "And that's why I can do this."

And he kicked his child between the legs.

"Get out," he said. "And don't come back."

That was when Dave passed out.

He came around some time later.

The pain had stopped.

On the outside, at least.

So with a groan he got up and started walking.

And within minutes heard voices coming towards him.

He wondered if he should hide.

But after everything he had lost tonight, he no longer had the energy.

Then he realised something:

The voices were coming from in front of him, not behind.

Someone was heading into the estate.

He stopped.

Saw a two-man camera crew heading towards him.

"Hey there!" said the lead man. "Fancy doing an interview? We're making one of those "benefit" shows. We're going to show the whole world what it's like to spend your life stuck in one of these places... in six forty-five minute episodes."

"Hey, come on, man," said his colleague, pulling at his arm, dragging him away. He looked Dave up and down, saw the cuts and the blood and the despair. "I don't like the look of this one. He's weird."

If you think that I'm weird, Dave thought, fighting the urge to laugh for fear that he would not be able to stop once he got started, then wait until you see the estate. He turned to watch the two men walk past him, thinking, good luck with your show, boys.

Then he put the place where he had grown up behind him and he never looked back.

NINE TENTHS
Jay Eales

Prologue

"But it's not my birthday for another week!" Sarah protested, though not too much at the prospect of an early present.

"I know," Marcus said, "I just wanted to surprise you." He had a lunatic grin as he grabbed both her hands and led her onwards, paying no attention to the street furniture strewn in his path as he backed up the pavement. From time to time, he would jig Sarah's arms up and down to encourage her using the medium of dance, enhanced by occasionally slipping on a discarded pizza box, or tripping over a chained up bike. Every so often, he would glance back over his shoulder, sizing up any substantial obstacles coming up. He particularly eyed up a battered old metal bin with '68' daubed on it in magnolia paint, rubbish overflowing its boundaries and leaving the lid parked atop it at a rakish angle.

"So... what have you got me?" Sarah could no longer hide her curiosity.

"Patience! It's just a token of my *luuuuuuurve*, baby!" Marcus suddenly let go of Sarah's hands and skipped around her, making her turn on the spot to keep facing him.

"Where'd you get all this energy from on a Sunday morning, anyway?"

"I'm just high on life. That and the three espressos I necked before I woke you."

"Ah, that explains why your pupils are spinning," Sarah said, "Anyway, don't change the subject. You were about to spill the beans about my prezzie?"

Marcus looked down the road again, "Nearly there," he said. He continued to cajole her along the path with a succession of hit and run kisses wherever he could find some exposed skin. Sarah continued to make mock protestations at her boyfriend's hyper behaviour, but her eyes were gleaming. They passed number 66, and Marcus spotted the bicycle chained to the street light outside the front door, and could not resist giving the bell a quick pump. A couple of curtains twitched at the nearby houses where the residents were already up and about, but nobody was looking for a confrontation, even with a mostly harmless looking Tigger-like twenty-something who was nine stone nothing ringing wet.

"You're an idiot," Sarah said, as Marcus continued to caper around her like a court jester.

"Yeah, but I'm your idiot," Marcus shot her a camembert grin.

"Who else would have you?" Sarah ruffled his hair fiercely, before pushing back his unruly cowlick. It took three attempts before it would stay.

Marcus took the opportunity to swoop on her again, nibbling at her collar bone and across her bare shoulder to the nape of her neck, brushing aside her hair to better reach his target, and making a series of 'mmn-mmn-mmn' noises as he did so, until he was standing behind her. He put his hands over her eyes and nudged her forward again, as they approached 68.

"Careful!" she said, as she stumbled blindly on, and Marcus adjusted his grip so that he covered her blindfolded with just his left hand. Sarah heard Marcus rummaging around in 68's dustbin, dislodging and pushing aside bin bags in search of something. She caught the sour tang of spoiled foodstuffs from more than a few days earlier. Luckily, the weather had been pretty mild or they would have been able to smell it all the way down the road at their flat. Students, she assumed, surprised that they had put out the rubbish at all. Marcus gave a small triumphant grunt as he hauled something free from the bin. At such an early hour on the Sabbath, and without a triple-espresso stimulant to help, Sarah could not fathom what it was that Marcus was doing, until he took his hand away from her face and got her to turn around to face him. He had his right hand behind his back, still hiding something from her.

Before Sarah could comment, Marcus brought out his prize with a flourish, presenting it to Sarah with a courtly bow, and adopting a poor cod-Shakespearian accent: "For you, milady! Tis nought but a trifle, the merest token of my undying affection." Sarah automatically took the proffered gift, a bouquet of flowers, amazingly, still wrapped in protective cellophane, and with an attached message card, slightly crumpled from their extended stay in the dustbin. It would have been a lovely arrangement, had it been six or seven days earlier, when the flowers had been freshly cut and purchased. Whereas today, they were more tired than Sarah was, wilting and shedding petals at the merest movement of her hands. Any fragrance that the flowers might once have produced had long since been overpowered by the aroma of rotting fried chicken remains and cigarette ash from their proximity in the bin. Marcus had eyeballed the discarded flowers while passing on the way to the corner shop for milk the previous day, and the whole crazy plan was born fully formed by the time he had arrived back at the flat.

"I'm… overwhelmed," Sarah began to speak in Marcus' cod-Elizabethan manner before thinking better of it, and wrinkled her nose at the pungent odour instead. As she held the flowers up for closer examination, she read the message card, "Who's Lizzie?" She raised an eyebrow in mock outrage. "Is that your… *strumpet?*" With a theatrical flourish, she tossed the bouquet into the road between two parked cars. "Here's what I think of your harlot's cast-offs!" She giggled as the flowers shed petal confetti as they arced through the air.

"Ah, that…" Marcus said, pausing for thought as he leant forward to retrieve the discarded gift, "Obviously… Well, *obviously*… it's my new pet name for you!" He held up one hand in supplication and he stretched between the cars into the road, and so did not even see the car that struck him.

1

"His eyes are open!"

Marcus blinked at the cold white light, feeling the detritus of sleepy dust in his eyes. He made to raise a hand to wipe it away, only to find tubes taped to his arm, and let out an involuntary yelp of alarm. In front of him, he could see a lot of movement, but his vision was blurred, and the women in front of him were strangers.

"Marcus?" One of the women, the one with a halo of blonde hair framing her face, leaned in to give him a cautious embrace. He accepted it. "Marcus? It's Sarah. You were in an accident."

Marcus pulled back against his pillow and looked around

him, blinking rapidly as he tried to clear his vision, but recognising the room he was in as a nursing ward, with pale green curtains instead of walls on two sides. At the mention of the word 'accident', the other woman, the one that Marcus now recognised as wearing the uniform of a nurse, put her hand on Sarah's arm.

"Sair…" he attempted to speak, but the dryness of his throat made it difficult to get the word out, "Ahh… Cuh huv… wor?"

Sarah turned to the nurse and said "Oh, could you get him some water, please?"

"Of course," the nurse said, but she squeezed Sarah's arm a little tighter, "Sarah, it's probably best if you don't tell him too much about the accident for a while, okay?"

"**'m noh fuk'n deff!**" Marcus spat at the nurse, his face flushed and veins pulsing at his temples.

Sarah stood open-mouthed at Marcus' outburst. She immediately felt the need to apologise: "I'm so sorry! He's not like this normally…"

"Don't be silly! He's been through a lot, Sarah," the nurse shrugged it off, "He's bound to have a lot of pent up emotion rattling around in that noggin! Better out than in."

"But still," Sarah continued, "I don't think I've ever heard him swear like that."

"We get a lot worse than that most weekends," the nurse laughed as she parted a curtain to go in search of a water jug, and to notify the duty station of the change in Marcus' condition.

"Back soon," she said with a smile through the gap in the curtain, before pulling it back across to maintain their privacy.

Sarah returned her attention to Marcus, taking his hand, and rubbing the back of it with her thumb sympathetically, while trying to avoid the needles taped in place, drip-feeding him with saline and glucose. Mistaking it for him returning her hand-holding gesture, Sarah did not see that Marcus had balled his hands into fists. But she did not miss his parting comment, his eyes firmly fixed on the curtain.

"Cunt."

2

The doctor's office had an imposing amount of wood panelling on view. Enough to build a small ark. Sarah's expression was grimmer than ever, and she kept tugging at her sleeves, as though her cardigan had shrunk in the wash.

"What I'm trying to say, Miss Ford, is that Marcus has suffered an extremely serious head trauma, and it is astonishing that his physical recovery has been as accelerated as it has, in just a few months..." Doctor Rothkiss exhibited his most practiced sympathetic air, but he had never been terribly good at it, and it mostly came across to people as vagueness and barely-concealed irritation.

"It's not his physical health I'm worried about," Sarah butted in, "It's his personality! He doesn't remember anything from before the accident. Well, not anything, but he only seems to remember things after I remind him," Sarah was on the verge of tears, unconsciously stretching her cardigan completely out of shape, "He's not the man he used to be."

"Miss Ford. Take a moment to calm yourself, if you would. As I've tried to explain to you in our previous consultations, Mister Hales has had a life changing experience. It's not unusual for there to be some memory loss. I can't in good conscience promise you that it will return in time, though it is not unheard of." Rothkiss shifted uncomfortably in his seat, as Sarah continued to sniff. He nudged his tissue box forward, encouraging her to take one.

"He's so angry all the time. I don't know what to do for him," Sarah finally took a tissue, if only to stop Rothkiss from pushing them at her in lieu of anything more helpful.

"While it is more common to find hostility coming out in patients coping with a physical injury – perfectly normal behaviour when frustrated by limited mobility issues – I imagine that not being able to remember your childhood can also be a burden. Personally, I get into a right old tizzy just trying to recall where I left my car keys! Perfectly normal." The Doctor attempted a warm smile, not entirely successfully.

"Is this *normal*, Doctor?" Sarah stuck out her left arm and rolled up her sleeve at him, so that he was confronted with her bruises. And the scabbed over rings where Marcus had stubbed out his cigarettes on her. "Before the accident, he didn't even smoke!"

"Good grief!" Rothkiss said, for the first time properly looking at Sarah, and showing genuine emotion, "He did this to you? Have you spoken to the authorities?"

"No!" Sarah said, "I don't want him arrested! I just want him back. Back as he was…"

"Miss Ford – Sarah, you are endangering yourself if you remain in the home with him, if he's capable of doing this to you."

"You told me there was no reason why he shouldn't make a full recovery, Doctor! I thought that if I… if I could just hold on, he'd come back to me."

"Sarah! I never promised he'd be exactly as he was. I could never do that. I can only give a diagnosis based on past case histories. In some cases with similar injuries, similar degrees of brain damage, the patients achieve full mobility and life returns to more or less as before, but there are always examples where the results are less favourable." Rothkiss stood up and moved around to Sarah's side of the great oak desk, as Sarah pulled down her cardigan to cover the accusatory weals on her skin, the point made well enough.

"You've heard of Foreign Accent Syndrome? It's where a head injury or other trigger can cause an otherwise healthy individual to completely lose their native accent, sounding as though they have become French, or Japanese, or some other nationality. Just one tiny part of the brain, starved of oxygen just so," he pinched thumb and forefinger together to demonstrate, "and it can cause a catastrophic change. We're still learning all the time, but as much as we know today, it can still sometimes feel as though we're blindly thrashing about in the dark."

"It's like living with a completely different person. Sometimes, he doesn't even look like Marcus any more. I keep thinking it's a nightmare, and that I'll wake up, and he'll be Marcus again. It's my fault. If I hadn't thrown those bloody flowers into the road."

"You can't think like that, Sarah. If Marcus hadn't gone to pick them up. If the driver hadn't been using your road as a rat-run shortcut. If, if, if. You're not to blame. Nobody is. Not for that. But *these*," Rothkiss pulled back Sarah's cardigan sleeve, bringing her injuries back into the light again, "*these* are down to Marcus, and nobody else."

"They're not the worst of it," Sarah said, and Rothkiss took a sharp breath.

"He didn't…" His words trailed off into silence, not wanting to anticipate Sarah's next words.

"Oh, nothing physical. It's all his mindgames. He'll sometimes start talking like Marcus, the *real* Marcus, and it gives me hope. I think it's over at last, and then I see him sneer. It starts in his eyes before it reaches his mouth. That's when he laughs. He gives me hope, then he snatches it away, and I fall for it. *Every. Single. Time.* I don't know who he is, but he isn't Marcus."

"Sarah, I'm not your GP, but I really think you should let me refer you to one of my colleagues."

"You think it's me? That *I* have the problem?" Sarah pushed Rothkiss away and stepped back from him.

Rothkiss cut off her retreat, "I think that Marcus needs help, but you need it too. It's a lot of pressure that you've put yourself under, but you don't need to do it alone."

"It's not him. Why won't you believe me? He looks like Marcus, and talks like him, except when he thinks I'm not watching. But it's not. *He's* not."

"Sarah! Will you listen to yourself? If we were living in the Middle Ages, you'd be burning him as a witch. Or possessed by the Devil! This is not rational thinking!"

"Rational? He went to sleep Marcus Hales and woke up… I don't know who."

3

He never touched her again. Not physically, anyway. But her mind, on the other hand… He had ways of getting into her head that no psychologist could untangle, no matter how many referrals she took up. He had her conditioned, and played her guilt like a Stratocaster. Guilt over her part in making him the man he had become. For his own amusement, he started to bring other women back to the flat when Sarah was home. For the most part, once he got them inside the door, one look at Sarah sitting there, and they were away again. A bit of no-strings attached infidelity was one thing, but most lost the taste for it when the injured party was standing in front of them. Most. He would email her links to XXXTube videos of him fucking other women in their bed, but they did not achieve the desired effect he was looking for. After the first one, she stopped opening them. So he sent them to her friends. Bingo. Isolated from any relationships outside of the flat, Sarah had no respite from it.

One thing that Sarah did pick up from her sessions with the headshrinker, was that she stopped thinking about him in ways that set alarm bells ringing with the medical professionals. Or at least, she stopped talking about it. She found coping mechanisms. She never called him by name. She did nothing to anger him, but no longer rose to his baiting. Like a toy he'd grown bored with, he dropped her, and mostly found his pleasures outside. Mostly.

He had done such a good job on her, whispering poisonously in the night, that she was still tied to him, unable to just pack her things and leave. It was nothing to do with fear that he might come after her. She had always had a stubborn streak, and would not give up when she set her mind to a task. As a girl, she nursed a duck with a broken wing back to health. Sarah's father told her he would put it to sleep humanely. It would not suffer, he promised. But she set her jaw, and even then, he knew better than to argue with her. So it was he who went to the vet and browbeat them into giving him antibiotics for the bird, and Sarah made Quackers her pet project. In some altogether creepier symbiotic manner, 'Marcus' was her new pet project. Like the duck's wing, the car accident had broken Sarah and Marcus, and she would knit them together again, no matter who tried to get between them. Or who made any attempt to offer help.

And then one day, like many a bully, he took it too far. He crossed the line that must not be crossed, and something ignited in Sarah. A purifying flame. A moment of clarity. The scar tissue that had formed around her under the barrage of mental torture was now her armour against his forked tongue. His barbed accusations could not penetrate her chainmail. The guilt he had traded as currency was spent. There was no more to be had. Lying prone in their formerly shared bed, with her kitchen knife to his throat, he looked into Sarah's eyes, and she into his. Something passed between them; some moment of revelation, and then they were free. Without a single word passing between them, or any form of protest – the blade remained in Sarah's hand, but it was unnecessary – he quickly threw on jeans, boots and a zip-up hoodie, and left.

Sarah watched through the Venetian blinds at the bedroom window. He did not even slam the door as a parting 'fuck you' gesture, but as he stood under the street light, he looked up at the window, right through her. Nothing of Marcus remained. Sarah drew back into the shadows, but saw him pull up his hood, shrouding his face within the night. And then from somewhere within, he summoned up an unnatural wail. It was the urgent yelp of a mating urban vixen, the hiss of steam escaping from a pipe, a crying polecat struggling with razorwire, the drone of an insistent car alarm; it was all of these things and none of them. It bounced around the houses for a minute, causing Sarah to shudder involuntarily. As the last echoes faded away, another voice picked up the refrain. And more. And yet more, both nearby and distant. As he loped off into the darkness, he was not alone.

Epilogue

Sunday morning. Just after eight o'clock. Sarah counted off the street lights, one every other house. She clutched an envelope in one hand and a single white rose in the other. A fresh one, this time, kept overnight in some water. As she approached number 68, she noticed that the new tenants had retired the old metal bin in favour of a wheelie-bin and a regimented set of different coloured recycling bags. Going up to the next street light, Sarah rifled through the pocket of her coat, and withdrew a couple of plastic gardening ties, which she used to affix the flower to the lamp at her eye-level. When she was sure it was firmly attached, she opened the envelope and brought out a photograph of Marcus with her in happier times. Both of them were making bunny ears behind the other's head. She lost herself in memories for a few seconds, letting the emotion well up in her, and then took out the remaining item from the envelope, a prewritten Sherwood Florist message card, and fixed them both to the flower with ribbon through punch-holes she had prepared earlier. She admired her handiwork, sniffed back the tears as she kissed her forefinger before touching it to Marcus' image in the photograph. Job done, she turned and went home, without looking back.

'Lost to me now, but I'll remember you always. "Lizzie" xxx'

ENVELOPES
Craig Herbertson

An ethereally pale hand puts ink to the envelope, a used polystyrene chip tray scuds against a rusted rail, evening stars orb the earth to echo the scattered glass of a vandalized car as a shadow figure throws the butt of a dead cigarette to the dirty pavement. It rolls towards the old door. It's a bleak evening, as usual.

*

The Church Hall where the Commune of Spiritus and the Veil met each week smelt of stale cabbage and boiled potatoes, a peculiarly revolting combination that gave Julia Ashton a faint headache. The flaking plaster on the ceiling and the worn and stained planks on the poorly polished floor merely supported the impression of abject poverty. The office to the left of the stage was no less oppressive: A yellowed windowless wall dominated by a single portrait of a dour septuagenarian, apparently the founder of the movement. His bleak face overshadowed the small room, stacked high with old bound books and musty folders that spilled like fossilized cataracts from the pre-war filing cabinets.

Julia swept the blond hair from her neatly oval face and unconsciously shielded her eyes from the portrait. There was something sinister and overwhelming in the expression. The narrowed eyes of the gowned figure lent a shabby oppressive weight to the room as if he was the reluctant overseer of its decay. She coughed and glanced from the portrait to its twin – the old man behind the broad walnut desk, Mr. Hutching, who fondled a brown envelope between his thin fingers and peered myopically at her through the lenses of his bifocal spectacles.

"You say you received this from our institution Miss Ashton?"

"Yes, it came three days after my father's funeral. I think

three days. I didn't open it until… It was a traumatic time."

"Quite. And what were the contents of the missive?"

"Well, nothing. There was nothing inside. Only the address of the sender."

"So you came to us, the Commune of Spiritus and the Veil?"

"Well, yes. I'm here. I couldn't understand why it had been sent. It was empty. Then I looked up the address and read something about your work. Somehow it seemed strange."

"Some are called," said Mr. Hutching emphatically. He gave her the kind of look that many men gave her – but in this case Julia sensed that her physical attractiveness was not the immediate inspiration. She got to the point.

"But who sent the letter?"

Mr. Hutchings gave a cryptic look. "Indeed, Miss Ashton. I wonder about that too." He examined the faded writing on the envelope and handed it back. "We are a small society. I know all the members on the temporal plane. None writes in this old fashioned script. Did anything strike you about the writing?"

"Why, it did seem familiar. Let me see." There was a long silence.

"It's very like – but it couldn't be – it's very like my mother's writing."

Mr. Hutchings waited for the implications of this to impact.

Julia stared at the old man in disbelief. "It couldn't be…"

The door opened. Julia turned. A young man, tall, bearded, wearing dark trousers and a white shirt stood on the threshold.

"Ah, Mr. Dent. Everything prepared? Meet Miss Ashton. She's had a bit of a shock."

Mr. Dent nodded curtly. "They're more or less all here. I think we can begin the service."

Behind him in the large hall, Julia could see people, mostly women, seated in rows. Some bowed in prayer. An older lady, clad in a black evening dress, was standing on the stage, perfectly still. She appeared to be in some kind of meditational trance. The woman even from a distance emoted a strange charismatic power. Suddenly, Julia felt the world spin around her. The events of the past few weeks, her father's failing health, his lingering death. It was all too much. She buried her head in her arms and began to silently weep.

There was a long pause. "There there," said Mr. Hutching.

"You came by bus didn't you? Mr. Dent... Peter will take you home."

As the old Ford fiesta trundled through the wind swept streets the red brick houses seemed to lean inwards. A constant reminder of bitterness, mediocrity and the hard life. Julia's father, lungs destroyed by the factory, had been too young to die. Now she was alone. She glanced at the driver, Peter Dent, a Londoner up at Manchester University finishing his PHD in Archaeology and Ancient Calligraphy. He was well dressed in a quiet way, perhaps a year or two older than her twenty five.

"You don't seem the type for this spiritualism thing?"

"Despite appearances it's an interesting field. If I may say so you don't look the type either. What is it you do?"

"Acting, modelling."

"Well, you're certainly a good looking girl. Glamorous work?"

"Everyone thinks that but it's a struggle. Castings, interviews. Not well paid unless you get lucky. And there are...pitfalls."

"I can imagine," said Peter tersely. "So what brought you to Spiritus and the Veil? The envelope?"

"Yes, father died and then it came. It looked like mother's handwriting and she passed on years ago. It was a shock."

"That's what I mean about Spiritualism. It's an interesting field. There are fakes of course, back alleys, chancers. But lots of surprises, contradictions, the thrill of the inexplicable. I've had some baffling experiences. So you're not alone in that."

"Mr. Hutchings seemed to think it came from beyond. At least that's what he implied."

"Who knows?" said Peter. "It's certainly a mystery." He thrust the car through a red light and entered the warehouse complex where the new flats rose out of the gloom in a series of anonymous squares. "I don't know my way around here. It's all changed..."

"You can let me out here."

"I'd be a bit concerned. I don't want to be a pompous fool but this is where the street walkers hang out. Not ideal."

"It's not a problem. I know the girls on sight. I walk home most evenings."

"Well, if you're sure. Look. Here's my card. You've had a

195

shock. If there's anything you need just let me know."

Julia took the card. She watched the old car until it retreated from sight. He had seemed like a nice guy. She was used to much worse. It was a short stroll along the pedestrian path that rose just above the canal. She never took the canal walkway. Girls and their punters often used it for knee tremblers. Drug addicts and muggers frequented the walkway but they avoided the well-lit street because of the ubiquitous police presence. Julia lit a cigarette. There were three girls clad in ostentatious clothes not far from her door. One looked about fourteen. The other two girls were slapping the younger. In the midst of the scuffle the young thing ran off to a volley of cursing. As Julia got out her keys she recognized her friend Amy.

"Got a light, Julia? Christ they'll be pimping ten years old next. Frigging cheek." Amy was the same age as Julia but, under the mask of face paint, the cocaine and the hard life had stolen ten years of her life.

"How's business?" said Julia. She didn't want to know but it was expected.

"Awful. A punter hit me." She showed the small bruise. "How's the modelling?" There was trace of envy in the voice. They had gone to school together and had started in the same casting agency. Amy had less luck or so Julia once thought.

"It's going downhill. Younger girls, better looking, no work. You know how it is."

"Don't give up," said Amy quietly. "Or you'll end up like me." She looked at the black canal waters beyond the railings and shuddered.

Alone in the cramped flat Julia switched on the answerphone.

The model agency had cancelled two jobs. There was a casting for the latest range of underwear for a small boutique but there would be at least thirty applicants and it was in Birmingham. Extra work on the latest soap opera at sixty quid a day but no guarantees and the producer was a known philanderer. Julia switched off the machine and lay on the single bed. For an hour she stared at the ceiling, seeing in the wrinkled damp patches a reflection of her own future. She looked at the unopened bills on her desk. She looked at the brown envelope with the familiar writing. She thought of Amy and began to cry.

On Wednesday evening Julia spent some time over her

wardrobe. She picked a casual black frock and an old leather jacket, stockings, plain black shoes and her lucky handbag. After an hour of careful attention to her face she felt ready. The doorbell rang. Peter was waiting on the step. He was decidedly handsome and there was a certain light in his eyes which she had long recognized. He walked to the car and opened the door for her. He said nothing until they had passed the city centre.

"I'm glad you rang. I was hoping you would."

"I've never attended a spiritualist meeting."

"Sit with me. You'll be fine."

She smiled.

Mr. Hutchings greeted them both at the entrance where he was handing out leaflets. There were around fifteen people in attendance. The same woman was standing in silence on the stage. Peter led Julia to the back of the room. A few minutes passed in which all Julia could hear was the sound of wheezing breath and mumbled prayers from an old gent in the next row. She found herself very aware of the strong masculine smell of Peter whose legs touched her own.

Suddenly, with a jarring explosion of sound the woman on the stage began to cry out. There was a babble of confused words and then Julia began to pick out halting sentences.

"Yes, it's Dame Farin…"

"She's a wise woman from the thirteenth century, her Spirit guide," whispered Peter. Julia was about to laugh but he seemed sincere.

"She has a man with her. He has kind eyes. An old man but vital. Vital! You have something for Joan. Is there a Joan here?" There was a stifled sob.

"Joan. Everything is fine. His name begins with an H… Harry. Yes, Harry. Harry is well and sends his blessing. I'm seeing an attic. There is an old box, like a music box. Harry says the jewellery is in the box. You must sell it wisely. Use the money for the hospital." The sobbing became uncontrolled.

"Joan's husband," said Peter quietly.

The voice became confused garbled. Then rose stridently. "I have a Jack here. Does anyone know Jack? He's a man of about fifty with black hair."

Julia shuddered but said nothing.

"Jack sends his blessing. He's very happy in the next life. He

197

wants his…daughter to be happy too. He says…'trust'. No, it's fading. 'Trust' I think."

Later, as they drove home Julia spoke. "My father was called Jack but… I couldn't answer. I just couldn't. Was it him?"

"Who knows?" said Peter. "Certainly I don't. But these coincidences they mount up. Look, have you eaten?"

They stopped at a curry house where Peter ordered a vindaloo and a vegetarian masala. As he stabbed into the meat he expanded on the principles of spiritualism. "We mostly agree that there is an Infinite Intelligence who governs all things. The nature of this 'God' if you like is beyond our understanding but what seems to be clear is that personal identity survives physical death. It's like a progression from one room to the next. We know the room is there but we just can't see."

"Beyond the veil."

"Yes, precisely. We get hints and we seem to be able to commune with the spiritual realms beyond, but who really knows?"

"Mr Hutchings seems to have no doubts."

"Well, I'm more of a sceptic, and while the Commune of Spiritus and the Veil is sound enough in its own way I prefer more individual methods. Hutchings isn't – well, I hate to be snobbish, he has a basic talent – but he isn't educated. My studies at the university." He gripped Julia's hand. "They'll be finished soon. I have a sinecure at the university, a probationary post on a three year stipend. I'll be relatively well off. I'd like to branch out. Investigate. I'd need help with some extra work in spiritualism. A companion to take some of the burden."

Julia let his hand remain in hers.

"I'd love to know if my father was truly happy beyond this life," said Julia. "I'm not sure about the abstract theories."

"But you could learn. You're bright as well as extremely attractive."

Julia smiled quietly and felt the inner glow of hope.

"I'd like to try."

"Look," said Peter releasing his hand. "It's quite simple really. The soul has a life apart from its corporeal envelope. The inner being exists eternally. That's obvious. This corporeal envelope is prey to lusts, to desires, to corruption and decay but the inner soul, within the envelope of the body, that must go on. Do you see?"

Julia listened, her eyes never leaving those of Peter, observing every enthusiasm, every mannerism. It was late when they left.

There was only one street walker outside her apartment when they returned. Peter had wanted to accompany her to the door but Julia was no fool with men. It was not yet time. As she drew out her pack of cigarettes the girl approached her furtively.

"Love, was Amy a friend of yours?"

"Yes," said Julia.

"They found her yesterday in the canal. Some bastard murdered the poor thing. I wasn't here. I never saw who she picked up. They'll never find the bastard. They never do because they couldn't give a shit."

Alone in her tiny apartment Julia stared at the ceiling. She had no one but herself. No living relatives, no friends. Only Peter. The police would investigate the murder. Maybe they'd think it was Peter. He had been there about the time. Best say nothing. Like all events in the underworld, Amy's death would sink to the bottom of the canal along with the old bikes, the needles and the used condoms.

When they left the meeting on the following Wednesday Julia was visibly upset. She had explained about her friend to Peter but no one else. Still, the old woman had given her messages. One from her father and one from a newly 'passed' girl. A girl too young to die, who found it difficult to accept the truth of her situation. There was no blessing. Only a desperate appeal to 'keep safe.'

Outside in the pouring rain, Peter stared at Julia from beneath his umbrella. "But was it her?" said Julia. "Was it Amy? I don't know what to think."

"Look," said Peter firmly. "I want to show you something tonight. I think it will help. It's to do with my work. These people, Hutchings, the spiritualists, all of them are well intentioned but they are grasping in the unknown. I have something that can really help you. It's not proof but well… you have to see it."

The car took them up to the North where the low hills gave way to the bleak moorlands and the jutting crags. The rain had stopped by the time they reached ridge of a high hill. They both got out into the quiet and still air. To the south Julia could see the great sprawling city of Manchester lit by bracelets of traffic lights, cars like fireflies winking in and out of existence. The air smelt crisp and fresh after the rain.

Peter took a wooden box a span in width from the trunk of his car. He tucked it under his arms and gripped Julia by the waist. "See that hillock. There's a circle of standing stones there. Incredibly ancient. Only I know of them. They're not actually visible but I observed the patterns on the grass and I'm trained to spot these things. I've been experimenting. I have what I think is the final proof and I'd like you to share it with me. Can you take this blanket in the boot? If we need to sit down for a bit. It's wet."

Julia nodded. She could think of other uses for the blanket. It was time.

They walked through the wet grass, the eerie hills rising around them. In a low declivity they halted beside a weather beaten rock. Julia spread the blanket on the grass as Peter laid down the box. He smiled at Julia and they embraced. He kissed her and then held her away from him. He stared at her for some moments and then turned to the box. "Stand in the centre. Three yards away, just beside the rock."

Peter was fumbling over the box. Julia didn't move. A strange fanciful expression played on her beautiful face.

"You see, Julia, I've found out what it's all about beyond the veil. These fools at Spiritus and the Veil are all interested in the soul, the passing spirit, but me…" He turned, in his hands two meat cleavers. "I'm only interested in the envelope."

An ethereally pale hand puts ink to the envelope, a used polystyrene chip tray scuds against a rusted rail, evening stars orb the earth to echo the scattered glass of a vandalized car as a shadow figure throws the butt of a dead cigarette to the dirty pavement. It rolls towards the old door. It's a bleak evening, as usual.

TUNNEL VISION
Tim Major

It's not dark but the school is so empty it feels like night.

Miss Henson must still be in the staffroom. In there, the teachers sit on saggy red sofas instead of classroom chairs too small for their big behinds. It smells a bit like cigarettes and a bit like the seaside.

The classroom feels massive with nobody but me in it. When I was little I thought teachers lived at school, but now I'm ten and old enough to know better. But I'm standing in the middle of the room and it feels empty at the edges.

I swing from side to side in Miss Henson's padded chair. Seeing the classroom from this angle gives me a queasy feeling, like looking down at your own street from above. I look over at my seat. I'd be facing Miss Henson if she was sitting where I'm sitting and I was over there. There's another wave of sickly surprise as I imagine my own face looking up at me.

I shake my head to clear it, like in a cartoon. I came in early for a reason. For a moment I think I've lost the envelope but there it is on the desk, mixed in with the exercise books and worksheets as if it needs opening and marking.

I hear a thump to my right. A dark shape appears against the glass panel of the door to the playground, wobbling as whoever it is shakes rain from their coat. I jump out of the teacher's chair, whip the envelope from the desk, run to the side counter and slip it into the tray marked Anita S.

*

Anita hasn't sent me a card. I almost wish I could take mine back, but it's propped up in front of her and she's been talking to Debbie about it, all excited. My cheeks glow as she reads the poem aloud again, even though it's nothing soppy: *Roses are red, violets are blue, Some poems rhyme, But this one doesn't.* Pretty funny. She doesn't read out the bit underneath where I'd written

201

something about love. I wish I hadn't written that, but it's just what you do.

After break-time a card has appeared in my own tray. Anita must have had it all along but just didn't think to come in early like I did.

She sits directly behind me with her back to mine. I'd have to turn to speak to her, but since break-time I hadn't turned around once. What happens next? Two people sending Valentine's cards to each other, that means something, right?

My face aches from the glowing and the keeping still. I thumb the edge of Anita's card where it sticks out from my maths workbook.

I have to speak to her. We're boyfriend and girlfriend now, or something.

I only manage to half-turn. "Hey Anita? Thanks for the card. But you know that honey is spelt H-O-N-E-Y, not H-U-N-N-Y?" I'm speaking much louder than I'd meant to. "'Hunny bunny', that's what you wrote."

Anita doesn't say anything. I turn fully but all I can see is red hair.

"Who says I sent it?" she says quietly.

I turn back to look at my workbook.

*

Anita doesn't speak to me for the rest of the morning. At lunch-time, even though it's not raining any more, the school fields are muddy and out of bounds. The playground seems tiny and there's nowhere to stand that's out of sight of Anita and Debbie and their friends. They keep glancing over to where I'm standing with Mousey.

"Cylinders: eight," Mousey says.

Anita doesn't look nearly so pleased about the Valentine's card now. I'm sure her friends are laughing at me.

"Cylinders: eight," Mousey says again.

I glance at my own Top Trumps card and back at Anita.

"Come on then. Hand it over. There aren't any others with eight cylinders."

I hand over the card without even checking to see which it is. "I'm sick of Top Trumps. It's stupid."

Mousey shrugs. "I don't even like cars. What is a cylinder in a car, anyway? Johnny's got Top Trumps with Marvel superheroes on."

I can't stand the looks I'm getting from Anita's friends. I push Mousey in the shoulder with the palm of my hand. "Tig! And no tigging the butcher."

"There's no-one else playing," Mousey says, rubbing his shoulder. "So who can I tig?" But I'm already halfway down the playground.

The game draws in other boys until there are twelve of us hurtling around the playground and paved area beside the school doors. Anita's eyes follow me, making my cheeks sting with heat.

Today I'm all limbs and speed. Soon I'm the only one left untigged. The other eleven shout and groan as I slip away again and again. They close in but I duck and weave. My winding, zooming route takes me towards Anita's group but I turn away even as I run toward them. Casual and cool.

When my head thwacks against the wooden post of the doorway awning, like a ball against a rounders bat, it's the surprise that takes me down, not the pain. I lurch backwards and hit the ground. Eleven boys tig me all at once with shouts of "Pile on!", and Anita's face disappears in the gaps between the bodies.

*

After lunch-time we're marched to the tiny music room. It's too hot with twenty of us in there and our glockenspiel-and-maracas version of *Yellow Submarine* makes my ears ring. I stay at the back, shaking my maraca only when Mrs Pearson looks my way. I'm sleepy. I raise my hand, waiting for the teacher to notice me.

"Mum, I need the loo."

Anita and Debbie turn, but it's not just them laughing, it's almost everyone. What's so funny? Has Anita shown my Valentine's card to them all?

The tiled bathroom feels small but it's not the room that's narrow, it's my view of it. I lean on the sink. The cold ceramic is shocking against my palms. The edges around my reflection in the mirror are hazy. I can't see anything outside the shaking image of myself looking back. It's not blackness exactly – there's just nothing there. I look left and right. The rest of the bathroom appears, bit by bit, as the circle of vision follows the movement of my head.

I leave the bathroom on shaky legs and take my place at the back of the music room.

I should say something to someone.

I can still hear quiet sniggers. Mrs Pearson shoots me a look which is partly annoyed, partly worried.

I'm telling nobody.

*

I leave as soon as the bell rings, stumbling through the gate and ignoring a hello from Mousey's mum, who comes to meet him every day because she thinks he's still a baby. I keep looking straight ahead, partly to stop the sickly feeling from spreading, and partly because everything at the edges is getting more invisible all the time.

Aldenham Road seems too long to bear. I take the cut along Roxby Avenue, past the place where an older boy once stopped me on my bike, said he had a secret to tell me, then leaned in close and spat in my ear. I cross to Lealholm Way and the embankment that I once worried was haunted, where me and Mousey sheltered from a lightning storm, certain we'd be struck and not minding.

Mrs Lilley from next door doesn't notice anything wrong when I ring the bell to collect the house key. And then I'm home, alone, heavy and dim.

The house is all corridor, just tiny circles of clear vision surrounded by mist. My head is like an enormous iron wrecking ball balanced on my body. I stagger up to my parents' bedroom, feeling the way. I look into the full-length mirror on the wardrobe door and something ghostly looks back.

I don't believe in God. It's all just stories. At the mirror, I pray to God, or something. Then I sit on the edge of the bed to rest.

I've always liked the wallpaper in here. The brown is broken up with curled vines, a pattern that repeats every five leaves upwards and three side-to-side. If you know where to look, there are faces in the spaces between the vines. Berries for eyes, wisps of stalks for mouths. One is laughing, one is worried, one is

204

jealous of the others, I don't know why.

"You know what this is?" the worried one says.

I stare.

"It's bad," he says, without moving his stalk mouth.

The jealous face nods without nodding. "It's bad, really bad." I don't know why he seems so jealous about that.

I look for the happy face. I can only see vines and leaves.

I'm dying. This is what it feels like. Soon I'll only see a pinprick of light ahead of me and then even that will close in and everything will be black, or just nothing, and then that'll be that.

I'm only ten. People don't die aged ten. But I'm dying all the same.

Why aren't mum and dad home from work yet? Where's Michaela, my sister? Even she would do.

Mousey once said that if he knew he was dying, he'd kill as many people as possible before he snuffed it. If he was going to die then they could too. He'd read about making a bomb from washing powder and it couldn't be all that hard.

Mousey's a nutcase.

But I'm dying and I'm on my own and nobody's home and I'm hungry too.

I'm back downstairs without knowing quite how I got there. I'm not all that hungry after all, just sleepy.

But I'm ten years old. I don't want to go to sleep.

The sunlight through the kitchen window makes me wince but wakes me up a bit. I fumble with the handle to the back door. The air is cold in a good way, because my face has got all fiery again. I stumble on one of the broken slabs that dad laid out ready to crazy-pave the path. Out in the garden the hazy nothing around my circle of vision seems even stranger. The bright greens and oranges bleed into blindness.

I try not to think about mum and dad and Michaela. They'll cry for ages, but what do I care? I won't be there to see it.

A scuffling sound comes from the shed. I'm not on my own after all. I open the door to see Michaela's rabbit, Roderick, looking up at me. He's as white and ghostly as I was in the mirror. Rabbits don't live long and he's already six. But I'm dying today and Roderick might live for years yet. Is that fair?

Dad promised I could write my name in the wet cement. Tomorrow.

My eyes sting. I heave one of the loose paving slabs into the air. It's thick and heavy and digs into my fingers at the jagged edge.

I lurch into the shed and raise the slab over Roderick's head. Then I drop it on him and there's no going back from that.

Back inside, I crawl up the stairs and into bed. The thought crosses my mind to leave a goodbye note but I'm very sleepy now and I don't have a pencil.

*

The glow of light through the curtains and the noise from the street tell me that it's still afternoon, not morning. I hear the front door close and then mum and Michaela talking.

My bedroom's big again. It's as though I can see everything all at once – not just what I'm looking at but things around the edges. Things and things and things instead of hazy nothing.

I'm not dead, or dying. I'm ten years old and I'm going to get older every day.

I hear the back door *thunk* open, then the door to the shed.

Seconds pass.

Michaela screams.

LIFE IS PRESCIOUS
MJ Wesolowski

Marney stares without speaking for just long enough for me to know that something's wrong.

Her eyes are wide and bulge from rings of black kohl like an old cartoon; she mouths the first two words, leaving out the last; leaves it hanging in the air, an almond shape between her lips.

"What?" I snap. "What's up? Why are you looking at me like that?"

I feel sudden anger; a nest of snakes unfurling in my stomach.

"What does it say?" Marney's voice is careful. "Life is... what?"

My first instinct is to clap my hand to my neck to cover it, as if I'm swatting a midge. Instead, I roll the cling film back up, feeling it tickle my earlobe. Marney peers closer.

"Let's have a proper look."

I can feel her breath on my neck.

"Nah, get off!"

This time I'm careful to place my hand gently over it, hiding it from view. It feels like sunburn, like when I was a kid and we were in Minorca. The tops of my feet were the worst, it felt like someone had stamped on them for three solid days and nights. My granddad was the only one I'd let touch me with the after-sun.

"Jay?"

My phone buzzes.

I turn away from Marney and start walking. Fuck this.

"Jay!"

Marney's voice is a wail, spiking with the middle vowel of my name in a pitch-perfect high-C. I keep going. My heart is thudding, thundering and I can feel the anger getting larger like a red balloon inflating behind my eyes. I want to punch something, boot a wall; kick in one of the betting shop windows. It's a shit hole round here anyway, no one'll care.

"Jay!"

I don't even know where I'm going, it doesn't matter. All I'm focussed on is the pavement in front of me, its angles jutting out at me like a hundred little frowns; around the rusty yawns of the manholes. When I was a kid I used to jump on them with two feet; granddad's hand in mine, heaving me up into the air, the unbreakable grip; clank.

"Jay!"

"What? Fucking what?"

I spin round and the anger trickles out of me; my balloon burst, all that red fury dribbling out of my sleeves and disappearing between the cracks. Dripping on the bears that don't get me anymore. I'm too big now and granddad doesn't walk.

Marney looks a little bit scared; her eyes are wide, like a child's; a little girl playing dress-up. There's a hole in her tights and her knee pokes out. She's drawn a smiley face on it in sharpie.

"Sorry." I say and hang my head. My fringe smells of Dax Wax.

"Let's have a look."

I let Marney turn my face with one finger. Her nails are painted in different colours, red and green and purple. She's wearing the plastic liquorice allsorts ring I got her. She stares at my neck like it's a wound.

"Life is... precious..." she says.

"Yeah."

She goes to say something else and stops again. I redden and mumble

"I know. I should have told you... I..."

"It's not that."

"But I just wanted to get it quick... while I was in the moment... before I wussed out..."

"I know."

She puts her arms round me; little twiglets in black hoodie sleeves. I rest my chin on the parting in her hair.

"I know it looks a bit... common on there, on my neck... a bit... but it's..."

"I know why," she says, and in that movement I bubble with a burning love for her that rattles through me with the force of a high speed train.

208

"I tried the other place, the one you went to but they asked for ID and anyway... I didn't have much money and..."

"It's not that, Jay... it looks good. Honestly."

Marney got hers back in year ten, a little black rose on the Karate chop part of her hand. She thought her mum wouldn't notice.

 I didn't see her for a month.

"It's just..."

"What?"

The anger's gone. I lean down, catch a whiff of my own BO and press my arms into my sides. We probably should get going; this part of town's not the sort of place you want to hang about in for long; a concentrated hub of charity shops and broken windows. I jump slightly as I catch the eye of a pale-eyed bloke folded up in a doorway. He gives me a meat-coloured grimace. One yellow peg.

"Come on." I take Marney's hand and we start walking. I kick out at a one-legged pigeon that's coo is a smoker's cough as it flutters up to perch on a windowsill above us, black with grime.

"Don't," Marney says. "Poor thing."

"Rats with wings."

We walk in silence for a bit, past the Indian food shops, great piles of gulab glistening like orange baubles. My stomach growls.

"We getting the 22?"

"Uh-huh."

We stop at the bus stop because it's there. The 22 goes past Marney's mum's and on to Honeysuckle House, the square four storeys that cling like a limpet to the edge of town. Granddad's room looks out onto the bypass. He won't watch the telly.

"You going to show him?"

"Course I am."

Marney squeezes my hand but she's still got a funny look betraying her face.

It stinks of exhaust and the road brims with cars, shuddering along; why anyone bothers trying to drive in town is just stupid.

"Give us another look."

I bend down and the edge of the cling film trembles. I take a quick glance at my phone, it's been buzzing like a fucking mad thing since I posted up the pic. I got the tattooist to take it, my hands were shaking too much.

37 notifications

Fucking hell. Not bad.

"Jay."

I put my phone back in my pocket; Marney goes fucking spare if I check it too much when I'm with her. "What?" There's something in her voice. Some trepidation. She shows her teeth, little white stubs in a tiny smile. "What?"

"It's just... Jay... he's spelled it wrong."

"Eh?"

"Your," she gestures to my neck, "your tattoo... life is precious... he's spelled precious wrong."

No. No way. She's having a joke, a laugh with me. Winding me up.

"Get out!" I waggle my hand at her in a sort of wave. No idea what that was.

"Jay! Seriously. There's an S in it."

"Yeah. And what? Of course there's an S in it!"

"No, I mean an extra one."

"Bollocks."

"Jay!"

"My precioussssss."

I do my best Gollum voice. Normally it makes Marney squeal. Not now. She's looking at me like a mum, stern. I want her to stop, to tell me it's a joke. Marney doesn't do jokes like that, maybe that's why it seems so real.

"Give up," I say.

My phone buzzes again once, twice. I push the urge to check it to the bottom of my battered converse.

"No. Not at the end. In the wrong place, after the E."

"What?"

My phone's going again; it's like a little electric heart down there.

"Jay, he's spelled it wrong. You need to go back!"

Buzz-buzz-buzz.

Horror begins descending like a massive black fucking cloud. The whole world seems suddenly lighter. This can't be real; it can't be me this is happening to. Marney's still staring at me. I slam my hand on the pole of the bus stop.

"Shit... you're serious? Shit…"

With the same ringing hand I clasp my neck, hard, palm over the cling film so it hurts. Fucking idiot. The anger's back. Cheeks red, I turn away from a bunch of kids clattering down the street in flapping white robes and velvet hats on the way to the mosque. Their laughter sounds like its heading straight at me, stupid idiot can't even spell.

Shit.

My phone's still buzzing. I don't want to even look. Fucking hell, I'm going to have to delete my account now; all day I've been on about it, under the desk, *'FOUR HOURS TILL INK'*, what an idiot. The whole sixth form will be pissing themselves.

"You need to go back! Get him to sort it out!"

"Yeah, I know."

"It's fucking stupid, Jay, how dare he just do that? It's not your fault."

"Yeah..."

"You can get your money back, you need to ask for your money back, Jay. It's stupid... it's..."

Anger explodes through me at Marney's outrage on my behalf.

"Oh, really? Well good fucking thinking! Well done! I'd have never thought of that my fucking self!"

My words are like a slap; Marney's face pales and her mouth opens. An old fella glares at me from across the road.

"Look!" I pull a crumpled bit of paper from my back pocket.

Four hours, the entirety of a fucking double art lesson it took me to draw out and I've spelled it wrong, how could I have been so stupid? I think back to the bloke in the tattoo place; big fat fucker with a beard, he had a fake canister with anti-bullshit spray written on it and he had shown it to me and I'd laughed.

He probably couldn't even spell his own name.

"What's that?"

I say nothing; wait for her to work it out. My design is still streaked with the blue transfer ink, 'Life is precious.' I think of the whine of the tattoo machine, the pain, like being burned; the pride when it was over, all gone.

"Doesn't matter." Marney is shaking her head. "Doesn't matter, he should have known, he should have seen it. You need to go back."

I play out walking back into the tattoo place, up those stairs, the citric reek of ink and disinfectant, the light head; death metal grunting away on the stereo. He had them everywhere, his hands, fingers, neck, scalp. I imagine him picking up that canister and laughing, the rest of them falling about, their beards and flesh-tunnels flapping. Fuck that.

"It doesn't matter."

I rest my head against the bus stop. The metal is cool and rough. I can't look at Marney, this is my default, all my fault; something else I've gone and ruined.

"Come on!" She grabs at my arm and I shake her off.

"Leave it."

"Jay."

"Leave it!"

"For fuck's sake!"

This time I really do explode, my right arm shooting out in a galvanic, flailing motion. I'm thinking as the back of my hand makes contact with Marney's cheek.

No-no-no, sorry-sorry- sorry. Shit!

But that doesn't stop it. In torturous slow motion, I feel her skin against the back of my hand, the edge of those tiny teeth against my fingers, hear the gasp of a passer-by. Pigeons rattling like bones up-up away into the sky.

"Sorry, shit, I'm sorry!"

The anger's gone again, dissolved, kaput, the world is horribly silent and all that's left is Marney stood there in front of me, one hand clasped to her cheek.

"Marney... I'm sorry... I..."

I stretch out my hand, her eyes are wide, a terrified rabbit; I feel grotesque, a shambling monstrosity, a terrible ogre.

"Jay! You... you..."

"I didn't mean to... I'm sorry! It was an accident!"

She knows, she must know... I'm not that sort of guy, it was an accident.

The world is stood still and I can feel everyone looking at me, their eyes, their hate. I want to cry.

"Jay?"

And I'm away, fuck it, forget it, I'm away back the way I have come, scattering pigeons and children in my wake. My heart is hammering again and I know that if I stop I'll fall. The city looms around me in a collage of fading grey and cuboid sandstone; the stench of piss and bin bags, grease between cobbles reflecting the dying sunlight and all I can think of is what my granddad would have thought of me if he'd seen that. Seen me lash out.

What a fucking massive failure.

When I reach the door of the tattooist, I'm out of breath. Squid Ink. There's about a million more stairs a million times steeper than before and they'll be closed in a bit. A manhole clonks as I step backward and I choke, keep my tears from spilling out at the last second. I want to punch the wall, I want to punch myself.

"Hey."

Jesus Christ.

I turn around again, fight or flight mode re-igniting. There's no cars here, just cobbles, those huge green council bins that stink like the dead in summer. A steady drip-drip of liquid from somewhere. It used to be a nice part of town round here, my granddad says, butchers, fishmongers, bakers. Now there's just rusted metal shutters, the back end of Wilko's and old graffiti. No one even bothers sticking up fly posters anymore round here.

"Hey, you!"

Two of the council bins create an impromptu corridor which leads into a blackened doorway, a burned out mouth in the bowels of the building. Someone hunched in there. Two milky eyes peering from the gloom.

My preciousss.

"Sorry, mate." I turn away, my senses crackling with adrenaline, stomach clenching and unclenching like a fist. I don't need this, any more aggro. I just want to go home.

"Hey!"

The voice is cracked, tinged with a lilting accent, Welsh perhaps? He doesn't sound drunk but that counts for nothing.

"I've got no change on me, mate, sorry." I pull out my phone and replace it quickly. Rookie mistake.

I remember my best mate Colm when we got on the wrong bus on the way back from a party a few years back, trying to avoid two lads who were giving him stick, by looking at his phone. One of them just got up and snatched it out of his hand. Colm's even skinnier than me and these lads were from the Brocklands estate, old man's faces, perma-scowls, fingers black with grime. Dead eyes. What were we going to do about it?

213

"I don't want your change."

I can hear the man now, shuffling, scrabbling around in that doorway like an old spider. I need to get out of here.

"It's either up those stairs or back the way you came."

I turn back, stare between the bins; there's a stink like soil and salt and something else, like the smell in your hair the day after a bonfire.

"Or in here, with me."

"Right!"

I'm actually laughing now. Maybe I'm losing my mind.

"I'm not going to hurt you, son."

"I suppose you're just going to show me some puppies are you? Bum me to death."

I don't give a shit anymore. I turn to face him. This motherfucker might have a knife, a rusty syringe dripping with disease.

Bring it.

"Funny aren't you?"

His voice comes from somewhere rough and reedy deep in his chest; a straggly beard, black tongue curling around a single tooth. He's stood still beneath the bins, looking at me with those eyes, pale blue and milky, not really looking at me but past me. I realise the poor old fucker's blind.

"Shit, sorry, man." I fumble in my pocket and find my bus fare. "Here, get yourself a..."

I give out a strangled sort of yelp as an explosion of feathers clatters past my head and I duck. A scrawny city pigeon, one pink foot curled into an agonised claw alights on the man's shoulder.

I'm starting to feel properly scared now; the buildings around us are tall; pipes and rusted fire escapes clinging to them like the fossils of some ancient ribs. I'm looking for a camera. A friendly policeman, anything. No one comes round here.

Buzz-buzz-buzz.

My phone. I reach for it slowly, so he can't hear.

"I wouldn't look at that if I were you," he says, and the pigeon on his shoulder ruffles its feathers and makes a coughing, cooing noise.

"Why not?"

"Trust me, son, just wait."

214

This is bullshit. I need to go back, find Marney, to sort all this out. What am I even doing here in town?

"Here."

The change for the bus is still in my hand, I walk toward the man, holding it out before me. The pigeon shifts, hopping on its one good foot. "Get yourself something to eat."

I get as close as I dare. The man doesn't move, he's hunched, both hands gripping the sides of the bins and I notice with a terrible sort of heave in my stomach that his arms are long, far too long, the jacket he's wearing is much too big, it pools around his feet; a filthy leather trench coat that is splayed out like the wings of a ragged bat. One leg flops lifelessly below him, one stands straight, mirroring his slate-coloured familiar.

"You're in something of a conundrum, I would say, son, aren't you?"

The pigeon hops again and cocks its head at me. Its eyes are black. Something inside tells me it was the one I tried to kick what seemed like hundred years ago.

Don't. Poor thing.

A little ripple of guilt.

"I just want to go see my granddad."

Why did I say that? What the fuck does he care? I'm losing my shit here. The pigeon ruffles its feather and attempts to shift its weight onto its withered foot. I hiss in empathy.

"Poison, that." The ragged man lowers himself into a sitting position between the bins with his too-long arms; his legs just crumple beneath him and I realise one is false, the other is just an empty trouser leg stuffed into a shoe.

"What?"

He cocks his head at the bird.

"Poison, acid. They put it down on window ledges, places where pigeons aren't welcome. It burns up their feet. Cheaper than laying nets or spikes. They save that sort of thing for people."

I remember the anti-homeless spikes outside Selfridges on the news, stone benches, sloped bus stops. That mosquito thing they put up round the offy to keep teenagers away.

"I'm sorry..." I don't know what to say. I hold out the money again, maybe he didn't know what I was doing. Those twin, bluey-milky eyes look past me but I can sense he sees something;

my eyes keep flicking back to the bird. No. That's just not possible. The coins chink together in my hand, on purpose.

He ignores me.

"So many ways to drive out the things we don't like."

One gnarled finger, unnaturally twisted, arthritis, has to be. It looks like the other fella in Granddad's home, Stan his name is; his thumbs bent outwards the wrong way, I couldn't turn away from them.

"You can drive birds, people from the habitats you created for them because you don't like the way they look. You can pretend to everyone that everything is clean and sparkling... Not so easy to get rid of our mistakes, to go back and change them, is it?"

Life is prescious

Jesus Christ, what an idiot I am. My fear has more or less dissipated and a pang of sorrow rips through my stomach.

Poor thing.

I shake my head, forgetting again that he can't see me. This doesn't seem to bother him.

"But what if you can?"

This time, those eyes seem to stare directly into my own. The pigeon flutters and coos. I can hear the road muffled by the buildings, aeons away. The stench of the bins hangs in the still of the air, hot black plastic and rot.

"What do you mean?"

My phone buzzes again and I go for it, hand slithering into my pocket. The pigeon clatters through the air toward me and I duck; its brittle feathers against my cheek.

"Jesus fuck!"

"I told you," the man says. "Don't look at that yet."

"Why?"

That anger is coming back now; what the fuck is going on here? I need to call Marney, need to find her; I need to go back.

"Look man," I say. "I'm sorry but I have to go..."

I need to get away from here, from the reek of the bins. I can feel it alighting on me like some hideous fog. There're so many shadows down here, the buildings block out the sky; time stands still. I begin to turn away.

"It was for him, wasn't it?"

"What?"

The sorrow, the empathy for the man has been replaced with an icicle down my back.

"What did you just say?"

He grins, his single fang jutting up from those too-red gums.

"Life is precious. That's what he used to say, isn't it? That's why you got it done... for him."

The icicle turns into a full-on deep-freeze. The world swims in and out and my heart is crashing around my ears like waves.

"What?"

I turn back, hand clasped to my neck.

"What if you could take it back?"

His grin is horrific, a rictus leer and I want to run, to sprint away from this murky shadow land and back into the light, the smell of exhaust, the bright windows of the betting shops and takeaways.

But I don't, my feet, my legs don't seem to want to move, they are stuck here, wedged between the ancient cobbles; the drifts of litter.

"What do you mean?"

The pigeon alights into the air and I duck instinctively. It's not me it's after this time; I follow the bird's trajectory as it flies up over my head and hovers, flapping for a few seconds by the entrance of the tattoo studio. A metal shutter where the staircase used to be; a swollen squid in spray-paint filling it like the confines of a tank.

"What if you could take it back?"

My mouth is moving but nothing comes out; I want to say this is mad, this is insane, that I need to get away from here, from this broken man with his trained pigeon, that this is some scam, some elaborate way of getting something from me... money? He didn't want my money... what does he want?

"What if it never happened?"

Now I turn around and approach him; one foot before the other through the filthy little walkway between the bins. Up close, the man is even more grotesque than before; somehow he looks less human, more like some sort of prop from a bad horror film - his skin is wrinkled and looks loose, as if it is too big for his skull. He smiles, calm; his pale, blind eyes gazing up, just past my eye-line.

"What do you mean?" I say. "What do you mean: 'what if it

217

never happened'?"

He points with one of those terrible fingers to my pocket. It takes everything I have not to flinch; it must be the shadows, the lights playing a trick with my mind, but that finger is too long, it has too many joints in it. The skin is pale, dead.

"If you look at your phone now," his voice is a gurgle. Black water down a black drain. "You'll see what's happened."

I don't want to. Something prevents me from moving.

The man goes on.

"That photo, that mistake your 'Life is prescious' tattoo has already been retweeted over fifty times; shared on Facebook by just about everyone... how long until it goes viral? Minutes? Hours? Days? How long before you're the laughing stock of the online world?"

A fear, hard and heavy and full has fallen over me, pulling my stomach down through my waist and into my legs. It seems so strange this ragged, deformed man talking like this but I know he's right, I know it. As if in answer, my phone buzzes again.

"Maybe you already are?"

"No..."

But it's possible, it's horribly possible, this stark realism scythes through me. I want to vanish, to disappear below the earth, somewhere cold and quiet.

The man points his finger again, hairy, twisted with at least four, maybe five joints in it. "...your mates, your mates' mates, their mates sharing that picture... who knows... maybe someone knows a journalist, maybe someone's got a friend at a paper, a TV channel... how long before that phone won't stop ringing? Until the whole world is laughing at you? Until you can't go out the house. Life is prescious scarred on your throat for the rest of your life."

The heavy fear is bubbling, seething, teeming now; my breath rattles in my chest, quivers through me. I think of all the photos I've shared; fat people, people with bad haircuts, girls with streaky fake tan, people dressed in full football kit. Idiots, dickheads, cunts, morons - they didn't seem real, those people, too stupid, too ignorant, I almost hated them. Now I'm one of them. Life is prescious. Jesus, now I'm one of those people.

"But what if I could make it all stop, what if I could take it back?"

218

"How?" I can't believe I can speak, that the words can even come out. I'm not here; I'm miles away, looking down on me like the pigeon that is peering at us from a sill of one of the black windows above.

"How will you take it back? That's not possible..."

He shrugs and his shoulders are all wrong somehow; pointed, too high. There are things moving beneath his clothes, ripples riding up and down his chest. I want to be sick.

"You have to make a choice," he says." I'll give you one chance. That's all. One chance. To take it back."

"And why should I believe you?"

He chuckles at this and the movements beneath his clothes twitch with a nightmarish galvanism in tune.

"You can take your tattoo back." And now his eyes narrow, mouth twisted up to one side; I can see teeth now but right at the back, far too far back, rows and rows of little daggers. "Just like you want to take back that slap... but, like everything... there are consequences..."

The pigeon flaps down from its perch and onto the cobbles before us, hops back and forth on its scarlet foot, making little burr sounds.

"And what happens if I agree?" My phone is buzzing again and again and again. I want to pull it from my pocket and smash it on the ground. "What's the price?"

The man's smile remains, the movements beneath his rags are worm like, thick as snakes, it's as if he's been formed together by something fluid, lots of smaller, writhing things. He raises that too long arm and as his sleeve pulls back I see his skin is pale, rough, almost scaly. Crabs' legs I think, like the crabs me and Granddad used to see when he took me to the fish quay when I was a kid. Maroon, spikey, almost furry, twitching crabs legs, that's what his fingers are like, but pale, the colour of sour milk.

"What are you?" I say.

"Do you really want to know?"

I don't say anything. I can't.

"This is your chance to make it go away," he says and there's another sound coming from him, a muffled clicking, the sound of more of those terrible crabs' leg fingers unfurling, uncoiling from beneath his clothes. My heart is hammering again; his form, this form he's taken, this disguise which isn't even a very good one, is starting to slip and whatever's under there, beneath that skin, beneath those clothes, whatever's under there, I would do anything not to see it. This needs to be quick.

"You know the price."

Into my head comes a thousand happy memories; the beach, the fair; too hot chips on my tongue, tomato ketchup and the smell of pipe tobacco, the shouts from a football pitch, my hand in his.

'Life is precious.' Granddad always said, "Life is precious, Jay, make sure you live it." I think of him crumpled in his chair in the too-hot day-room staring out at the bypass, the dying flicker of recognition that takes longer and longer to ignite.

"You know the price," the terrible man says again from his hollow between the bins.

I nod.

The pigeon flaps its wings and lifts itself into the air above us.

"Put out your hands," he says.

This isn't real, this isn't happening, it's a dream. I'm looking down on us again from somewhere high up, on this sorry corner of town. My hands tremble as the pigeon descends; it feels like bones and dust between my fingers, a steady thud-thud of life.

"Stop its misery." The man's face is flopping to one side, the skin like a bad Halloween mask; the arms from beneath the sleeve is pale scales, wiry hairs rising from it, too many fingers. I look down at the pigeon cooing gently in my hands.

Poor thing.

"Stop its misery."

His voice is like water dripping through some underground echoing drain; a smell is ringing from him, salt of the sea and something rotten, some terrible black fungus. The bird looks up at me, its expression almost quizzical. Get on with it then.

"What if I don't?"

"One day," he says, "one day everyone will have their fifteen minutes, everyone will find the spotlight. Will this legacy be yours?"

I close my eyes. I think of Granddad, the good times, the happy times, the times when it was just him and me, the precious times that will stay in my heart till the day I die. I feel my fingers find the pigeon's head, its throat, the creature is almost skeletal, no flesh, just feathers.

He fought in the Second World War, my granddad did. There's a scar on his hand where a sniper caught him. "It opened up in a perfect little circle," he used to tell me. "Never even felt it till afterwards."

I remember when the EDL marched in town; his disgust. "I shot and killed a man, you know, Jay," he said. "Ended someone's life, a boy like me, a boy lost his life because he was German... I killed a boy like me because I thought we could stop hate like that...'

Life is precious.

He can't remember where he got that scar now. I point at it and he looks at me with the terrified eyes of a child.

"He saw things in the war he would never tell any of us," my mum told me once. "Things he could never forget."

Life is precious.

"I'm sorry," I say and twist. The pigeon gives a spasmodic flap of its wings and I drop it, hear it flump, lifeless on the pavement. There's a sound like a sigh before me and a hiss like fizzy liquid. I open my eyes.

The bins, overflowing with swollen black bags; cans and newspapers and flyers, old chewing gum trodden between the cobbles. Slate coloured feathers and a few baby-white ones fluttering to the ground.

I'm crying now, tears blurring my vision, but I know he's not there anymore, just an empty black place where something once sat and a dead city pigeon with a withered foot.

Stop its misery.

I turn and begin to walk back out of the alley and onto the main road. The cars are still chugging along, inch by inch, and a light rain has begun to fall. I feel only half-real and pull up my hood, blocking out the flashing lights of shop windows and the twinkle of music.

There's someone up ahead, a figure leaning against the bus stop; hood pulled up but I'd recognise those torn up tights anywhere. I nearly stop when she sees me.

"Marney... I'm..."

"Come here."

She opens up her arms and I step into them slowly, tentatively.

"Marney, I'm sorry... I..."

"Shh."

She holds me and I rest my chin on the parting of her hair. Apologies are thrumming through me, twisting up my tongue.

What if you could take it back?

"Are we going up there," she says, nodding at the bus stop, "on the 22?"

"Yeah," I say. I don't want to say any more, still not entirely sure if this is real.

Marney squeezes me tighter and I can feel her shoulders shaking. This is fucked up; what is going on? There's a terrible black maw opening in my stomach. I clap my hand to my neck.

No cling-film, nothing.

The rain is drumming on our hoods now. I reach into my pocket and slide out my phone. Marney usually goes wild if I look at it too much when I'm with her.

Not today though. Not today.

78 notifications

That maw opens further. My mouth is dry. The road is starting to clear and the cars are passing by a bit quicker; the faint tang of sweat, breath on my face as a man on a bike hums past us, thin tyres sluicing through the rainwater.

I tap the screen, tongue like a dried out slug. Rain already spattering on its surface.

Stop its misery.

Most of them are wall posts, some are private messages. I tap the latest one.

Hope ur ok m8. Thinkin of ya.

Gimmie a shout if u wanna chat bro :)

Sending *hugs* xxxx

I give a great hiccupy sob and feel Marney hold me tighter.

In the distance, the number 22 bus shines its headlights like two bright eyes through the rain.

I was that sniper, that was me, stood before some burbling monstrosity in the alley behind Wilko's; I made a choice and my aim was true. He never stood a chance.

There's a message from Colm.

Got some good memories from when we were kids and your granddad took us fishing mate :) Never forget them days eh? Gimmie a bell bud, yeah? :)

My granddad used to tell me something else too, he used to tell me that when he looked down and saw that wound, where that bullet had passed through his hand, he realised then that life was precious.

"I was a cynic like you, Jay," he used to say. "Life just passed me by but it was that moment when I realised that life is precious, that even against all the odds, even if you do things you regret, you have to face up, go and just live it."

I think of him sat in that chair, staring out at a road, memories fading, life winding down.

You have to go and live it.

We pay our bus fares and sit at the back, scrunched up together, staring out at the streets, people with newspapers over their heads, protecting their hairstyles from the rain.

I pull Marney tight to me, so I can feel her heart beat, faint but full of life thudding against mine.

Dual tattoos.

Living.

CANVEY ISLAND BABY
David Turnbull

The sky hung low over Canvey, full of rain heavy cloud that made what was left of the afternoon daylight appear coarse and grainy. It had been like this for weeks, a shroud of persistent dampness, occasionally accompanied lethargically swirling mists that clung to the houses on the estate and glowed moodily beneath the streetlamps.

Patsy pulled the hood of his parka tight. His felt face raw and wet from the drizzle being blown inland from the estuary. Splashing through puddles on the uneven pavement he hurried past the little amusement park, shut for the winter, sodden tarpaulins covering the rides, gaudy paintwork at the entrance flaking away and in desperate need of a touch up.

Head down against the squall he took the stairs up to the floodwall two at a time.

The wrought iron gate creaked on salt rusted hinges as he passed through and onto the concrete walkway. The wind slammed hard against him. He turned slightly so that the full force was no longer in his face and plunged his shivering hands deep into the pockets of his parka.

It was an hour before sunset and there was not another soul to be seen. The tide was out, revealing a serpentine ribbon of rocks and muddy sand, strewn with sloppy strands of green river weed that lay in some places in tangled verdant heaps. A smell of decay clung to the beach and the wind was full of its festering stench.

To his right he could just make out the massive mechanical cranes at Tilbury's new container port, to his left, the mile long pier at Southend, tracing its way forlornly out into the gloomy waters. On the other side of the estuary the tall chimneys of the oil refinery on the Isle of Grain were belching out huge columns of grey smoke that kissed the churning boil of the clouds. A dredger went past; engines humming in baritone, agitating dirty water into white spumes.

Patsy skittered down the sloping wall that dropped from the walkway to the beach. Gravel crunched noisily beneath his boots. Crouching low he began to search amongst the detritus washed up on the shore, sometimes slipping on the green slime of the weed, the stink gagging at the back of his throat. He stepped closer to the water's edge and sank ankle deep in cold mud, his jeans becoming dark and splattered in filth.

As day grew ponderously darker he spied something where the water was ebbing and flowing against the slight camber of the shoreline. Pulling down his hood he cocked his ear and listened. A white gull went wheeling overhead, dipping low and coming in to land on the floodwall. That was a good sign. He'd heard that seagulls were drawn to the area where there was an appearance.

Pulling his hood back up he ploughed sloppily through the mud till he reached the object. His disappointment so was palpable he actually felt a sharp pain radiate across his chest. It was nothing but a piece of wood, smooth and rounded from rolling and bobbing in the water. He picked it up, turned it over a few times and then tossed it as far as he could into the estuary.

"Shit!" he yelled in frustration. "Shit! Shit! Shit!"

*

By the time he reached the flat the drizzle had turned to a downpour. His parka was drenched. He took it off and draped it over the radiator in the corridor, stuffing the hood down the back to hold it in place. The rain had washed most of the mud from his boots. He unlaced them and placed them on the doormat. Then he unbuckled his belt and shook himself out of his filthy jeans.

He shuffled into the living room in his boxer shorts and sweatshirt, wet socks leaving grubby footprints on the faded linoleum. Chloe had her dressing gown on and a blue towel wrapped in a turban round her head. She was painting her toenails, feet up on the coffee table. There was a grease stained pizza box on the table, beside it a crushed lager can. The ashtray was overflowing with dog ends.

"Nothing again?" she asked.

She didn't even bother to look at him.

225

Patsy shrugged.

"It wasn't for the want of trying."

Chloe turned her attention from her nails to the television. A repeat of the *Jeremy Kyle Show* was running. "This is getting embarrassing," she said.

Patsy sighed. He was no mood for another argument.

"Is there anything to eat?"

Chloe tapped the pizza box with her left foot.

"I saved you some."

Patsy groaned.

"I've been freezing my nuts off down at the floodwall for the last two hours. Something hot would be nice."

"You can heat it up in the microwave."

Chloe's attention remained firmly fixed on the television. Patsy was about to say something else. Without even looking at him she held up her hand. "Shut up, would you? They're about to announce the lie detector results."

He felt his fists clenching. His knuckles turned bone white. He hated the way she treated him. A bit of respect wouldn't go amiss. With a grunt he grabbed the pizza box.

There was only about a third of the pizza left. He misjudged the timing on the microwave. The cheese and the pepperoni were like rubber, impossible to chew. The crust was so hard it hurt his teeth. "Maybe I should pack my bags and piss off to London," he called from the kitchen.

"Maybe you should," Chloe shot back.

He heard the volume on the television go up. The couple on the *Jeremy Kyle Show* were screaming at each other about the lie detector results.

*

Patsy lay awake with his eyes closed against the darkness. Beside him Chloe was asleep with her mouth open, breath rattling noisily at the back of her throat. In his mind he kept going back over the events of the annual Boxing Day party at the club.

There had been the usual raffle; meat cuts and bottles of wine, a hamper with a big tin of assorted biscuits and jars of chutney and mustard. Then came the main event - the draw to see who would become surrogates in the coming year.

All the young couples gathered in a huddle in front of the stage. Chloe was half cut, arm looped through his as she swayed unsteadily at his side. Geoff Burns, the club President spun the tombola with a vigorous enthusiasm. When it came to a halt, Maggie Dean, the club Secretary, plunged her cheaply bejewelled hand in and pulled out a ticket.

Everyone winced as she reached for the microphone, causing ear-splitting feedback to screech from the speaker. She tapped the mike with her many ringed fingers and series of dull thuds echoed through the hall. "Can you hear me at the back?" she asked.

"Yes," they roared in response.

Chloe whooped and held up her half pint of lager; sloshing most of the contents down the sleeve of the new blouse he'd bought her for Christmas.

"It's a blue ticket," announced Maggie.

Silence descended as she unfolded the ticket.

"Number thirty-five," said Maggie. "Three and five. Blue ticket, thirty-five, who's got blue ticket thirty five?"

Patsy watched Chloe open her hand and felt a little spasm twist in his stomach when he saw the number on the wet blue ticket that was stuck to the clammy sweat of her palm. "Me!" she screamed. "It's me. Number thirty-five. I've got it."

The crowd parted as she made her way to the stage.

Patsy hung back.

A huge cheer erupted when Maggie confirmed the validity of the ticket. Things got a bit crazy. People were slapping him on the back and holding out their hands for him to shake. Numerous pints of lager were lined up side by side along the bar for him.

Party poppers and streamers started going off. The disco kicked in – loud, thumping music and bright, flashing lights. Chloe was out on the floor, dancing and laughing with her mates, guzzling down lager like there was no tomorrow.

Patsy managed to slip outside. He needed some fresh air. The knot in his belly was getting tighter. When he was eleven his cousin Yvonne and her husband had won the raffle. He remembered going round to their house a month or so later and recoiling in horror at the grotesque and hideous thing that squalled and squirmed in the crib.

*

He was awake by four fifteen, out the door by four thirty. By five he was clocking in at the depot. By five forty the pickers had loaded his van. A quick cup of coffee from the vending machine and he was revving through the gates by five forty five.

His head was full of minute slots and delivery windows, short cuts and rat runs.

His route took him down into Colchester and then various drops on a convoluted return to the depot. He headed out for the A12, windscreen wipers swinging hypnotically back and forth against the driving rain. *Crisps, cola and confectionary to corner shops, cafes and convenience stores*, he chanted in time to their motion. The firm delivered other stuff too, but a while back some drivers on a work's do had drunkenly devised the tongue twister and it had stuck ever since.

Patsy was one of the lucky ones, still on the old job and finish contract. By two in the afternoon he was back in the depot. By two twenty he'd completed his paperwork and swept out the van. He was out the gate by two thirty and back at the flat by ten to three. He made himself a peanut butter sandwich and a mug of tea and slumped heavily down onto the sofa.

No sooner had he switched on the television than Chloe arrived.

She was dressed in a bright pink tracksuit with the words *Hot Stuff* embroidered in fat, chunky letters across the chest. Her hair was pulled back into a severe ponytail, eyebrows plucked to narrow black scars, lip gloss applied over lipstick that was so red it gave her pale complexion a sick, almost ghostly look. In one hand she held a cardboard container into which two McDonald's cappuccinos in tall paper cups were wedged. In the other was a McDonald's take out bag.

"I thought you'd be down by the floodwall by now," she said, spidery false eyelashes narrowing over her green eyes.

"Give me a chance," he replied. "I only just got in. I'm knackered."

"The sooner you find one the better, then," she said.

The smell of the French fries was making his stomach rumble.

"Some of that for me?" he asked, nodding at the bag.

228

"No it's not. My sister-in-law is coming round. My brother and her were surrogates a couple of years ago. She's going to give me some pointers. We're going to watch *Loose Women*."

Her eyes wandered covetously to the television, then back to Patsy.

Patsy took a bite from the peanut butter sandwich and rose to his feet.

"What if I don't find one?" he asked.

He saw her hand close around the McDonald's bag.

"You'd better," she said. "This is getting really embarrassing."

"I mean what if, for once, there isn't one to find?"

"There will be. There's always one."

He reached for the mug of tea and took a long gulp.

"Maybe not this year."

Her pale cheeks turned red. He saw spite darken in her eyes.

"Did you hear that Toby and Becca split up?" she asked. "I used to go out with Toby." She dropped the McDonalds bag onto the coffee table and snapped her fingers noisily in front of his nose. "I bet I could get him back like that. I bought the raffle ticket. Do you think anyone would care whether it was you or Toby that was the surrogate?"

Patsy laughed at her.

"That little shit? He's hardly even five foot tall."

"He's big in other ways," she shot back. "Ways you can only dream of."

He felt like slapping her for that.

"Maybe I should just pack my bags ..." he started.

She cut him short.

"Change the record, Patsy. It's getting boring."

He slumped back down on the sofa and huffily folded his arms.

"How about I sit here all afternoon and stuff my face with cheeseburgers, while you go down the floodwall?"

Chloe sighed and shook her head as if she was looking down at a complete idiot.

"The men do the searching, Patsy. The women do the suckling."

"What law says it has to be that way?" he challenged her.

With another sigh she placed the tray with the two coffee

229

cups down on the table.

She wedged her hands beneath her beasts and jiggled them crudely about.

"The law of fucking nature, Patsy. The law of fucking nature."

Patsy felt his fists clenching again. He rose to his feet and barged past her.

"That thing," he grunted. "That thing you want me to find. That's not natural. That's anything but natural."

"Grow a pair of tits," she called after him. "Because you'll never grow a pair of balls!"

*

He sat on one of the benches on the floodwall, looking out to the choppy waters of the estuary. The rain had stopped but the sky was still dreary and grey. His parka smelt fusty, his boots were still damp inside. His jeans were crusted in streaks of black mud.

It had occurred to him that morning that if he did eventually find one he wouldn't be able to bring himself to touch it with his bare hands. So he'd pilfered a pair of orange gloves from work. They were stuffed inside the pockets of the parka.

Unable to muster the will to go down onto the beach he rested his elbows on his knees and bowed his head. After a while he became aware of someone sitting down beside him. "You'll won't find nothing moping around up here," said a throaty voice.

Patsy looked up. His granddad had a tartan scarf wrapped tightly around his neck and woollen hat pulled down over his ears. The cold air was making the old scar on his left cheek deepen to a dark purple. He removed a thermos flask from the plastic bag he was carrying and handed it to Patsy.

"What's this?"

"Bovril," replied his granddad. "Thought you might be in need of some fortification."

Patsy unscrewed the lid and inhaled the beefy steam. He poured some of the dark translucent liquid into the little cup, blew on it and then took a long sip. It settled nicely in his belly.

"It's been three weeks," he sighed. "And not a sight. Chloe's pissed off with me. I'm pissed off with myself."

230

His granddad started puffing on an electronic cigarette.

"You got any full fat smokes?" he asked.

Since his GP had cajoled him into packing in his forty a day habit he'd taken to referring to real cigarettes as full fat smokes.

Patsy took another sip of Bovril. "You know I don't smoke."

His granddad slowly exhaled vapour down his nostrils.

"These are shit," he complained. "They're like low alcohol beer. No fucking point to them."

"Better for your health," said Patsy.

His granddad laughed.

"A bit of tar on the lung never hurt no-one."

Patsy emptied the cup and refilled it from the contents of the flask.

"I think your doctor might have something to say about that."

"Doctors? What the fuck do they know?"

Patsy drank some more Bovril. The old bugger was a wind up merchant. He wasn't going to give him the satisfaction of rising to the bait.

"Three weeks is nothing," said his granddad, after they'd sat in silence for while.

Patsy turned and looked at him.

"You know Jack Ferris?"

Patsy nodded

"The gas fitter? The one that does boiler repairs on the side?"

"Him and his wife won the raffle back in 1975. He didn't find anything till Easter."

"Easter?"

Patsy felt his heart sink.

"Some years it just takes a bit longer, that's all."

"Has there ever been a year when there was anything."

"Not since the flood of '53," came the reply. "That was the first year."

Patsy had heard this hundreds of times.

Every kid on the estate had grown up with it.

"The first one was found nestling in the weeds after the flood," his granddad went on, "I was fourteen at the time. A bit of a tearaway, even back in them days." He chuckled to himself and then fell serious again. "A couple took it in, Dan and Mary Brentford. It was an ugly little fucker and no one knew what it was. But everyone agreed we wanted to keep it hushed up."

Patsy closed eyes.

Who'd have thought something as simple as Bovril could taste so satisfying?

"There was a lot of journalists coming down the island," his granddad continued. "People had drowned in the flood and some other folk had to be evacuated from their houses. They were sniffing around for stories. Of course one of them went and got wind of what had been washed up on the shore. It started getting mentioned in the papers."

"The Canvey Island Monster," said Patsy.

"That's what they called it."

Patsy attempted to pick up the story and finish it off.

"So this bloke who worked as a porter down Billingsgate brought home a rank old anglerfish and laid it out on the beach…"

His granddad snatched the story back before he could say any more.

"Down came the press with cameras and what not. And the mystery of the monster was done and dusted. It was just a mouldering anglerfish that was washed in by the storm. End of story and good riddance to the lot of them."

"But every year since then one has turned up on the beach," said Patsy.

His granddad nodded.

"And every year it's down to a local couple to look after it. We keep it to ourselves. Our secret. No business of any other fucker."

Patsy shook the Bovril dregs from the cup and screwed the lid back onto the flask.

"Why are you telling me? I know it already."

"Because you need to understand your responsibilities, boy."

Patsy wondered whether Chloe had put him up to this.

"I don't see why we have to be responsible for them. Have you seen how disgusting they look? Monster is the right word, if you ask me."

"We look after their little 'uns because they're us."

"Us?"

"We live on the land and they live in the estuary - but they're our kin, Patsy. Blood of our blood."

This was new. He'd never heard this before.

"What are you going on about?"

His granddad stared out to the swell of the estuary.

"The flood of '53 wasn't the first," he said. "They knew it wouldn't be the last. That's why they built the floodwall. But there's been a community living out here since long before Roman times. The land was flatter then, no buildings and stuff. Floods would come, ruin all the crops and wash away the huts. People got drowned. Women and children got drowned.

"So here's what I reckon.

"They evolved, Patsy. They became... What's the word?"

"Amphibian?"

"That's it. They took to living in the water. It's deep out there in the middle."

"Bollocks," said Patsy and shook his head.

"You got a better explanation, boy? The way I looked at it, when the flood tries to swallow you up you either evolve or die."

Patsy shrugged his shoulders.

His granddad rambled on.

"But then we started dumping all sorts of shit into the Thames – chemicals, and sewage, and other stuff. And maybe they got sick. So sick all they could produce was a single offspring once a year. And that poor little mite was so sickly itself it needed help to make it strong enough to survive."

"So maybe we should just leave them to die out," suggested Patsy.

His granddad leapt to his feet and started to berate him.

"Is that how you was fucking brought up?" he challenged, the scar on his cheek growing even darker. "Is that how your mum and dad brought you up? To turn your fucking back on your own in their hour of need?"

This was the belligerent grandparent that Patsy remembered from childhood. The one who always seemed to be involved in pub brawls. The one who thrived on confrontation with the neighbours. The only adult he knew that was forever nursing a black eye or a cut lip. He watched his wrinkled and liver spotted hands clench into a pair of tight fists and wondered if that mannerism might be hereditary.

"Steady on," said Patsy. "I was just saying."

"Well don't say, boy. Get off your fucking arse and do your

duty."

Patsy heaved a sigh. He stood up and handed back the flask. His eyes scanned the coastline, peering down to the rocks and weeds. It started to rain again. He jumped down from the wall to the beach.

*

He stayed on the beach till well past sunset; brooding about the way his granddad had spoken to him, tensing up when he thought about all the pressure Chloe was putting him under. The tide came in, foaming up the stone strewn camber to the edge of the floodwall. He was buffeted by the wind and lashed by the rain, damp and shivering.

And still he found nothing.

When he reached home he stood by the living room door, listening to see whether Chloe's sister-in-law was still around. All he could hear was the television - the title music for the *One Show* echoing against the walls. Unable to face another confrontation he went straight to bed.

He was surprised when Chloe came to the bedroom half an hour or so later. He heard her undressing in the darkness. She slipped quietly under the duvet, pressing her bare breasts to his back, hand reaching over to tickle the hairs on his belly with her fingers.

"I'm sorry," she whispered and kissed him twice on the shoulder.

When he turned to face her she clamped her lips urgently over his. Her tongue slipped into his mouth like a wet fish. It had a sour taste of lager about it. Her hair smelled of cigarette smoke. She smothered him in kisses, sharp fingernails digging into his back and his buttocks.

Eventually they made love. His heart wasn't really in it, but for a little while he convinced himself that they might have turned a corner.

*

The rest of the week dragged by. The weather didn't improve. Dank, cloud filled days, made worse by tedious bouts of sleet and drizzle. He did his rounds, was home by three, ate an unsatisfying snack and went down to the floodwall.

He watched the dredgers go past and the smoke billowing skyward from the refinery chimneys. He saw gulls wheel beneath the swollen belly of the clouds. He searched the beach and found nothing. Everything felt as monotonous and predictable as the bland greyness that filled the sky. There were days when he felt as if he was drowning.

Chloe was incessantly on his back, berating him and belittling him. They bickered endlessly. He clenched and unclenched his fists till the joints on his fingers ached. He found a text from Toby on Chloe's phone. A few simple words, seemingly in response to something she'd sent. *I'm fine. How R U?* Maybe it was all perfectly innocent. But he suspected she was hedging her bets, laying down a marker.

He pondered on what his granddad had suggested to him. He began to think that it might be true, that the locals and those hideous things that inhabited the estuary shared a tainted bloodline. It made sense. Everything about his life and the ties that bound him ever tighter to his supposed responsibilities seemed increasingly grotesque.

Saturday came.

He awoke with a start at four twenty and cursed his body clock for never allowing him a long lie whenever his weekend off came round on the roster. For half an hour he listened to Chloe's rhythmic snoring, wondering why they'd ever hooked up in the first place.

She'd insisted from the outset that she was out of his league. Maybe for him that was the initial attraction. Punching above his weight and all that. Now she was full of spiteful put-downs and he was full of reciprocal resentment. He felt his fists clench beneath the duvet. There was a monster brooding inside him, straining to be unleashed, ready to wreak havoc and mayhem.

He slipped out of bed, picked up his crumpled clothes from the floor and dressed in the corridor. Fifteen minutes later he was on the floodwall. It was still quite dark. He could see streetlights through the hazy fug, twinkling on the Kent side of the estuary. When he looked in the direction of Southend he could make out the headlamps of a single vehicle passing along the coastal road. He speculated as to whether it was one of his workmates out on his weekend round.

He sat on one of the benches. It was damp. It didn't bother him. He was probably going to get wet anyway. For a long time he simply stared straight ahead of him. When it got a little lighter he stood up, yawning and stretching, resigning himself to the prospect of another wasted search and another ear bashing from Chloe.

Then he noticed the gulls, a little way along the beach, just where the water was lapping the camber - four of them, white wings flapping as they hopped and screeched around something that lay in the mud. He retrieved the stolen orange gloves from his pockets and pulled them on. His heart began to pound. He could feel the sweat prickling on his brow.

He jumped from the floodwall to the beach and strode purposely ahead, yelling at the gulls and waving his arms. They ascended massively skyward, squawking ill-tempered irritation. Sure enough a tiny thing was lying there, little legs and arms pummelling the air. His mouth felt dry. It hurt to swallow. He stepped cautiously closer, then baulked and froze on the spot.

It was resting nakedly on a twisted nest of weed. Its jellyfish flesh was so transparent that he could actually see the jagged blue veins and pulsing crimson muscle beneath. Its fingers and toes were webbed, dark little pointed talons on the end of each digit. The diagonal slits of the pink gills slashed on either side of its neck quivered grotesquely as they opened and closed, opened and closed.

Bile rising in his throat he forced himself to take a step closer. The thing turned its bulbous and hairless head in his direction. The membrane of its eyelids blinked vertically across its black, bugged out pupils. It meowed like a cat and when its mouth opened he could see the rows of tiny shark-like teeth that filled its maw.

His granddad was deluded. Nothing human could ever have evolved to become like this. And yet its limbs and the proportion of its head to its torso looked unsettlingly like those of a human child. He picked up a flat stone. Tested its weight. Felt his fingers curl maliciously around it.

Who would ever know if he smashed its ugly head in right there and then?

Something, a cold and certain sense that he was being

236

watched, made him turn his head and look out to the estuary. Several yards out, somehow managing to maintain a fixed position against the seaward flow of the current, an object bobbed hazily just above the water. It looked like a head and shoulders. In the early morning gloom it might have easily been mistaken for a seal.

Patsy knew in his heart that it was something else entirely.

It was observing him. Waiting to see exactly what he'd do. He couldn't see its eyes, but he could feel their malevolence. A cold shiver washed over him. Fear engulfed him in a cloying embrace. In a moment of panic he dropped the stone and walked swiftly to the thing that squirmed in the nest of weeds.

Hurriedly he unzipped the front of his parka and picked up the creature, glad of the gloves, retching slightly at the noxious odour it exuded. In one swift movement he had it cradled against his chest. It clawed at his sweatshirt, bug eyes blinking back and forth as it keened and coughed gluey streams of snot through flared nostrils.

Shuddering and sick to the stomach Patsy turned his attention back to the estuary. The head and shoulders paused momentarily and the uncanny stillness made him hold his breath. Then it dipped beneath the undulating billows and was gone.

*

He had to ring the doorbell seven or eight times before he heard Chloe shuffling along the corridor, grumbling and cursing. He felt her scrutinising him through the spy-hole. "What the fuck?" she complained. "Do you know what time it is?"

"Just open the door," he called back. "I forgot my key."

He heard her undo the latch.

She squealed in delight when she saw what he had nestled inside his parka.

"Give it to me," she said, holding out her arms. "Is it a boy or a girl?"

Patsy gave a shrug and handed the thing to her.

"It's a girl," she said, cradling it in her arms. "I can't believe you didn't check."

She turned and walked slowly to the living room, rocking the

237

monstrous baby back and forth. Patsy went to the kitchen and put the kettle on. He heard the thing let out a series of tremulous bleats that raised gooseflesh on his arms. Then it fell silent.

When he entered the living room with a mug of tea in each hand Chloe had it pressed against her chest, hand resting gently around its hairless skull. The sound of its greedy, wet slurping turned his stomach. When he placed one of the mugs down on the coffee table he saw that its teeth were clamped firmly to the pale flesh of her right breast. A trickle of blood was running down, staining her open nightdress.

"Does it hurt?" he asked.

"Nips a bit," she replied. "But I reckon I'll get used to it. I'll need to start drinking Guinness to keep up the iron in my blood."

Patsy blew on his tea. His hand trembled as he brought the rim of the mug up to his lip. "Is there anything you want me to do?" he asked.

The creature released its grip on her breast and turned to the sound of his voice, bug eyes watching him, strands of gelatinous, blood stained saliva hanging from its narrow lip. Then it turned back and sank its teeth into her once more. Chloe winced and stroked its head.

"You've done your bit for now," she told him. "I've been texting my sister-in-law. She's going to come round at lunchtime. It's her turn to buy, so she's bringing a KFC bargain bucket."

The monstrous little thing pummelled her with its little legs, sharp claws shredding her nightdress and furrowing jagged scratches into her belly. She didn't seem to notice. "You should go down the club," she said. "My bother's going to be there. He's rounding up all the other blokes. Maybe you could buy your granddad a pint."

*

Patsy forced open his gummy eyelids and squinted at the digital display on the bedside clock. Twenty to nine – a long lie in at last. But it was only because of the effects of his twelve-hour binge. A sharp pain throbbed in his head. His sandpaper tongue felt swollen against the roof of his mouth. Going to the club had been a huge mistake. He'd been there from midday till midnight.

Word of his successful find had spread like wildfire across the estate. He was the hero of the hour. It was like Boxing Day all over again. Everyone who came through the door wanted to slap his back and shake his hand. He was wedged into one of the alcoves with Chloe's brother. Pints and chasers kept appearing on the table, one after the other. Guys who'd been surrogates in previous years sat down beside him to share sage advice and wildly exaggerated anecdotes.

"Told you that three weeks was nothing," said his granddad when he arrived.

Patsy offered to buy him a pint.

"Keep your money in your pocket, son," said his granddad. "It's my round."

Somewhere around six or seven, when he was bleary eyed and slumped in the alcove, someone brought him a huge portion of cod and chips in a polystyrene container. They were so drenched in vinegar it made his eyes water. He wolfed the lot down, wiping his greasy fingers on the front of his shirt.

Big plans were hatched for the May bank holiday. They'd all go down the front with Patsy when he released the creature back into the estuary. Then they'd have a slap up breakfast of bacon, eggs, sausage, tomato, black pudding, beans, fried bread, mushrooms, the fucking works. When their bellies were good and full they'd hire a minibus and go and blow a month's wages at the casino in Southend.

Patsy felt sickened by the very idea of it all. Sicker still by the thought of having to live in the same house as that blood sucking little parasite till May. He didn't let it show. He just guzzled beer and whisky till he was oblivious. At one point the entire club started chanting his name like the crowd on a football terrace.

"Patsy! Patsy! Patsy!"

He staggered up onto the table and waved his arms around in fey triumph.

A fight broke out in the car park between his granddad and this guy who was twenty years his junior. Patsy recalled the guy screaming like some schoolgirl that he'd bitten straight through his lower lip when his granddad had hammered his jaw with an upper cut.

The club steward brought out the first aid kit and inexpertly administered some Germolene and an Elastoplast. Granddad

239

and the guy were cajoled into grudgingly shaking hands. Everyone filed back inside. The guy bought them all a beer. There was a singsong. Patsy threw up in the toilets.

Staggering drunkenly home in the darkness he devised a plan to rid himself of the creature. He'd sneak in and snatch it from the wooden cot he'd assembled at the foot of the bed a month ago. Then he'd take it down to the floodwall and sling it back into the estuary where it belonged. It could sink or fucking swim for all he cared.

But when he reached the bedroom the cot was empty. The creature was sleeping near the edge of the bed. Chloe had her arm slumped over its peculiar little body. There was no way he could remove it without the risk of waking them both.

Dejected he undressed and slipped unsteadily under the duvet. Chloe was snoring. The room was full of the sulphurous stink of the creature. He drifted in and out of sleep. The creature awoke and started to bleat. Chloe stirred and pulled it to her. She let out a strangulated cry of pain and he knew its teeth were closed around her flesh. When he heard the creature slurping greedily he started to cry in stifled sobs.

Now the smell in the room was twice as bad as it had seemed when he was drunk. He looked at the clock again. Ten to nine. *I'm done*, he thought. *I've done my bit and I'm done with all of it.*

He eased himself out of bed and dressed as quietly as he could. On tiptoes he crept around the room, packing clothes and socks and underwear into a backpack. At the bedroom door he turned and looked down at the sleeping creature. The bed sheets were stained from the oily secretions that were oozing from its pores. Its chin and nostrils were darkly caked in Chloe's blood.

He held the handle down so the door would close in silence. Chloe's phone was on the coffee table. He sent a text to Toby – *Call Me* and added an X for a kiss at the end. That would be enough.

In the kitchen there was an old teapot, stuffed with ten and twenty pound notes. They'd been saving up to go to Ibiza once their fostering duties were done. Patsy folded the notes into the pocket of his jeans. He wasn't going to be anybody's mug. If Chloe wanted a holiday, Toby could damn well pay for it.

Outside, the clouds had finally dispersed. The sky was clear and blue. A coating of frost sparkled on the pavement. It was melting fast. The sun felt warm on his back. He walked the mile and a half to Benfleet train station. At the machine he used some of the money from the teapot to buy a one-way ticket to Liverpool Street.

As he waited on the platform, inhaling the crisp Sunday morning air, his headache began to recede. He wondered if Chloe had stirred to suckle her hideous blood-guzzling ward. The train came. The carriage doors hissed closed behind him and it actually felt like closure. There were monsters on Canvey. But he wasn't going to be one of them.

OUR WRITERS & ARTIST

Shaun Avery writes crime and horror fiction in a variety of different mediums and has been published in many magazines and anthologies. He has won competitions with both prose and comic writing, and was recently shortlisted for a screenwriting contest. He lists as his biggest writing influences Bentley Little, Garth Ennis, and the late greats Richard Laymon and Ed McBain. He has a love of heaping satire into his work, probably inspired by large amounts of time spent watching the TV show *South Park*, with particular sarcastic scorn normally directed towards the twin modern day obsessions of surgery and celebrity. A lifelong fan of the graphic novel medium, he recently co-created a self-published comic called *Spectre Show*, which can be found here:

> *http://www.comicsy.co.uk/dbroughton/store/products/spectre-show/*

The Great Estate is his longest publication to date, and he enjoyed the process of creating it so much that he has several other novella-length works planned.

Stephen Bacon lives in South Yorkshire with his wife and two sons. His stories have been published in *Black Static*, *Cemetery Dance*, *Shadows & Tall Trees*, *Postscripts*, *Crimewave*, *Terror Tales of Yorkshire* and *Murmurations*, and several of them have been selected by Ellen Datlow for her *Best Horror of the Year* series.

His debut collection, *Peel Back the Sky*, was published by Gray Friar Press in 2012

Please visit him, or get in touch, at:

> *www.stephenbacon.co.uk*

Charles Black is the editor of the *Black Books of Horror* anthology series and owner of Mortbury Press. His fiction has appeared in *Weird Tales*, *Nemonymous*, and *Best New Zombie Tales*. Parallel Universe published *Black Ceremonies*, a collection of his stories earlier this year.

> *http://www.freewebs.com/mortburypress/*

Adrian Cole began writing at the tender age of 10, although he wasn't ready to submit professionally until he was much older – at 19. His first published work was a ghost story for IPC magazines in 1972, followed soon after by a trilogy of sword & planet novels, *The Dream Lords* (Zebra, US) in the 1970s. Since then he has gone on to have more than 2 dozen novels published and many short stories and his work has been translated into a number of foreign editions.

He writes science fiction, heroic fantasy, sword & sorcery, horror, pulp fiction, Mythos and has had two young adult novels published, *Moorstones* and *The Sleep of Giants* (Spindlewood, UK)

His best known works are the *Omaran Saga* and *Star Requiem* quartets and these have also been published recently as ebooks under the Gollancz SF Gateway imprint and are also being released as audio books (Audible).

His most recent novel is *The Shadow Academy*, sf from Edge (Canada) and the anthology *Nick Nightmare Investigates* (Alchemy UK) which collects the first arc of stories about his hard-boiled occult private eye, who confronts the various minions of Lovecraft's Mythos, as well as other monsters and horrors in different, bizarre locales.

He has been nominated for various awards and has appeared in *Year's Best* collections and is currently enjoying success with new macabre stories, several of which are shortly due for publication. *Late Shift* is one such story.

A native of Devon, he lives in Bideford with his wife, Judy, and enjoys frequent dips in the sea and an occasional bike ride up into the forests of the local area, about which the less said, the better.

For more information, visit
adriancscole.com

Andrew Darlington: The first thing Andrew Darlington
had published was the poem *Anthem For A Lost Cause* in Barnsley-based 'underground'-arts magazine *Sad Traffic* (no.5, May 1971). It was also the first poem he'd ever written. It name-checks Homer's Odysseus, and the Edgar Rice Burroughs 'Martian Tales' establishing the recurring technique of using the

trash Junk Culture of cheap pulp SF (and loud Rock 'n' Roll) to reference personal issues – the 'lost cause', of course, being himself! Over 3,000 published items follow, extending across a widthband from Music Journalism to Erotica, from closely-researched historico-features on Science Fiction to interviews with culture icons William Burroughs, the Kinks, Kurt Vonnegut, Stone Roses, Byrds, Craig Charles, Peter Green (Fleetwood Mac), Robert Plant (Led Zeppelin), Cabaret Voltaire, Carolyn Cassady (Kerouac's lover), EC Tubb, Jack Dee, and many more (a selection collected into *I Was Elvis Presley's Bastard Lovechild*, Headpress, 2001). He was born 18th September 1947 – to coincide with the Roswell UFO Incident in New Mexico, and pubesced through the fantastic graphic-strip exploits of 'Jet-Ace Logan' (a SFictional hero he later scripted for). Fiction was the first form – in New English Libraries *Stopwatch* anthology (edit: George Hay, January 1975) through multiple magazine and hard/softback appearances around the world (including German and Flemish translations) to the 2015 *The Mammoth Book Of Sherlock Holmes Abroad* (edit: Simon Clark, 2015). In fact, space restrictions mean that elaboration of the Alternative Cabaret 'Stand-Up Poet' work, the vinyl records as part of UV Pop, editing 'Ludds Mill' alternative-arts magazine, and the 'Don't Call Me Nigger: Sly Stone & Black Power' biography (Leaky Boot Press, 2014) and etc will have to wait for elsewhere. His website is:

> *www.andrewdarlington.blogspot.com*

Jay Eales was born among the dying embers of the Swinging Sixties, in a rural Northamptonshire town where the Co-op was (and remains) King, and almost every family was in thrall to the boot and shoe industry (May it Rest In Peace). Jay has written, edited and published a variety of prose and comics, mostly under the Factor Fiction imprint, especially *The Girly Comic* and *Violent!* comic anthologies. He was News Features Editor for the award-winning *Borderline – The Comics Magazine* between 2002 and 2004, and co-organised Caption, Britain's longest-running comic convention between 2006 and 2011. He is currently the Graphic Novels Reviews Editor for the British Fantasy Society. His comics have been published by Constable & Robinson, Image Comics, Accent UK, Futurequake Press and Borderline

Press to name but a few. His prose has appeared within the pages of anthologies from the likes of Obverse Books, Murky Depths, Hersham Horror, Dog Horn Publishing, Rainfall Books and The Alchemy Press. His first novel progresses in fits and starts. If you simply must know more, then *www.factorfictionpress.co.uk* is a fine place to start.

Kate Farrell lives in Edinburgh. She was an actress for over thirty years, a career that spanned everything from Chekhov to *Chucklevision*. Her favourite role however was as Mrs Lovell in *A Guilty Thing Surprised,* adapted from the story by Ruth Rendell.

As Kate is pathologically indisposed to describe a happy ending, she now principally writes 'contes cruels' wherein bad things happen to bad people; sometimes the innocent suffer too. Several of her short stories have been published: in Charles Black's *Black Books of Horror*, Paul Finch's *Terror Tales*, *The Screaming Book of Horror* and *Best British Horror 2014*, both edited by Johnny Mains. Her first novella *My Name is Mary Sutherland* was published by PS in 2014, and a collection of her stories *And Nobody Lived Happily Ever After* is due out later in 2015, to be published by Parallel Universe.

She has won awards for some stories, also one sonnet and one haiku, and the opening chapter of her *novel Or The Cat Gets It* won the Linen Press award for their Beginnings Competition. For further information check out the website:

mynameiskatefarrell.com.

Gary Fry lives in Dracula's Whitby, literally around the corner from where Bram Stoker was staying when he was thinking about that character. Gary has a PhD in psychology, but his first love is literature. He is the author of many short story collections, novellas and novels. He was the first author in PS Publishing's Showcase series, and none other than Ramsey Campbell has described him as "a master." Gary warmly welcomes all to his web presence:

www.gary-fry.com

Walter Gascoigne is a writer of short fiction. He began

writing at the young age of 40 while attending college for a Bachelor's degree in English and Creative Writing. Mr. Gascoigne has written several dozen short stories which are bizarre, horrific, and thought provoking in nature. He has been published in *Centrique Magazine*. Walter's haunting narration can be heard on the hour long radio program *Speaking of Our Words*, which airs monthly on his hometown radio station WGTD, several of which can be found on YouTube. His influences include, Edgar Allen Poe, H. G. Wells, Ray Bradbury, Richard Matheson, Katherine Dunn, Stephen King, Neil Gaiman, as well as many others. An avid reader and voracious devourer of all things horror, his ambition is to have his works situated on library shelves next to his favourite authors. He enjoys public speaking and has given performances in several local events, including the Olio Storytellers Collective, where his narrative of revenge earned him the eternal mistrust of several women in the audience. Walter is a member of The Kenosha Writer's Guild, which sponsors many of the activities he participates in. His greatest achievement is his lovely daughter Katie, who gave birth to his adorable granddaughter Addy. Mr. Gascoigne is a lifelong resident of Kenosha, Wisconsin, where he resides in his two-story mansion, with his two trouble making cats.   You can contact Mr. Gascoigne at his e-mail address *fritzwhistle@yahoo.com* or listen to his frenzied rantings on YouTube, by typing in "Speaking of Our Words".

Craig Herbertson, musician, songwriter and author was born in Edinburgh, Scotland in 1959. His first short story. *The Heaven Maker*, was published in 1988 in *The 29th Pan Book of Horror Stories*. He is author of two novels, *School: The Seventh Silence* (Immanion Press) and *The Death Tableau* (Black Horse Books) one collection, *The Heaven Maker and Other Gruesome Tales* (Parallel Universe Publications) and many short stories, two of which received honourable mentions in Ellen Datlow's *Best Horror of the Year*. In a review of *The Heaven Maker and Other Gruesome Tales* Stewart Horn of the BFS, said "a satisfying read. A well written mix of the literary, the trashy and the darkly humorous. A fine addition to any horror lover's library".

As a musician, Herbertson has appeared before Diplomatic Ambassadors and Attaches from Ireland, Great Britain, Australia and Canada, multinational firms in venues ranging from The Usher Hall in Edinburgh to the opening of the Ryan Air terminal in Frankfurt. From a Mississippi river boat in New Orleans to Irish bars, restaurants, five star hotels, folk festivals, theatres and clubs but he is a prolific reader and has always maintained a love of Horror.

His debut novel *School: The Seventh Silence* was reviewed by Black Abyss: "Craig Herbertson has created a marvellous fantastical adventure with a deep and dark undercurrent". His short stories have received critical acclaim in the genre: *Soup* published in *The Fourth Black Book Of Horror* and edited by Charles Black: "Quite possibly the most beautifully written example of cannibal torture porn I've ever read!" -Demonik, Vault of Evil.

Craig Herbertson lived and worked for over fifteen years in Manchester, England, the setting of the novel *The Death Tableau* a stark account of a descent into occultism and also the short story published here: *Envelopes*.

Benedict J Jones is a writer from south east London who mainly works in the crime/horror genres. His first story was published in 2008 in *One Eye Grey*. Since then he has been published in a multitude of genre magazines, websites and in several anthologies. His debut novel, *Pennies for Charon*, featuring three-time loser Charlie "Bars" Constantinou, was released in late 2014. This followed up a collection featuring a novella and ten short stories entitled *Skewered; And Other London Cruelties*.

Mark Patrick Lynch lives and writes in the UK. His short fiction, mainstream and genre, has appeared in print anthologies and journals ranging from *Alfred Hitchcock's Mystery Magazine* to *Zahir*. His book, *Hour of the Black Wolf*, is published by Robert Hale Ltd in hardcover and FA Thorpe in paperback. A novella, *What I Wouldn't Give*, is available for ereaders. His next

book from Robert Hale Ltd is *No Fire Without Smoke*. You can find him online at:
markpatricklynch.blogspot.com.

Tim Major lives in Oxford with his wife and son. His love
of speculative fiction is the product of a childhood diet of classic Doctor Who episodes and an early encounter with Triffids.

Tim's horror novella, *Carus & Mitch*, was published by Omnium Gatherum in February 2015. His short stories have featured in publications such as *Interzone, Perihelion, Every Day Fiction* and the *Infinite Science Fiction* anthology. He blogs about writing and reading at
www.cosycatastrophes.wordpress.com
and you can follow him on Twitter @onasteamer.

Franklin Marsh has had several stories in *Filthy Creations*
magazine. His story *Last Christmas (I gave you my life)* appeared in the *Black Book of Horror*. A further two stories have appeared in the 3rd and 4th volumes of the *Black Books: The Lake* and *All Hallow's Even*.

David A. Sutton lives in Birmingham, England. He is the
recipient of the World Fantasy Award, The International Horror Guild Award and twelve British Fantasy Awards for editing magazines and anthologies (*Fantasy Tales, Dark Voices: The Pan Book of Horror* and *Dark Terrors: The Gollancz Book of Horror*). Other anthologies are *Phantoms of Venice* and *Houses on the Borderland*. He has also been a genre fiction writer since the 1960s with stories appearing widely in anthologies and magazines, including *Best New Horror, Final Shadows, The Mammoth book of Merlin, Beneath the Ground, Shadows Over Innsmouth, The Black Book of Horror, Subtle Edens, The Ghosts & Scholars Book of Shadows* and *Psychomania*. He is the proprietor of Shadow Publishing, a small press issuing collections and anthologies such as *Horror! Under the Tombstone, The Lurkers in the Abyss and Other Tales of Terror* (by David A. Riley), *Tales of the Grotesque: A Collection of Uneasy Tales* (by L. A. Lewis, edited by Richard Dalby) and forthcoming, *Creeping Crawlers*, edited by Allen Ashley. His short

stories are collected in *Clinically Dead & Other Tales of the Supernatural* and *Dead Water and Other Weird Tales.*

David Turnbull is a member of Clockhouse London Writers. His short fiction has appeared in numerous magazines and anthologies as well as being read live at Liar's League London and The Solstice Short Festival. His most recent anthology inclusions are *Beware the Little White Rabbit*, Leap Books and *We Can Improve You*, Boo Books. He can be found at:
www.tumsh.co.uk

MJ Wesolowski is a writer, former chef and former secondary school teacher from Newcastle-Upon-Tyne. He currently works for New Writing North as a group leader for Cuckoo Young Writers, a creative writing group for young people.

His short horror fiction has been published in *Ethereal Tales* magazine, *The Midnight Movie Creature Feature* horror anthology (May December Publications 2011)and the *22 More Quick Shivers* anthology (Cosmonomic Multimedia).

His début novella, *The Black Land*, set in the Northumberland countryside was published by Blood Bound Books in 2013 and has been given a five-star review from New York Times best-selling author Carsten Stroud.

MJ Wesolowski has stories forthcoming in the *Selfies from the End of the World* anthology (Mad Scientist Journal 2015) and the *Onyx Neon Shorts Horror Collection 2015.*

His first ever book, written and illustrated at age 11 was entitled 'Attack of the Killer Flytraps' and whilst his writing style has possibly matured since then, his themes and content almost certainly haven't.

MJ Wesolowski spent some years in Lancaster studying linguistics and now lives in Newcastle-Upon-Tyne with his family. He spends the majority of his time locked in his study surrounded by vintage taxidermy and plastic monsters, listening to black metal and occasionally doing a bit of writing. He blogs about horror, the supernatural, books and other strange things here:
https://mjwesolowskiauthor.wordpress.com/

Joe Young is a professional freelance artist and writer with excellent rates and a cheeky grin. He's an Englishman living in Frankfurt, Germany without the usual wife, children, cat or dog, but with his amazing and very forgiving fiancée whose flexibility enables him to concentrate on writing and illustrating full-time.

A former Circus Clown and full-time responsibility dodger Joe always wrote for pleasure until his best friend nagged him into sending some of his work out. Joe has since been published in The Exaggerated Press: *Wordland 2: Hi Honey I'm Home*. Haunted Waters Press: *From the Depths*. Zoetic Press: *Non-Binary Review*, and in the *Journal of the British Fantasy Society* as both Writer and Reviewer.

Artistically his previous successes include a couple of sell-out art exhibitions in the UK as well as mural work for special events. Recently he adopted the Adobe Creative Cloud Suite as his weapons of choice, working on his own projects as well as creating book covers and illustrations for independent publishers.

His artwork can be seen in/on an ever expanding array of publications including several editions of Morpheus Tales as well as cover illustrations for *Goblin Mire* by David A. Riley and *Kitchen Sink Gothic* from Parallel Universe Publications. He has created spoof advertising artwork for Nat.Brut's magazine *SALE* and has various other works in progress. Joe also had art featured in LifeTime TV/DeviantArt's campaign promoting the TV series *The Witches of East End*.

He has written several articles for *Another Dimension* and can also be found on Jim McCleod's *gingernutsofhorror.com* where he is a regular contributor and movie reviewer.

Joe loves his fiancée and his job to ridiculous degrees and is always up for new challenges.

You can contact Joe via:

novelillustrations@yahoo.com

Or check him out here:

www.novelillustrations.com

https://www.facebook.com/MrJoeYoung

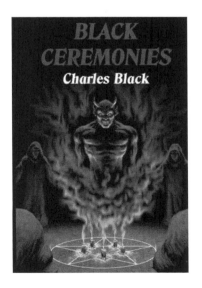

HIS OWN MAD DEMONS:
DARK TALES FROM DAVID A. RILEY
ISBN: 978-0-9574535-8-6

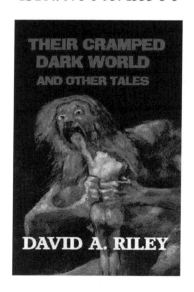

THEIR CRAMPED DARK WORLD
by David A. Riley
ISBN: 978-0-9574535-9-3

THE HEAVEN MAKER AND OTHER GRUESOME TALES
by Craig Herbertson
ISBN: 978-0-9932888-2-1

GOBLIN MIRE
by David A. Riley
ISBN-10: 095745354X

THINGS THAT GO BUMP IN THE NIGHT
edited by Douglas Draa and David A. Riley
ISBN-10: 0957453566

CLASSIC WEIRD
selected David A. Riley
ISBN: 978-0-9574535-3-1

MOLOCH'S CHILDREN
by David A. Riley
ISBN: 978-0993288814

And coming soon:

AND NOBODY LIVED HAPPILY EVER AFTER
by Kate Farrell

Check our website:
http://paralleluniversepublications.blogspot.co.uk/

Made in the USA
Middletown, DE
15 August 2015

Spread the word so others can benefit too!

If you enjoyed this journal, please leave a review on Amazon. I'm a freelance writer with no "big marketing company" backing me, so I would greatly appreciate your review, and it will only take you a few minutes.

Here's how to submit a review:

1. Go to Amazon and in the "BOOKS" category, search for:

   Positive Affirmations Journal: 100 Journal Writing Prompts
   (be sure the author is Susan LaBorde)

   Click on this book title to go the detail page.

2. In the Customer Reviews section of the page, click on **Write a customer review.**

3. Then just write your review, and click **Submit.**

Thank you in advance!

Peace,
Susan

---

www.MakeAVisionBoard.com

Visit us on the web to learn about more ways to create a better life for yourself:

- Find out what a vision board is and how to make one.
- Get topic ideas and learn about Gratitude Boards.
- See options for vision board apps and software.
- Explore our "Being, Doing, Having" blog for more about affirmations, happiness, limiting beliefs, mind power, the law of attraction, quality personal growth resources and much more!

http://makeavisionboard.com

Notes ...